MW00615738

# Point of Impact

a novel by
Clair
M. Poulson

Copyright © 1988

All Rights Reserved.

No part of this book may be reproduced in any form whatsoever, whether by graphic, visual, electronic, filming, microfilming, tape recording, or any other means, without prior written permission of the author, except in the case of brief passages embodied in critical reviews and articles.

This book is not an official publication of The Church of Jesus Christ of Latter-day Saints. All opinions expressed herein are the author's and are not necessarily those of the publisher's or of the Church of Jesus Christ of Latter-day Saints.

ISBN: 1-55517-403-5

v.2 K24C

Published by: **Bonneville Books**

Distributed by:
925 North Main, Springville, UT 84663 • 801/489-4084

CFI    Publishing and Distribution Since 1986
Cedar Fort, Incorporated
CFI Distribution • CFI Books • Council Press • Bonneville Books

Cover design by Corinne A. Bischoff and Sheila Mortimer
Printed in the United States of America

To my daughters, Kelly Ann, Amanda, and Mary. They are an example to me. The creation of Darcy in this book was inspired by them and their lives.

# Foreword

IN WRITING THIS BOOK, I relied heavily on nearly three decades of experience in the criminal justice field. As a patrolman on the road, as a law enforcement administrator, and finally as a justice court judge, I have been, at times, almost overwhelmed by the needless tragedies I have witnessed. Some of the saddest tragedies have affected me and those I love the most in a very personal way.

This book portrays a problem that I have observed in our society, one that involves youth, alcohol, and driving. I do not profess to have all the answers. I doubt that anyone does. And it was not my purpose, as I wrote this work of fiction, to either provide legal solutions or place blame. Rather, I have tried to create more of an awareness of this very complex problem as I see it.

The only solution lies in our homes and communities. Prevention is the key. Somehow, if we could instill in our children, our grandchildren, and every young person, an understanding of the dangers associated with drinking and driving, the problem would decrease in magnitude. This novel is an attempt to help both young people and adults to personally relate to the issues and emotions involved with the massive problem of drunk drivers and the consumption of alcohol in general.

Please be aware that any similarities in this work to real persons or events is strictly coincidental. I created the characters from my own imagination with the intention of pointing fingers at no person, group, profession, or organization. Nor is it my intention to bring up old wounds from those who have suffered, although I realize that could be a result of this work. If it is, please accept my apology. My purpose in writing this novel is to entertain while creating an awareness of one of the most serious maladies of our society. If I can make people think and want to do something to help prevent some of these problems you will witness in this book, then I have succeeded.

# Chapter One

HER ARMS FULL OF BOOKS, Darcy Felding stepped lightly from the school bus. Her little brother darted past, shouting, "I'll beat you home, Darcy!" He streaked off the pavement and up the lane before she could respond to his eager proposal.

The bus pulled away in a smelly cloud of diesel smoke as Darcy stood at the road's edge watching Nate, a fond smile lighting her face. He slowed to a walk and looked back expectantly. "Hey, come on, Darcy, don't you want to race me?"

"Sure, but I can't today. My arms are too full of books."

Nate started back toward her. "I'll take half of them, then it'll be even," he said with a mischievous grin.

"All right," she agreed reluctantly, not wanting to dampen the competitive glint in a pair of dark green, eight-year-old eyes.

Several cars passed by on the highway behind her. Suddenly, Nate's eyes bulged and he shouted, "Look out, Darcy!"

The approaching roar of an accelerating engine and suddenly blaring horn punctuated Nate's warning, and Darcy lunged from the pavement, slipped in the loose gravel at the road's edge, and fell. Her books flew from her hands, releasing several loose papers into the backwash of Shad Cleverly's red Ford pickup.

"Darcy!" Nate screamed in alarm. "That truck almost hit you!"

With tears of embarrassment stinging her eyes, Darcy began to gather up her books. "I'm fine. Grab those papers, will you please?" she asked.

Without a word, the little boy spun on his heels and tore down the road to rescue his sister's papers. When he returned, he was all grins and presented Darcy with a sadly crumpled handful of school work. "I think I wrinkled 'em a little, but I got 'em all for you," he announced proudly.

Darcy tried to smile. "They'll straighten out just fine. Thank you, Nate," she said, tossing her head just enough to send long chestnut hair sailing over her shoulder.

"Still wanna' race?" he asked hopefully, reaching for some of her books.

"Not now, Nate. I bruised my knees and skinned my hands when I fell. Maybe another time, okay?"

His grin was replaced with a look as black as a boy his age could muster, and he asked, "Who was that, Darcy? He was aiming right for you. If you hadn't jumped he would of hit you," he said as they started together up the lane toward the house. "Was it Shad?"

"Yeah, it was Shad."

"I thought he liked you. He could of hurt you!" Nate said with venom.

"He'd never do that, Nate, and you know it. He was just showing off. He's really a good driver," Darcy scolded.

"Well, I hope Randy gets him. It'll serve him right for driving like that."

Randy Hutchins was a trooper with the Utah Highway Patrol and their uncle, their mother's youngest brother.

"Nate! He doesn't usually drive like that. He doesn't need a ticket," Darcy said, glaring at him.

Nate lapsed into a moody silence, giving Darcy a chance to reflect. Shad Cleverly, like herself, was just beginning his senior year in high school. They had dated off and on since the Junior Prom.

A star on both the football and basketball teams, Shad was very popular with the girls. A shock of curly black hair that was usually partially covered with a baseball cap, almost always worn with the beak shading the back of his collar, added almost irresistible charm to his dark face. Most of the girls, including Darcy's friends, considered him cute.

Darcy, whose friends insited she was one of the prettiest and brightest girls in the school, liked Shad with his athletic build and "Clint Black" features. Her friends said that she "drove him wild" and that was okay with her.

"Darcy, is Shad still going to be your boyfriend?" Nate suddenly asked.

"Of course! Why shouldn't he be?" she said angrily, surprised at Nate's question. "What makes you ask such a dumb thing?"

"He tried to run over you," Nate said in a slightly broken voice, his eyes dropping to the dusty road at his feet. "He made you get hurt!"

"Oh, Nate, he didn't mean to," she said testily. "It was my fault for jumping like I did. He would never have hit me. That's the way guys are, Nate. Anyway, I'm not hurt that bad."

"I bet Mom and Dad won't like it," he responded.

"Darcy glanced angrily at him. "Nate, let's just forget it. Mom and Dad don't need to know. And I don't want Shad to know I fell, either. He'd feel bad, so don't you go telling his little brother."

"Oh, come on Darcy. It won't hurt nothing if I tell Billy," Nate pouted. "He won't say nothing to Shad if I make him promise."

A cool September breeze stirred the dirt at Darcy's feet and tugged at her blouse. She hunched forward, hugging her books in frustration. She knew Nate, and the more she begged him not to say anything to Billy, the more likely he was to do just that. It would be best to drop the whole thing right now.

"Are you going to the football game tomorrow?" Nate asked after a long period of silence.

"I suppose so, why?" she asked, frustration still evident in her voice.

"Billy says Shad's the starting quarterback this year."

"That's right. And he's really good, too."

"If he's such a good player," Nate said suspiciously, "then why ain't he at practice today? Billy says the team practices right after school every day."

"I don't know," Darcy mumbled. Nate had made a good point. Shad was supposed to be at practice. The thought gnawed at her as Nate handed back her books and opened the front door to the Felding home.

*

"You better slow down, Shad," his new friend, Todd Albright warned. "That uncle of Darcy's loves to pick on us high school kids."

"Oh, Randy Hutchins won't bother me. He knows Darcy's my girl, and he wouldn't do anything to upset her. She's sort of a favorite of his, you know," Shad said confidently.

"I don't know," Todd said with a shake of his head. "He has one fast patrol car, and if he saw you driving so fast, he'd punch that car of his and crawl right up this old pickup's tailpipe."

Shad glanced nervously in his mirrors and let up on the gas. "I've almost got my Trans Am rebuilt and ready to go. I guarantee it'll blow everything off the road between here and the state line, including Hutchins' patrol car!"

"Yeah, maybe, but if I were you, I'd keep an eye out for him, especially after he hears how you scared his favorite niece," Todd said with a chuckle.

"She'll never tell. She likes me too much," Shad said smugly. "Anyway, she wasn't hurt or anything."

"Are you sure? I looked back after we'd passed, and I thought it looked like she'd fallen down," Todd revealed.

Shad jerked his head around. "Are you sure, Todd? Gee, I would never hurt her, you know that, Todd. I was just giving her a thrill. I'll give her a call later—turn on the old charm, you know. Tell her I'm sorry—truck sort of got away from me or something. Then I'll ask her out to the game tomorrow."

Shad slowed down as he talked and pulled off to the side of the road. Then, jamming the gas peddle to the floor and cranking the steering wheel, he laid a black arc on the pavement and shot toward town.

Only after he had regained his seating did Todd comment. "Don't you think it might be a bit embarrassing asking her to the game, old buddy? She's bound to ask why you're not playing in it."

"So?"

"So you know how Darcy is. If she finds out the coach suspended you from the team for a week for drinking, she won't even speak to you, let alone go out with you anymore," Todd said.

He had hit a nerve. Todd just might be right. If Darcy knew he was hanging around with Todd and drinking a little, and that's all it was, just a couple of cans every now and then, why, she'd be terribly angry. He couldn't believe they'd been caught. He hadn't been drinking all that long and had been discreet about it, and yet the coach had somehow found out. Todd, on the other hand, had been drinking for years, and this was the first time he'd ever got in trouble for it.

"Got ya worried, ain't I," Todd snickered.

"Yeah. Darcy'll be mad. If she finds out, I'll have to promise never to touch the stuff again, or she'll not even speak to me. I'd rather she didn't know." He was thoughtful for a moment, frowning. "Hey, I got it," Shad said in a sudden burst of brilliance.

"Got what?" Todd asked.

"I'll tell her that the coach wanted to give some of the younger guys a chance to play tomorrow, so he gave me and you the game off," he said brightly.

"I don't know, Shad. She's awful smart, you know," Todd cautioned.

"She'll believe me, and she'll go," Shad retorted angrily, knowing that Todd was right but not willing to admit it. He really liked Darcy and would hate to lose her, but on the other hand, a lot of the guys were drinking a little, and he didn't want to be left out of the gang. Anyway, he liked the stuff.

"Guess we'll see," Todd said.

"Yeah, I guess so," Shad mumbled. He was worried. "Let's drive by the field and see how the practice is going. I'll bet the coach is wishing he had me about now."

Todd glanced at him but said nothing more.

❄

"Would you mind setting the table, Darcy?" Sharon Felding called from the kitchen.

"In a minute, Mom. I'm right in the middle of a trig problem," Darcy answered, biting the end of her pencil as she concentrated.

A few moments later, she laid her notebook and badly-marred pencil aside and slowly entered the kitchen. She was still worried that Shad would find out about her bruises and scrapes, and she didn't want that. She knew he hadn't meant for her to fall.

"Set the dining room table tonight, dear, and include four extra places."

"For whom?"

"Randy, Sandy, and the boys."

"Oh, good," Darcy said, her mood suddenly brightening, and she began to cheerfully pull dishes from the cupboard.

Randy Hutchins was one of Darcy's favorite people. Her mother's youngest brother, he had spoiled Darcy from before she could remember. And even though, at age twenty-three, a pretty school teacher had successfully put a ring on his finger, he never ceased to fuss over Darcy like he had when he was twenty-one and fresh off a mission, and she was a starry-eyed ten-year-old.

No one could quite measure up to Randy in Darcy's eyes, and no one was more proud than she when he was hired by the Highway Patrol. Darcy had even had to fight off a wave of jealousy when Sandy first noticed Randy's short blond hair, broad shoulders, wide grin, and shiny black boots.

A very happy couple, Randy and Sandy had two boys now, ages two and three, and Darcy was spoiling them just as properly as her Uncle Randy had always spoiled her.

When the doorbell chimed a few minutes later, Darcy answered the door. As was his custom, Randy smiled down at her and said, "My good-ness girl, I do believe you're prettier every time I see you."

Darcy blushed, as she always did, and then said, "But I'll never be as pretty as Sandy."

That same statement, when Darcy was only thirteen, had been the stroke of brilliance that had won the heart of her new aunt.

"Hi, Darcy," the oldest Randy Hutchins look-alike said from his posi-tion near his dad's knee.

"Hi, Scotty," she said, bending to pick him up and waiting to receive his overly generous kiss on the lips.

"Come on in, you guys," she said with a laugh, wiping the excess moisture from her mouth and smearing the pale red lipstick she had so painstakingly applied that morning.

As soon as the door closed, the younger of the look-alikes demanded equal time and left Darcy with more fresh slobber on her face.

Dinner was a cheerful, laughter-filled affair, as it always was when Randy and his family were there. They were not yet half-finished when the phone rang. Mrs. Felding scurried into the kitchen to answer it and then called out. "It's for you, Darcy."

"Hello," Darcy said into the handset after her mother had disappeared into the dining room.

"Hi, Darcy. How are you?"

"I'm fine, Shad," she said cheerfully upon recognizing his voice. "What are you doing?"

"Feeling bad," he said softly. "That's why I'm calling, Darcy. I wanted to apologize. I didn't mean…"

"I'm fine," she interrupted. "What happened, anyway?"

"The accelerator pedal got stuck when I was passing a car up the highway from your lane. It scared me so badly that I leaned down and tried to pry it up with my fingers. That's when I accidentally swerved toward you. I honked the horn to warn you when I saw you standing there. I'm really sorry," he said.

Shad sounded sincere, and Darcy was glad there was a good explanation for what had happened. Now that she knew he wasn't just showing off, she would put Nate in his place if he opened his mouth when he shouldn't. "It's okay, Shad," she said. "But you better get your truck to a mechanic and get it fixed."

"I fixed it myself when I got home. It won't happen again," Shad said. "Did you get hurt? I really didn't mean…"

I know you didn't, Shad," Darcy said lightly. "So don't worry about it."

"Okay," he said, "but Todd said he thought you fell, and I was worried."

"Todd Albright!?" she exclaimed.

"Yeah, he was with me. He said he turned and saw…"

"Shad, you know what I think of Todd. He drinks! What was he doing with you?" she demanded, suddenly upset.

"Darcy, please don't be mad. Todd's not so bad. He just needed a ride home after school, and I was taking him there. But he asked me to take him for a spin after he got in my truck. I mean, you know, his parents don't have much, and he sort of likes my truck. I was just being friendly," Shad lied smoothly.

"Yeah? Well, okay. It's just that the guys he hangs around with are always in trouble," she said. "I just…"

"Just what?" Shad demanded defensively. "You don't think I'd go and do the kind of stuff he does, do you? Anyway, he's never been in trouble that I know of."

Darcy hadn't meant to upset Shad, but she could see that she had. It was just that guys like Todd had such different standards than she and Shad. She hoped Shad wouldn't ever do the kind of things Todd did, like drinking, but how could you ever be sure? She wondered.

"You still there?" Shad asked.

"Yeah," she answered.

"Okay. Well, hey, another reason I called is to ask you to the game tomorrow."

"To the game?" she asked in surprise. "I was going to go, but how can I go with you where you'll be playing and all?"

"Oh, didn't I tell you before?"

"Tell me what?" she asked suspiciously.

"I don't have to play tomorrow. We're playing such a lousy team that Coach Starr thought it would be a good chance to work the younger guys and give them some experience," he explained.

"Oh, so that's why you weren't at practice after school?" she asked.

"Yep. Coach gave some of us older and better players the week off, so I'll get to watch the game from the bleachers. I thought I'd told you at school."

"Not a word," she said lightly, feeling so much relief that she could have shouted. That Shad had not been at practice had worried her more that she'd cared to admit.

"So, what about it, Darcy? Why don't I swing by and pick you up about thirty minutes before the game?"

"Sure. Sounds like fun," she agreed.

"Good," he said quickly. "I'll be by to pick you up at four o'clock. Thanks, Darcy. It'll be a ball. I must admit I was a little miffed with Coach Starr at first, but it has been years since I was able to sit in the bleachers and watch a football game," he said with a laugh. "Well, I better go. See you at school."

"Was that Shad?" her mother asked as Darcy re-entered the dining room a minute later.

Before she could answer, Nate blurted, "Shad! He almost ran over Darcy with his truck today!"

"What!" Mrs. Felding exclaimed.

"Oh, he didn't either, Nate!" Darcy cried angrily. "His gas peddle got stuck was all."

"Then why was he laughing when you fell and he went by?" Nate asked impishly.

"Well, it was an accident. He didn't even know I fell. And he apologized," Darcy responded sharply.

"Is that the reason he called?" Darcy's mother asked.

"Yes, that and to ask me to go to the game with him tomorrow."

"How come he's not playing in the game?" Nate asked shrewdly. "I thought the starting quarterback always played."

"He has the week off, Nate," Darcy answered defensively.

"That's a new one," Randy said, frowning. "Why does he have the week off?"

Darcy's eyes met Randy's briefly. He was clearly puzzled. "They're playing a really poor team tomorrow, and Shad says the coach wants some of the younger kids to get some experience," she said haltingly. *That sounds really fishy,* she admitted to herself, and an irritating gnawing in her stomach started up.

But Randy just said, "Oh," and dropped the whole thing. She was grateful, but something about the look he gave her mom made Darcy squirm uncomfortably in her chair. It was almost like he knew something she didn't.

"Who was the other guy in his truck?" Nate asked.

Darcy could have clubbed him. "Just a guy he was giving a ride to after school," she answered evasively.

For the first time, Darcy's father spoke up. "Who was it, Darcy?" he asked.

"Just Todd."

"Todd Albright?" Randy asked quickly.

"Yeah, he needed a ride, and well, you know, he doesn't have much and Shad said he'd run him home," she explained, still wishing she could club Nate for getting the whole thing going again after Randy let it drop.

"Darcy," Randy said with a look of concern in his eyes. "I hope that Shad's not starting to run with Todd's crowd. There's a lot of drinking going on with those guys. And you do know Todd's dad is an alcoholic, don't you?"

Everybody knew that, but Darcy was getting defensive. "Shad just gave him a ride, that's all. Is that a sin? I thought we were supposed to do things for people who are less fortunate," she snapped, feeling her cheeks flush.

"You're right," her mother, said. "Shad's a nice boy. Now let's talk about something else."

But Nate wasn't finished yet. "You could'a got him today," he said to Randy, his green eyes shining. "He almost hit Darcy at the end of the lane. Made her fall and hurt herself. I even had to chase her papers."

"Nate. We've been over that," Darcy hissed. "He didn't mean to and I'm okay." Dismissing Nate, she turned her head and smiled at one of her little nephews. "Will you help me clear the table when we're finished, Scotty?" she asked.

The subject of Shad Cleverly did not come up again that evening.

❋

"I told you it'd be all right," Shad bragged to Todd as the two temporarily banished football stars each nursed a cold can of beer. "She believed me. And I really shouldn't be drinking with you. I really should quit drinking. At least, I've got to be more careful where I drink. I don't want to lose her," he added.

They were sitting in Shad's truck in a grove of trees beside the river, just a mile west of town. "And where will you get your beer?" Todd asked sharply.

"Oh, Todd, forget it. Let's just be careful not to drink around some of the other guys so much. One of them had to have tipped the coach off," Shad said. "I don't want them telling Darcy, too."

Todd snickered. "None of them talk to her, anyway. But I do have a hard time believing that she bought your story about the younger guys playing while we got the week off," Todd said doubtfully.

"Of course she did. She knows I'm the main man," Shad bragged. "By the way, where did you get this beer? You can't just go out and buy the stuff, can you?"

"Boy, are you the sheltered one. Time you got an education, Shad. A real one, I mean. I got this from the fridge. Dad won't miss a few cans. By now he'll be so plastered that he can't even see the TV. He don't care if I take it anyway. He lets me drink with him in the house sometimes...whenever Mom's not home. She really has an attitude. If she knew I was drinking his beer, she'd quit letting him keep it in the house, so I gotta be kind of sneaky. Don't want our source to dry up, do we?" Todd said, and he belched loudly.

"Have some manners, Albright, or you can't sit with me and my girl at the game tomorrow," Shad said with a grin.

"Gee, that'd be just terrible. What would I ever do if I couldn't sit by Miss Prim-and-Proper," Todd said, forcing another rude belch and wiping his mouth in exaggerated movements with the back of his freckled hand.

Shad groaned. "Oh, please," he said.

# Chapter Two

RANDY HUTCHINS ADJUSTED his gun-belt before pulling a ring of keys from his pocket. "Almost four o'clock," he said, glancing at the Timex on his wrist. "Time to go to work."

"I'll have your dinner ready at seven," Sandy said, and she kissed him lightly on the cheek.

"I'll be here if I can," he responded with an easy grin and turned to pat the boys on the head.

He moved toward the door. Sandy blocked his way with her slender frame and threw her arms around his waist, laying her head against his broad chest. "You be careful tonight, darling. I always worry when you switch to evening shift. You might get too sleepy."

"You always worry, period. The fate of being a cop's wife. I'll be fine, Sandy. I always am." His grin was in place, his face relaxed and unconcerned.

Sandy stretched upward and kissed him on the lips, lingering a little longer that she usually did, before letting him slide out the door. She waved and smiled as he backed his patrol car out of the driveway. He waved, grinned, and eased the white Ford down the street.

Randy liked his job. He loved people and took the responsibility he had to protect them very seriously. Nobody liked to get a citation, and Randy knew that. When he issued one, it was always with the hope that it would cause that driver to seriously consider the danger illegal driving acts put themselves and others in, and cause him or her to drive more safely.

He approached his job with the attitude that most drivers were good ones, conscientious and alert. However, he knew that just about everyone became a little careless at times and needed a reminder. Goodness knows, he'd had a couple himself in the past. What really concerned him were the few drivers who simply did not care.

The most dangerous, in his mind, were those who drove after consuming alcohol. The very first thing alcohol affects when it flows into a person's brain is judgment. And good judgment, when behind the wheel of a car, is one thing no driver should ever be without. The second most dangerous drivers were those whose judgment was already clouded. That kind believes that no matter how fast or recklessly they drive, they are still totally in control. Randy did not believe that. He felt that it was a very erroneous assumption and an especially deadly one when mixed with alcohol.

Randy drove by the high school football field at four-thirty. The game was in full swing, shouts, laughter and boos coming from the stands. He noticed Shad Cleverly's red pickup and remembered the previous evening. Somehow, hearing that Shad was with Todd Albright worried him. Not that Todd was a bad kid, as far as he knew, but Todd was known to run with a crowd of boys that drank. He just hoped Shad didn't have any thoughts of getting involved in that kind of behavior himself.

He smiled when he thought of Darcy. She and Shad did make a handsome couple. After a couple of passes around town, Randy cruised east, past the Felding farm, and several miles beyond. Later, he patrolled west for a few miles. Traffic was light and moving sensibly. About six-thirty he worked his way back to town. A few minutes later, the football game ended.

Randy spotted one of the city police cars parked near the Texaco on Main Street. He pulled up and chatted amiably for a few minutes. Then he noticed Shad's red truck pass and smiled at the sight of Darcy's rich chestnut hair in the center of the cab.

The other officer noticed, too, and commented. "Isn't that your niece with that Cleverly kid? Seems like they're together a lot lately."

"Yeah, she kind of likes him, Sarge," Randy replied.

The man he called Sarge looked at him through thoughtful blue eyes. He was near fifty and a veteran officer. Although his name was John Howard, Randy had never known him as anything but Sarge. He was a steady, honest, and shrewd cop—the kind that kept the peace in small towns all across the state of Utah. Years of police work had developed in him an almost unerring instinct for trouble.

When Sarge spoke, Randy always paid attention. He would usually learn something. "I'm concerned, Randy. Shad has always seemed like a good kid."

"He is. Pretty good family, too."

Sarge gave Randy one of those *are you sure?* looks. Randy grinned and said, "Well, his dad does have an attitude at times."

"I'd say. Ever give him a ticket?" Sarge asked.

"Tom Cleverly? No, I don't think I ever have."

"You'd remember if you had. I have, and it was not fun. He's a hard-headed coot. Doesn't think he can be wrong…ever. Hard worker, though. Makes good money. Maybe too much for his boy's sake," Sarge added.

"His wife's sure a sweet lady," Randy said. "They're in the same ward as Sandy and me. She's as faithful as they come."

"And Tom?" Sarge asked with a raised eyebrow.

"A once-in-a-whiler," Randy admitted. "But Shad usually comes."

"That's good. But I still worry about him. I've seen him with the Albright kid several times lately. And you know what the old man Albright is like," Sarge commented dryly.

"Yes, I'm afraid so. There's a sad case."

"So true, but I'm afraid his drinking has rubbed off on Todd. I've never actually picked the boy up for drinking, but I suspect that it's only a matter of time. At least that's what some of the kids are telling me."

Sarge was one of those officers who has a way with young people. They liked him, and he could extract information from them without their even realizing what was happening.

The older officer watched the street for a moment and then added, "Hear they both got suspended from the team for a week."

Randy looked at Sarge inquiringly. "Suspended?"

"That's what I hear. He hasn't been to practices for several nights. But he and Todd have been together a lot after school this week."

Randy sat back for a moment, recalling the conversation the previous evening at his sister's house. He was sure Darcy had said that Shad had just been giving Todd a ride home, although that certainly didn't explain what they were doing out past the Felding farm and during football practice. They both lived in town. Finally, Randy asked, "You're sure of that, Sarge?"

Sarge nodded. "The coach apparently caught them drunk the other night."

"Drunk! Shad?" Randy exclaimed. "Are you sure?"

Sarge nodded and Randy began to worry. This wasn't the Shad he knew. But Sarge was usually pretty sure of his information before he revealed it. Randy wondered if Darcy had any idea. He doubted it. She wasn't the kind to put up with her boyfriend drinking. At least, he didn't think she was.

"Keep your eye on him, Randy," Sarge advised. "The Albright kid has an almost unlimited supply of beer available to him. I hear his dad sees to that."

It was Randy's turn to nod, and his face grew dark. "If Shad drinks while Darcy is with him, I'll throttle the kid. For that matter, so will Darcy, if I know her, and I think I do." He glanced at his watch. "Sandy'll have my dinner ready in a minute, so I'm going to run home for a bite. Keep me posted, will you? If you keep hearing things about Shad drinking, I'll try to find a way to let Darcy know...if she doesn't figure it out for herself. I'll catch up with you again after dinner."

"Sure thing, Randy. I'll see you in a bit."

Randy almost got to finish his dinner before the phone rang. "Hope that's not for me, " he mumbled through a mouthful of meat-loaf.

Sandy answered it. "Yes, he's just finishing his dinner, Kerry," Randy heard her say, and he relaxed. The only Kerry he knew was Kerry Felding, Darcy's father. But he tensed again when Sandy asked, "Is Darcy all right?"

He was on his feet, reaching for the phone by the time she said, "I'll get Randy for you."

"Kerry, what's the problem?" Randy asked brusquely.

"Darcy just got home."

"Already?"

"None too soon! And only because she insisted," Kerry said, and Randy could feel the anger in his brother-in-law's voice. "She didn't want me to call, but I had to say something."

"What happened?" Randy asked, suspecting that he might already have an idea.

"She and Shad had a fight a few minutes ago. And she made him bring her home. She's in her room crying right now."

"What did Shad do? Darcy's not the fighting type."

"She can be," Kerry said. "Just ask her little brother."

"Yeah, but that's normal," Randy chuckled. "Fighting with Shad, that's not. I thought she liked him quite a bit."

"She does. And so do we. But she got her world shattered tonight," Kerry said. "I guess I shouldn't be calling you, because I don't want to get him in trouble, but when it comes to my daughter, I'm pretty protective."

"As well you should be. So what happened?" Randy pried.

I guess it was right after she saw you talking with Sarge. Someone pulled out in front of Shad and he had to stop kind of fast and..."

"Who was it?" Randy interrupted.

"She wasn't sure. An older lady was all she saw. But that's not the problem. You see, when he braked, a beer can rolled from beneath his seat."

"Oh, no," Randy murmured.

"Yes, I'm afraid so. And of course, Darcy asked Shad about it. He said he didn't have any idea what it was doing in his truck. But Darcy isn't dumb. She asked him if it was Todd's and he told her it wasn't, that Todd had only been in his truck that one time, and he sure didn't let him drink," Kerry explained.

"So what happened after that?" Randy pressed

"Well, I guess Darcy told Shad she didn't believe him, and he blew up. He said something to her about how he never locks his truck and that one of the guys must have put it there as a joke. She didn't accept that explanation and reached under the seat."

"Were there more cans there?" Randy asked.

"A couple. Anyway, she made him bring her home, then she called the coach. You know Darcy when she's angry. She told me that she was sure there was more to the week off for Shad than he had said, because the team got beat badly today."

"So she knows," Randy said with a sinking feeling.

"Knows what?" Kerry asked.

"About Shad being suspended from the team?"

"You mean you knew?" Kerry asked sharply. "Why didn't you say something? You know we'd never let Darcy go out with a boy that drinks. Not that she'd want to."

"Hold on, Kerry. I just found out a few minutes ago. Sarge told me right after Darcy and Shad went by," Randy said. "So what did the coach tell her?"

He suspended Todd and Shad for drinking. Darcy is crushed. It's one thing to learn that someone you care about is doing things you don't approve of, especially when you're being lied to, but it's another thing to quit caring. She's hurting, and I could kick Shad clear across town," Kerry said intensely.

"I thought Shad was talking about a mission next year," Randy said.

"He was, and it still isn't too late. I guess that's why I called you. Seems to me the best thing that could happen is for him to get caught drinking. Maybe at this point that's all it would take to get him to straighten up," Kerry said hopefully.

"Maybe. I'll try to keep an eye out, and so will Sarge and the city boys. I'll let them know. And Kerry, tell Darcy not to be upset if Shad does get caught. It's for his own good."

As soon as he had checked on the air again, Randy called Sarge on the radio. "You remember that kid we were discussing earlier?" he asked.

"Sure do," came Sarge's baritone over the air.

"I need to talk to you about him."

"I'm back where I was when you went to dinner," Sarge said.

"I'll be right there."

Randy told Sarge what had happened, and Sarge said, "We'll just have to keep an eye out for Shad. Now's the time to turn him back, before he gets to liking the stuff too much."

"Well, I better get out on the highway," Randy said. "I gotta earn my keep."

❊

"Why did you take Darcy home so soon?" Todd asked as he climbed into the pickup with Shad.

"She found one of your beer cans," Shad snapped.

"Our beer cans," Todd shot right back. "What did you leave them in the truck for?"

"I forgot. But they were under the seat."

"What was she doing looking there?" Todd asked.

"She wasn't. Some old lady pulled out of the Foodtown right in front of me, and when I hit the brakes, a can rolled out...right under Darcy's feet. Of all the luck!" Shad exclaimed angrily. "You know how she hates people drinking."

"Yeah, but she'll get over it."

"You don't know Darcy," Shad said sadly.

"Surely you didn't admit to drinking, did you?" Todd asked.

"Of course not. Do you think I'm an idiot or something?" Shad snapped. "I told her it must have been put there by some of the guys as a joke, but she didn't buy that for a minute."

"She'll get over it, I tell you," Todd said again.

"I hate to disagree with you, old buddy, but I don't think she will. I've really blown it big time."

Todd grinned. "Ah, come on, Shad. If she likes you, she'll still go out with you."

Shad shook his head. "She was really mad, Todd. She made me take her home right then. I think I'll call her later, but I'm not sure she'll talk to me."

"Hey, there are other girls, Shad. If she's gonna' be..."

"Todd," Shad interrupted angrily, "there's only one Darcy. I don't want to lose her."

"Then don't. Hey, come on over to the house. I'll bet I can find something that'll make you feel better. A good cold can of Bud is what you need right now," Todd offered.

"Sure, why not?" Shad said, slamming his fist into the seat. "She ain't my boss. I'll get drunk tonight and then make it up to her tomorrow. I ain't giving her up," he said fiercely as he jammed the gas-feed to the floor.

The pickup lunged into the street, and Shad, steering with one hand, laid a strip of rubber on the pavement for a hundred feet.

Todd ran into his house a minute later and came out with two six packs of beer. "Wow, that was close," he said.

"What was?"

"Mom nearly caught me leaving the house with this stuff. She don't like me borrowing Dad's beer," he said as he threw the beer on the seat and jumped in.

Shad put the truck in gear and shot into the street, laying another strip of rubber. "I better buckle up," Todd said with a laugh, "if you're gonna' drive like a maniac."

"Chicken," Shad taunted as Todd snapped the buckle into place with an exaggerated movement. "Me and this old truck are a team. I'll never wreck her, and you can count on that. Open me a can now, will you?"

An hour later, Todd said, "Shad, don't you think you better lighten up. You've had more than me, and I'm used to the stuff. You'll be sicker'n a dog in the morning."

"I can handle it," Shad said in a slurred voice. He and Todd had been parked by the lake drinking since leaving town. He started the truck again and backed around. Then he headed for the highway.

"Where we going?" Todd asked.

"I don't know, just around, I guess."

A few minutes later, as they streaked east past the lane to Darcy's home, Shad asked, "Think Coach Starr will let us play next week? After the thumping they took today, I'll bet he'll be begging for his quarterback."

"Probably," Todd agreed.

They talked about how important they were to the team and how badly they had been missed that afternoon, their heads swelling in direct proportion to the beer they'd consumed.

"Hey, what's that on the road ahead?" Todd asked a couple of minutes later.

"A cow, you idiot," Shad responded, keeping the accelerator down.

"Yes, it's a cow all right," Todd agreed as they raced closer.

"Stupid thing better move," Shad growled, still not slowing down.

"Just go around it," Todd suggested as if the creature were immobile.

"What did you think I was going to do?" Shad asked with a

chuckle, totally unaware of the damage inflicted on his brain by the beer he had consumed.

The cow, a large Hereford, was standing in the north lane. It spotted a tuft of grass on the south side of the road and, heedless to the rapidly approaching pickup, ambled toward it.

"Stop!" Todd yelled in alarm.

Shad's foot reacted considerably slower than it would have normally, and the danger itself was slow in presenting itself to his woozy brain. He finally jammed down hard on the brake, putting the truck into a screeching slide. Then, with a rending crash, the cow was lifted from the road. For a moment, it filled the windshield, which vaporized under the big animal's impact. Then it flew on over the cab.

Cursing and showered with glass, Shad tried to control the careening truck, but it was too late, and they slid up the road on four smoking tires. The pickup left the pavement sideways, and Todd screamed as the ground rushed up at his window. Then they were upside down. For a moment, the whole world was spinning as the truck continued to roll. Shad was thrown about in the cab like a ping-pong ball.

Finally, the truck stopped rolling and slid on its top through a fence, snapping wires like cotton thread. After what seemed like an eternity, the truck came to rest, still on its top, several feet into a recently harvested wheat field.

A terrorized scream continued to discharge from Todd's mouth. Shad struggled dizzily to find his friend in the crammed confines of the mangled truck cab. He finally realized that Todd was suspended from the seat above, still strapped to the seat by the seat belt.

"Shut up!" Shad growled as the reality of his plight penetrated his thick, badly banged-up skull.

Shad was lying on his side on the crumpled metal that used to be the roof of the truck cab. He attempted to get to his knees, but a searing pain in his right arm caused him to drop on his belly, smacking his already bruised face on the jagged metal.

"Shad! Shad! Help me! I'm stuck here," Todd was crying.

To Shad, it seemed like Todd was at least a hundred feet away, even though their faces were not more than a foot apart. Shad again tried to move, ignoring his injured buddy as if he were not even there, but pain shot through his body and everything began to fade. Both his pain and Todd's shouts for help grew distant as darkness mercifully enfolded him.

*

Trooper Randy Hutchins was a mile west of town when the call to respond to a one-car rollover came through. "The caller is on a cellular phone," the dispatcher reported calmly after giving the location. "There are injuries involved and we have dispatched an ambulance."

"Ten-four, I'm en route," Randy answered as he activated his overhead lights, flipped on the siren, and directed the shiny white Ford east with a surge of power from the big engine.

Several minutes later, as he raced past the lane to the Felding farm, he caught a glimpse of his nephew, Nate, riding his bike toward the highway, waving cheerfully with one hand. Randy raised a finger in acknowledgment but continued to concentrate on the feel of his racing car and on the highway ahead.

Two miles farther, Randy knew he was almost there by the knot of cars stopped alongside the road. He eased up on his speed, noting the mangled, bloody body of a large Hereford near the pavement. He flipped off the siren as he continued to slow down, finally parking where the flashing lights would give the most protection to the accident scene.

As Randy stepped from the car, a half-dozen people crowded around him, each attempting to give their version of the seriousness of the injuries sustained by the two young victims. In the distance, Randy could hear the wail of another siren and was silently grateful, as he always was, when he knew the skilled assistance of an ambulance crew was close behind him.

Pushing his way through the crowd of stunned onlookers, Randy finally got his first glimpse of the wrecked vehicle and his stomach lurched. The crumpled red remains of Shad Cleverly's pickup lay a short distance out in the field. He began to run, grateful that Darcy was home, but concerned about Shad and whomever was with him.

Several well-meaning Good Samaritans had pulled Shad from the wreckage through the cramped space that had been the windshield, adding, Randy was sure, more injury to the boy in the process. Shad lay unconscious beneath a dark blue blanket. Randy knelt beside him, checking quickly for vital signs. Shallow, labored breathing sent the distinct odor of beer into the young trooper's face. "There's another boy still in the truck," an elderly gentleman said, tugging at Randy's sleeve.

Pity and anger, fiercely contending emotions, surged through Randy as he stood and turned toward the wrecked vehicle. "Keep an eye on him for me until the ambulance crew gets here," he ordered the elderly man.

Two men lay on their stomachs with their heads, shoulders, and arms out of sight in the mangled waste of the red pickup's cab. "Young fellow in there," someone said helpfully. "He's hanging from the seat belt. Both doors are jammed and there's not much room to get in the windows. One of those fellows has a knife and is going to try to cut the seat belt."

"No, stop!" Randy shouted in alarm and roughly pulled the two men back.

"Hey, you don't need to get huffy, officer," one of them said angrily as he lurched to his feet, a pocketknife in his hand. "I was almost where I could have cut the belt!"

"Sorry, but if it isn't done right you could break the kid's neck," Randy said brusquely, remembering only too vividly an accident he had investigated a couple of years before.

The car had rolled similarly to this one, and a man and his wife had both initially survived the crash. But in his haste to free his wife from the seat belt from which she was suspended, he had dropped her on her head, breaking her neck. She was dead before Randy arrived.

Crawling to where he could see Shad's passenger, Todd Albright, who was moaning and calling weakly for help, Randy spoke. "We'll have you out in a jiffy, Todd," he said, aware as he spoke of the ambulance crew placing equipment beside him.

At the hospital, over an hour later, Randy watched as a frowning nurse drew blood from Shad's arm. Sarge joined him. "How is he, Randy?"

"He'll be all right. He was out cold for a while, but other than a broken arm, a bad gash on one leg and a few other cuts and bruises, he's in pretty good shape considering the kind of wreck he was in. Any word on his folks?"

"No. They're still not home and no one in the neighborhood has any idea where they might have gone this evening." Turning to Shad, who was conscious and glaring at Randy with undisguised hatred, Sarge asked, "Are you absolutely sure you don't know where your parents are?"

Shad swore, provoking a tart response from Sarge. "You act like you're mad at the world, kid. You should be glad you're not hurt worse than you are."

"Drunk driving!" Shad hissed. "Can you believe that? Randy thinks I wrecked because I was drunk. It wasn't even my fault. Any cop worth his salt could see that old cow caused the whole thing. And this idiot wants to arrest me for drunk driving!"

"That's right, Shad. This blood will tell me just how much you had to drink, and if it's too much, I will be charging you with DUI. And frankly, I think it will be too much," Randy said, trying very hard to be patient. "You certainly don't seem very sober right now."

"Hot shot cop! That's all you are. Any idiot can see it's not my fault. My dad'll sue you," Shad threatened.

Randy and Sarge exchanged tired glances and shook their heads sadly. But Shad wasn't through. The alcohol in him kept him shouting. "Bet you can't wait to tell Darcy. Well, it was all her and Todd's fault."

Randy turned to Shad again and asked with a scowl, "How's that, Shad?"

"Darcy thought that just because I had a can or two in my truck that I'd drank it. She wouldn't believe me," he said as tears filled his angry eyes. "And as for the beer, Todd got that for us!"

In the hallway a few minutes later, Sarge said, "I hope you can make it stick, Randy. The kid's angry and is throwing blame everywhere. That always scares me."

"I suppose he'll hate me for the rest of my life, but if I can help him before it's too late, it will be worth it." Randy paused for a moment, then he scowled again and said, "To think that Darcy was with him earlier. The Albright kid told me all about what happened. He's pretty shook up. He even admitted to getting the beer. He said that Shad hadn't drank very much at a time until tonight. He said it was all his fault. Maybe that was his own beer talking, but he seemed pretty remorseful.

"He even said they saw that cow in plenty of time, but Shad was going to shoot right on by it! Well, I am glad they weren't hurt worse than they are. Maybe this will put an end to their drinking," Randy concluded.

"I wish I could believe that," Sarge said as the two men left the hospital together. "How long will they be in here?"

"Only a day or so, the doctor thinks. I'll be referring Shad into Juvenile Court as soon as he is released. If I can't get him for DUI, I will charge him for reckless driving. I'll have the blood test by sometime tomorrow, and I really will miss my guess if he isn't quite a bit over the limit," Randy said solemnly as the officers parted. "Todd told me that Shad had downed over six cans in less than two hours!"

# Chapter Three

SHARON FELDING WIPED her hands on her apron as she hurried to answer the door. "I wonder who that could be on a Saturday morning," she mumbled to Darcy as she reached for the knob.

"Why Randy, what are you doing in uniform this morning? I thought you worked last night. Nate said he saw you pass by on the highway with your lights and siren going. Was there a bad wreck out there somewhere? Nate said he watched an ambulance pass, too."

"I'm afraid there was, Sharon. That's why I'm working this morning. It got dark before I finished all my measurements. I had to calculate the speed of the pickup that wrecked just a couple or three miles up the highway," Randy explained.

"Hi, Randy," Darcy said, looking up from her homework. "Was it anyone we know?"

"I'm afraid so, Darcy. I'm sorry," Randy said.

The way Randy spoke made the blood drain from Darcy's face. "Was it Shad?" she asked in a shaking voice.

"I'm afraid so. He hit a cow up by Jim Burrows' place, a big Hereford."

"Oh, so it wasn't his fault," she said, relieved. "He was so mad when I made him bring me home that I was...well, worried. Especially after I called Coach Starr and found out he'd lied to me about why he didn't play yesterday. Is...is he hurt badly?"

"He was hurt, but it could have been a lot worse. He has a broken arm and some cuts and bruises, but he'll be all right. The wreck was his fault, though. It was very much his fault. The cow was on the road, and it shouldn't have been, but Shad and Todd both saw it when they were still a quarter-mile off."

"Why didn't they stop and chase it off the road?" she asked, her hands trembling so hard that she had to close her book in order to keep the pages from rattling.

"They had been drinking," he said bluntly, ignoring the tears that instantly wet Darcy's eyes. "Near as I can figure, Shad was driving just over eighty when he finally hit the brakes, and by then it was far too late," Randy said with a touch of indignation.

"Ooh," Darcy moaned. "Coach Starr told me that Shad swore to him that he had only drank that one time and that he promised him it wouldn't happen again. Anyway, I thought it was all Todd Albright's fault."

"Not really, Darcy. Shad made his own decisions. And it has happened more than once. Even Todd admitted that to me. He also admitted that he got the beer for Shad."

"That Todd!" Darcy hissed. "He probably wasn't even hurt."

"Well, considering that the truck rolled two and one-half times and then skidded on its top another hundred and forty feet, he did come out in remarkably good shape," Randy said calmly. "Of course, he was wearing his seat belt. Shad wasn't."

"How bad is Shad's arm?" Darcy asked, fighting to keep from crying.

"It'll heal, but he's through as quarterback. Todd did get a slight concussion, a lot of bruises, and one cracked rib. Probably got that from Shad's head when they were rolling," Randy explained bitterly. "Stupid kids. They could both have been killed."

Randy paused while Darcy wiped her eyes. Then he asked, "Darcy, may I borrow your phone and call the hospital? The lab technician said he'd have the blood alcohol results on Shad by ten."

Darcy's eyes instinctively darted to the clock above the sofa. It was ten-thirty. She sat with her elbows on the table and her head in her hands while Randy made his call. She was scarcely aware of her mother pulling a chair out from the table beside her and sitting down. Darcy's long chestnut hair covered her book, and a smattering of tears streaked her mascara.

She cared for Shad. More than she wanted to admit. And despite his stupidity and lies, she felt terrible about him getting hurt. Now Todd Albright, he was another story. She didn't either like or dislike him; she didn't know him very well. He hadn't been to church for several years, and she never spoke to him at school. But she was angry with him, for it was easy to blame Shad's problems on Todd.

Todd's father was a drunk, and everyone knew it, but that was no excuse for Todd. His mother was a good woman and tried hard, but there was only so much she could do. She wasn't home much because she had to work to support Todd and his father. She'd heard her folks talk about that.

"Well, that settles it," Randy said, interrupting Darcy's brooding thoughts.

"Settles what?" Mrs. Felding asked.

"How I'm going to be charging Shad in Juvenile Court. His blood alcohol level was .11 percent. That's more than enough for DUI. I'll see the county attorney first thing on Monday and have Shad in court within a few days," he said, but he did not sound triumphant.

"And what good will that do?" Darcy asked angrily. "He's hurt and his truck is ruined and he can't play football. Isn't that enough?"

"What's this? A touch of temper? I'm sorry, kid, but it's not enough. If you really care for Shad, and I get the feeling that you do, then you need to understand that the worst thing I could do is overlook what he did. Maybe this will put a stop to his drinking before somebody gets hurt real badly...or killed."

Darcy flushed and came to her feet, brushing the hair from her face. "I suppose you're right," she said. "But he'll be angry with me. And...well...everybody will say it's my fault he's in trouble. If I hadn't made him take me home he would never have been drinking last night." She sniffled and reached for a tissue.

"Nonsense," Randy snorted. "You didn't make him drink, and nobody will blame you for that."

They were both right to a degree and both wrong as well. In church the next day, no one pointed a finger at Darcy, but in school on Monday, several kids were downright rude to her. They were only a small minority, but they taunted Darcy all day long.

Her friends rallied around her, though. The coach even singled her out and said, "I'm proud of you, Darcy, for having the courage to stand up to Shad when he was acting like a darn fool. Maybe you will be the difference for him."

"But you've lost your quarterback," she moaned.

"He was already lost, I'm afraid. I told both Shad and Todd that if I heard of just one more time they'd been drinking they would not play this season. Maybe this will serve as a lesson to the other fellows. If it does, then some good will have come from it."

Darcy felt somewhat better after that, and after school, she even approached her folks about letting her use the car to run into town and visit Shad at the hospital.

"Todd is home, but they had to keep Shad longer than the doctor thought at first. I think I should go see him while he's still there," she said, wondering how he would react to seeing her.

"Darcy," her father said firmly, "I think it would really be best if you just steered clear of Shad after this. After all, he..."

"But Dad, he's my friend," Darcy cut in. "We've had some fun times, and now that he's in trouble, is it right that I just pretend I never knew him, let alone dated him? Oh, he makes me really mad, drinking and all. He knows how I feel about it, and I don't think I'll ever go out with him again," she said. "But he is hurt and maybe I can cheer him up a little. I really am sorry about his accident, and I think that the least I can do is to tell him so."

Kerry put an arm around Darcy's shoulder and gave her an affectionate squeeze. "All right, sweetheart, you go and do that," he said quietly.

"Thank you, Dad," Darcy replied, and she hurried out the door.

The antiseptic smell and somber mood of the hospital nearly caused Darcy to lose her nerve. She was embarrassed to face Shad after the scene she had created when she made him take her home early on Friday evening. But she bolstered her courage and hurried on. Having already asked Randy Shad's room number, she swung quietly past the nurse's station and down the hall.

At the door, Darcy waited for an orderly to come out of the room, then she slipped quietly in. Shad's head was turned toward the far wall, and his broken arm was propped on a pillow, a cast all the way to his shoulder.

She was almost to his bed before he sensed her presence and turned his head. His brown eyes lit up at the sight of her, but he did not smile. She spoke quickly. "Hello, Shad."

"Hi, Darcy. Come to tell me you told me so?" he asked bitterly, the light in his eyes fading quickly.

"No, I just came to see how you're doing. I'm...I'm sorry, Shad," she stammered.

"You mean you're sorry you weren't there when old man Burrows' cow got in the road?"

"Shad, that's not fair. I'm sorry you had a wreck and that you're hurt," she said. "And I'm sorry about your truck."

"Not as sorry as old Burrows will be. Dad's already talked to his lawyer about suing him. The whole thing was his fault, you know."

Darcy felt a mixture of anger and bewilderment at the bitterness and lack of responsibility Shad was exhibiting. Perhaps even more, she was feeling hurt and betrayed, for she had trusted him, liked him...a lot. She tried to shove her feelings aside. She had come to visit with Shad, not to argue. "So, how are you feeling?" she asked awkwardly.

"Not so hot! Look at my throwing arm! The guys won't win any games now. That worthless old man. I can't believe he could do this to me."

"Well, maybe..." Darcy began.

"And that worthless uncle of yours!" Shad interrupted hotly, his voice rising. "I thought he was an okay guy. Boy, was I wrong. He came in today and told me he was sending me to juvenile court! My dad says we'll fight it. His attorney..."

"Shad!" Darcy sharply cut him off this time, her face flushing. "Leave Randy out of this. I didn't come to talk about the trouble you're in. I only came to say that I was sorry you got hurt. Maybe that was a mistake. I..."

Shad interrupted again. "I'd like to leave the ignorant know-it-all cop out of it, all right! He's the one too dumb to see that the whole thing was old man Burrows' fault, not mine."

"Shad Cleverly! You are so...so...stupid!" Darcy suddenly shouted in anger and frustration. "You and your precious beer! Well, it serves you right that you lost your truck and that you were hurt. I was feeling sorry for you, but not anymore." She began to sob in frustration and ran from the room, her face in her hands.

"I should never have gone to see him," she later told her mother. "He's blaming the whole thing on poor old Mr. Burrows and his cow! And on Randy! I hope I never have to speak to him again as long as I live."

❊

"They told me at the nurses' station that Darcy had been here. They said she left in tears, Shad, and for me not to upset you, too," Todd Albright said as he entered Shad's room an hour or so after Darcy had gone.

"Yeah, she was here but left mad. She just had to say that she tried to warn me," Shad lied.

"Did she?" Todd asked doubtfully. "Maybe she was right."

"Right? You were there, Todd! The whole accident was because Mr. Burrows let his cow out on the road."

"Gee, I dunno, Shad. Like you said, I was there, too, and I been thinking about this some. You really should have slowed down when we first saw it," Todd said reflectively.

Shad swore, and his face turned red. He shot Todd a look of genuine disgust. "You sound just like that stupid uncle of Darcy's!"

"Well, maybe Randy's right, Shad. Maybe we shouldn't have..."

"Get out of here!" Shad shouted. "I thought you were my friend. I can't believe this garbage you're talking."

"Sorry, old buddy. I know it's my fault, the beer and all, but like Randy told me, maybe we could both learn something. Think about it. Now, I'll go if you like, but I..."

"No, don't leave. Just knock off the crazy talk, man. So did you get to see Coach Starr?"

"Yeah. I'm off the team. He said you would have been, too, even if your arm hadn't got busted."

"Why that no good…"

"Cut it out, Shad!" Todd interrupted before the profanity started again. "Coach warned us. You can't say he didn't."

"Yeah, but what's a little beer now and then. That never hurt anybody!" Shad shouted.

"Are you saying all these bruises I got don't hurt?" Todd said angrily. "And that you feel just fine? And isn't this a hospital you're in? Come on, Shad, you know darn well that if you hadn't been drinking you could have stopped in plenty of time to avoid hitting that cow."

Shad swore again. "You really aren't my friend, are you?" he asked after his tirade had worn itself out. "You're nothing but a traitor."

"Mr. Albright!" A nurse stormed into the room, making Todd jump. "I distinctly recall telling you not to let our patient get upset. Twice in one evening is not good for him," she scolded.

"I'm sorry. I was just leaving," Todd said meekly.

"Yeah, you do that, you creep," Shad hissed. "And don't come back until you come to your senses. Next thing I know, you'll be running to Darcy's uncle and volunteering to testify against me."

Todd was really angry now. He had spent a long night of soul searching and then he'd had a long talk with his mother and another with Trooper Randy Hutchins. The wreck had scared him badly, giving him a much needed wake-up call. And besides that, he did not want to end up like his father. He had promised his mother just that morning that he'd slit his wrists before he'd ever touch another can of beer.

Todd had come to see Shad with the hope, even the mistaken belief, that his friend would see it like he did. After all, Shad had only recently started drinking, and it was mostly Todd's fault that he had. He had hoped that it would be as easy to convince Shad to quit drinking as it had been to get him started in the first place. He had also carried with him to the hospital the hope that he could help Shad to see that they should both face up to what they had done and take their medicine from the law.

He stopped at the doorway and faced Shad, ignoring the nurse who was still emphatically trying to shoo him from the room. "I'm sorry I ever gave you a can of beer," he said bitterly. "And I'm really sorry you feel like you do. Hutchins is going to give me a ticket for drinking. I'm going to go in and admit what I done, and then I ain't touching another drop of the stuff."

Shad moaned and the nurse stood bouncing from one foot to the other, but she let Todd go on. He said, "You are right about one thing, Shad; if you ain't man enough to admit that we both screwed up, then I just might be there to testify against you!"

Before the nurse could react and Shad could begin another tirade, Todd strode briskly up the hall. Ten minutes later, he found himself shaking in his tennis shoes while knocking on the front door of Darcy Felding's home. When the door swung open, he found himself face to face with the pretty girl he had so often referred to as Miss Prim-and-Proper!

He did not call her that now, or even consider it. For a dreadfully long moment, he didn't call her anything, just stared at her startling green, red-rimmed eyes and flowing chestnut hair. When he finally found his elusive voice, he called her by her name. "Darcy, can I talk to…to…you?" he stuttered.

For a moment she just frowned, and Todd almost turned and fled. At last she said indignantly, "I'm not sure we have anything to talk about, Todd Albright!"

"Please," he said with downcast eyes, taking hold of the door frame to keep himself from bolting. "There's something I just gotta' say."

"Well…a…sure, Todd. Come in, I guess," she said in a softer, puzzled tone.

But she had not even closed the door behind him before she swung to face him. "Did Shad send you?" she asked resentfully.

"Oh, no, Darcy! He don't even know I was coming," he said. Then before his courage gave way, he blurted, "I came to say I'm sorry."

Darcy had to search for her suddenly elusive voice. To ease her embarrassment, Todd turned and closed the door quietly behind himself while she propped up her sagging chin. Then he forged on. "I been really stupid," he said, noticing, as he spoke, her little brother peering through a doorway across the room.

Darcy noticed it, too, and found her voice in a huff. "Nate Felding! You get out of here this instant! Can't you see that Todd and I are trying to talk?"

As quietly as he had appeared, the little fellow vanished, and Darcy signaled Todd toward a spot on the sofa. "Sit down, Todd," she said with a voice that wavered with uncertainty. "I'm sorry I jumped to that conclusion. It's just that when I visited Shad a little while ago, he was not very pleasant."

"I know," Todd said, sitting as close to the exact spot Darcy had indicated as he possibly could. "I just got run off, too!"

"You did? By Shad? But I thought you two were friends now," she said with a trace of bitterness as she lowered herself to the sofa so close to Todd that he felt uncomfortable and eased farther away. With a jolt, it occurred to him why Shad was so crazy about her. She was gorgeous! And that scared him half out of his wits. Todd had dated very little, and now…

"How could he do that to you?" she asked when he failed to answer. "Or is he mad at you because you got him the beer? If he is, I don't blame him."

He slid over again before saying in a voice that grated with fear, "I wish he was mad at me for that, but he's not. He's mad because...because..."

"Because?" Darcy pressed.

Todd had a hard time looking into those beautiful green eyes. But he finally managed to meet her penetrating gaze and say in one long breath, "Because I told him I shouldn't have ever got him any beer and that I thought we shouldn't drink anymore, and because I said the wreck was our fault." Then, as Darcy's red-rimmed but magnetic green eyes managed to hold his gaze, he recounted for her his recent argument with Shad. He did not leave out a single thing. He even told her about his talk with Randy and his pledge to his mother not to drink again.

As he finished, Darcy's eyes, those stunning, bright green eyes, misted over with tears and she said in a voice so sweet that he thought he'd fall off the sofa, "Do you really mean it, Todd? You will never drink again?"

"Course I mean it," he said. "And that's partly why I came to see you. This whole thing is my fault. I gave Shad that beer Friday night. I got it from my dad, and I'm awfully sorry. It was a stupid, dumb, terrible thing for me to do, especially when I knew he was dating the prettiest...I mean...well, you know, that he was dating you. I shouldn't a been so darn thickheaded, I guess. But Darcy, when we hit that cow, and Shad's truck started to roll, I thought I was a goner for sure!"

"Oh, Todd, how horrible that must have been for you," she said sympathetically. She reached out and put a hand on his knee. And those eyes...

"Yeah," he said, thinking he ought to move over some more, but his back had already bumped up against the arm of the sofa. "It was pretty bad, all right. I didn't know if I'd ever get out of that truck. And from what I hear, if it hadn't been for that trooper..."

"You mean Randy?"

"Yeah, your uncle. If it hadn't been for him, I might of got my neck broke. Could of still got killed. But anyway, I don't wanna die, and I been thinking what a dumb bugger I been. I been thinking about lots 'a things."

He paused and Darcy asked, "What have you been thinking about, Todd?"

He didn't think she'd slid any closer, but he sure felt trapped. Not that it was entirely unpleasant, just something new and very awkward for him. "Well, I been thinking about drinking and stuff."

"What kind of stuff?"

Todd could swear that Darcy never once blinked those pretty eyes of hers. She just kept looking into his, and he began to wonder if she could see clear into the middle of that not-too-smart brain of his and read every thought he was having. "Oh, you know, stuff like church," he said, finally managing to tear his eyes away from her before she figured out everything he had stored between his fiercely burning ears.

"I haven't seen you at church for a long time, Todd," Darcy said, removing her hand from his knee and folding her arms.

"Been over four years since I was there. I'm still just a deacon," he admitted, suddenly noticing his hands which were wringing each other like a wet rag. He sought for a place to put them without touching Darcy. That would be too embarrassing. He finally managed to put them both near his belt. He stared at them as he added, "And now I messed Shad up. I'm sorry Darcy. I'm just no good."

When he looked up again, Darcy was smiling at him, and he honestly couldn't remember ever seeing a prettier sight. He flushed and his already burning ears and face felt like they were being attacked by an acetylene torch.

"You're a good guy," she said softly. "I think it takes a lot of guts to admit that what you did was wrong. Now if Shad will just..."

Her voice trailed off, and Todd said, "I want to help him. I owe him that and a lot more. But I don't know what to do. He won't even listen to me."

"I don't know either," she said. Then for a long time it was silent. Finally, Darcy spoke again. "They split the ward a year ago, Todd, but I'm pretty sure you're still in the same one as us. My dad's in the bishopric and has to go early on Sunday mornings. But when Mom and Nate and I go, we could pick you up—if you don't mind being seen with me, that is. A lot of the kids are really down on me right now and..."

"Oh, no, Darcy. I mean, yes. I mean most of the kids think it was good what you did. I'm the one that caused all the trouble. I don't think you should be seen with me, but...but..." he stammered, suddenly all confused.

"Sacrament Meeting is at nine," Darcy persisted firmly. "We'll pick you up on Sunday at quarter to."

"Oh, Darcy, you don't have to do that. I was thinking about going anyway," he said awkwardly.

"Good. It's settled then," she smiled.

Todd rose stiffly to his feet. "Thanks Darcy, for understanding. I've been a real jerk, I know. You're okay. So we're friends, then?"

"Friends," she said.

"Shad will be madder than ever," he added. "And I don't want him to think...well, you know, he don't like nobody..."

"I will be friends with whomever I like, Todd," Darcy broke in sharply. "And Shad has nothing to say about it. Nothing at all. He and I are through. And I won't change my mind about that."

Tears rolled freely down her cheeks, and Todd couldn't think of another thing to say. So he left, wondering if all that had just occurred was real, or if it was just the effects of that concussion he had suffered in the wreck.

# Chapter Four

IT WAS A COOL, overcast night. The half-moon played peek-a-boo with Randy's Crown Victoria as he cruised a lonely stretch of highway about twenty miles south of town. It had been an uneventful shift, and drowsiness was tugging lightly at his eyelids.

Randy pulled off the road and unwound his lanky frame from the cramped confines of his patrol car. For several minutes, he stretched and walked around, soaking up the still, cool beauty of the night. The air was saturated with the pleasant aroma of impending rain, and he inhaled deeply. The drowsiness fled and, refreshed and alert, Randy again tucked himself behind the wheel, put the big Ford in gear, and headed north.

It was well after midnight when he pulled into town. The only other car on Main Street was Sarge's blue patrol car. Randy whipped into the lot beside the Texaco and, a moment later, Sarge joined him.

"Howdy, Randy. Are you as bored tonight as I am?" Sarge asked with a sleepy grin.

"Yes, and loving it," Randy answered. "Haven't wrestled with a single drunk all night. Sometimes it just feels good to have a real quiet shift. After last Friday night, I could use a few."

"I can relate to that. Hey, speaking of drunks, how's the Cleverly kid doing?"

"Okay, but he's sure mad. So's his dad. Say's he'll sue Mr. Burrows and get every dime the old man has to his name. He'll have a hard time, though, because the cow he hit was not branded, and Burrows says it's not his." Randy allowed himself a smug smile. "And I can't prove anything different. Neither can Cleverly or his lawyer."

"It was along there by his place, wasn't it?" Sarge asked.

"Yes, but like I said, it had no brand. I even had a state brand inspector come take a look at her. He said it could be anyone's cow. Could have come from ten, fifteen miles away for all we know."

"But if it doesn't belong to Burrows, couldn't it be one of his neighbors that owns it? Surely you have some idea who the owner is."

"I don't have the foggiest, Sarge. And I really did make an effort to find out. I talked to every farmer within five miles of the accident. Nobody claims it."

"Well, I guess that's to be expected. Bill Cleverly can be plenty nasty when he wants. If I were old Burrows and it was my cow, I'd surely never admit it. So how does Cleverly plan to sue if ownership can't be established?"

Randy shrugged. "He won't get anywhere, that's for sure. I just wish he wouldn't back his kid like he is on this thing. Seems to me like the only thing that's come from his reaction so far is an attitude on Shad's part that it's okay to drink...and drive."

Sarge smiled. "I know you're right, Randy. No question about it, but wait until your boys are older. It's the most natural thing in the world for a parent to run to the defense of a child in trouble. Believe me, it really is. So don't be too hard on Bill. His storming around may be misguided, but I do believe he loves his kid and thinks he's doing what's best for him."

"Yeah, I suppose you're right, Sarge, but I can see him heading Shad in the wrong direction. All I want is to see the kid straighten up."

"So do we all, including his father," Sarge said.

"But think how we'll all feel if he backs the kid to the point that it gets someone hurt seriously or even killed some day. I wonder how Bill Cleverly would handle that?"

"I hope we never have to find out, Randy. Maybe Shad will follow his buddy's example and straighten up. It really surprises me, but I hear the Albright kid's got a whole different outlook now," Sarge said.

"It's really quite amazing. He even agreed that he would testify against Shad. I don't think they'll be friends anymore after that, though. Darcy was telling me that Todd came by last night. Shad had just cussed him out at the hospital and ordered him out of his room," Randy said, shaking his head. "I guess that at least it will be tougher for Shad to get beer now, because Todd said he won't be getting any more for him."

"Good, although if he wants it badly enough, someone will help him out. Speaking of your niece, how's she taking this whole thing?"

"She's upset, and she's mad. Even if Shad makes a turnaround, I don't think she'll have much to do with him again. Shad was pretty rough on her at the hospital."

"She went to see him?" Sarge asked, a little surprised.

"She really had a thing for him," Randy said. "But Shad finished that off. And I can't say I'm sorry. She's one fine girl, and she doesn't deserve to be treated like Shad treated her."

"How are the other kids taking it. I mean, is Darcy getting blamed?"

"By a few, I suppose, but most of the kids know that Shad messed up. And Darcy is a popular girl. She's smart and pretty. I'll tell you what, if I ever have a daughter, I hope she'll be just like Darcy."

Sarge grinned. "Not a little prejudiced, are you?"

"Well, yeah, I suppose I am, but..."

"I know, Randy," Sarge interrupted. "She really is a good gal. And pretty, too. My, I can see why that Cleverly kid was so taken by her." He chuckled.

❉

"See ya, Darcy," Jill, her best friend, said as Darcy prepared to board the bus after school on Friday. "See you at the game later?"

"No, I don't think so. I've got a ton to do," Darcy said evasively.

"I don't blame you," Jill said with understanding.

Darcy managed a grin at the pert redhead as she stepped through the bus door.

Darcy worked her way toward the back of the bus. A whimper drew her attention when she was only about half-way there. Turning her head, she spotted Nate, hunched over and crying. He was facing the side of the bus, his little body trembling.

She quickly slipped into the seat beside him. "Nate, what are you bawling about?" she asked impatiently. But when he turned toward her, she exclaimed, "Oh, no!"

The front of his shirt was bloody, and his nose was red and swollen. One eye was nearly shut, and a shiny blue circle about the size of a silver dollar was threatening to close it the rest of the way.

"Nate, what happened to you?" Darcy asked in alarm, dropping her books on the seat and putting an arm around his shaking shoulders.

"B...B...Billy..." he stuttered, and a fountain of tears gushed from his eyes, creating tiny pink rivulets down his bloody face.

"Billy Cleverly?" Darcy asked as she pulled her brother's head against her chest, oblivious to the stains being transmitted to her light green blouse.

"Y...y...yes."

"Did you get in a fight with him?" Darcy asked as she stroked his wavy brown hair.

The bus came to life and lurched into the street. One of Darcy's books slipped to the floor. As she bent to pick it up, Nate mumbled something unintelligible that she took for a yes.

"Why, Nate? Why did you fight Billy? You know what Dad and Mom think about you getting into fights at school," Darcy said with just enough sternness in her voice to turn up the tap on his tears. Her blouse was ruined!

"I h...h...had...to," he said as he sobbed, his little body shaking like a leaf in the wind.

"Why?" Darcy pried.

"Cause...cause he...he said...you was a s...s...slud!"

Darcy chuckled in spite of herself, but Nate seemed not to notice. "You aren't a...a slud, are ya, Darcy?"

"I don't know. I hope not. Sounds pretty bad." She chuckled, then said, "Are you sure that's what he said, or did he call me a slut?"

"Maybe. I dunno. I never heard it...before." The flow of tears slowed down and his little head lifted. "Darcy, what is a slut?"

"A bad girl," Darcy said simply.

"See, I told ya. I had to fight Billy. You're not a bad girl, Darcy. You're my sister, the best sister in the whole world."

Tears stung her eyes. She wasn't always as good to Nate as she should be, and here he was, bleeding and in pain from defending her honor. It was more than she deserved. "Thanks, Nate," she said softly. "I'm glad that I'm your sister. You're a pretty good brother, too."

Nate relaxed and the trembling of his limbs stilled. As they rode on, the two of them were silent amidst a chorus of laughter and chattering throughout the bus. Darcy felt badly, both that her own troubles had spilled over onto her little brother, and that Shad's brother would say such an awful thing about her. It did not take much imagination to figure where Billy got such a perverted idea as that. She wondered if she had ever really known Shad.

A few minutes later, as Darcy and Nate slowly walked up the lane, Nate confirmed what she had thought. "Billy said you was a slut, and he said he knew it was true cause Shad told him."

"Oh, he did, huh?" she murmured thoughtfully.

"Yup, and so I said Shad was a liar. That's when Billy punched me. So I had to hit him back and..."

"And you are both probably pretty sore all over," she interjected.

"But he got me the worst. I'm not nearly as big as Billy." That thought brought fresh tears, and Darcy put an arm around his shoulders.

"It's okay, Nate. I'm proud of you."

"Why? I'm not supposed to fight."

"I'm proud of you for being so brave and sticking up for me. But you don't have to do that again. You remember the little saying about words, don't you?"

"No."

"'Sticks and stones might break my bones, but words will never hurt me,'" she quoted. "Just remember that, and you won't have to fight anyone after this."

"Okay," he mumbled. Nate was thoughtful for a moment, then he asked, "Will I be in trouble with Mom and Dad? Billy hit me first."

"I know he did."

"And I didn't fight during school. It was after school while I was waiting for the bus to come."

"I think they'll understand, especially if you promise not to get in any more fights, even if someone says something awful. Okay?"

"All right, Darcy," Nate agreed with some reluctance.

A trip to the doctor resulted in a huge white splint over Nate's broken nose. The pain he was feeling when his father came in from chopping corn was more than sufficient reason to make him give a hard and fast promise to drop out of the elementary school fighting circuit.

By the time Randy dropped in with his boys the next day, Nate's right eye was swollen shut. "Gee whiz, Nate," Randy said with a twinkle in his eye, "if I didn't know better, I'd think you must of tangled with one of your dad's prize bulls."

"Nope, just with Billy Cleverly," Nate reported with a painful grin. Then once again he got to tell his story.

A short time later, he overheard Randy and Darcy talking. Randy said, "I just can't understand why Shad's so busy blaming everyone but himself for his troubles. You certainly aren't to blame at all."

"It's okay," Darcy said.

"It is not okay!" Randy argued. "It is not fair to you. And that little guy in there, why he's just like one of my own sons. And he's been hurt just because that darn Shad Cleverly is too stubborn to admit he made a mistake and quit laying the blame on others."

Nate swelled in spite of his hurts. He really did love his Uncle Randy. And right then and there Nate decided that when he was grown, completed a mission, and was out of college, he was going to be a policeman, just like Randy Hutchins!

✳

Sunday morning blew in with a stiff breeze and a hard rain storm.

The air was cool, and Mrs. Felding put another blanket over Nate. "I'm going to stay home with him today, Darcy. Sister Rayborne is going to take my class for me," she explained after coming out of Nate's bedroom.

"So I have to pick up Todd by myself?" Darcy asked, slightly alarmed.

"Yes, dear, but I'm sure he won't mind," Sharon answered with a grin.

"I suppose not, but he is rather shy, and I don't want to embarrass him," Darcy said.

She could imagine tongues wagging and eyeballs popping when she walked into sacrament meeting with Todd Albright. Actually, it would be sort of funny in a way, she decided and smiled. "Hey, where's Nate and your mom?" Todd asked when he jumped from the pouring rain into the Felding's old Ford.

It took Darcy all the way to the chapel to explain about Nate's fight and what led up to it. Some of Todd's shyness was swallowed up in his indignation over Shad's behavior, and he kept interrupting her story. "He called you a slut?" he asked at one point. "That really makes me mad! I could just about break his other arm!"

"He'll get over it, Todd," Darcy said, but his anger dissipated only when he walked beside Darcy into the chapel a few minutes later.

Darcy had slipped her arm through his and favored him with a reassuring smile when she felt him tense. She was a bit nervous herself as nearly every eye in the place turned on them. Then it seemed that everyone suddenly had the urge to visit. She was positive, as she was afraid Todd was, that they were the main topic of all the frantic whispering.

Darcy automatically headed for the place where her family usually sat during sacrament meeting. After sliding into the fourth pew from the back on the right side of the chapel, Todd leaned toward her. "I don't think this was such a good idea, Darcy."

"Don't be silly," she replied cheerfully, feeling anything but cheerful at the moment.

"But people will say things about you, Darcy. You shouldn't be seen with me."

"Why not?" she interrupted firmly. "We are friends. Remember, we agreed."

Randy, Sandy, and the Randy Hutchins look-alikes entered the chapel from the far door. Just then, Darcy saw them and succeeded in catching Randy's eye. He smiled, pointed her out to Sandy, and led the way across the back and up to their pew.

Darcy slid toward the wall and Todd followed. Randy entered ahead of his family and sat next to Todd. "Hello, Todd," he said, offering his hand.

They shook and Todd cleared his throat before saying, "Hello,

Trooper Hutchins."

"Randy's my name," Randy said firmly, but he accompanied his words with a friendly smile before shifting his gaze to Darcy. "Hi, Darcy. How's Nate this morning?"

"He's still pretty sore, but he'll be all right. Mom kept him home in bed today."

"That splint affair on his nose won't be there too long, and the swelling in his eye will soon go down," Randy whispered. "I suspect that's most of his problem."

Just then the bishopric walked in. Bishop Mark Olsen started up the steps to the stand, looking down over the slowly gathering congregation as he did so. He caught sight of Todd and Darcy, reversed direction quickly, and strode toward them. Darcy felt Todd shrinking as the bishop entered the empty pew in front of them. Darcy was grateful to him when he did not go straight to Todd. That would have been just too obvious. Instead, he shook hands with Scotty and Jeremy, taking time to fuss over how big they were getting and how handsome they were. Then he shook hands with both Sandy and Randy. Finally, with a big smile on his weathered face, he extended a calloused hand to Todd. Todd reached out tentatively and Bishop Olsen pumped firmly. "It's nice to see you, Todd," he said, then he turned his smile on Darcy. "Your dad told me about Nate's little scrape. He's tough. He'll be fine."

Darcy agreed, and then Bishop Olsen turned back to Todd. "Are you planning to stay for all the meetings, Todd?"

When Todd hesitated and looked toward Darcy, she answered for him. "Of course, but we were wondering about priesthood meeting," she said perceptively.

Todd nodded his agreement and she knew she had guessed right. Bishop Olsen understood his concern without it being spelled out for him and said quickly, "You can just come into the priests' quorum with me and the fellows your age."

"But...a...I'm only a teacher," Todd stammered.

"That doesn't matter. That's not a permanent thing anyway. You just come with me after opening exercises of priesthood meeting," he said with a warm smile and moved away, searching for more hands to shake.

A moment later, Darcy looked toward the far back door, but she didn't look for long. Shad was seated with his family on the back row, and he was glaring at her. "What's the matter, Darcy?" Todd asked, turning to look where Darcy just had.

He wasn't long in turning back either. "Oh, no!" he exclaimed. "Shad is really mad!"

"Too bad," Darcy said, leaning toward him. "That's his problem. I'm not exactly happy with him right now."

"Me either," Todd agreed.

Darcy looked toward the stand. Bishop Olsen was just walking up the steps to join her father and Brother Samson behind the pulpit. Bishop Olsen was a short, stocky man of about forty. An unruly shock of greying black hair contrasted sharply with his neat pin-stripe blue suit. His face was heavily tanned and bore an almost constant smile.

Like her own father, Bishop Olsen was a farmer. He lived two miles beyond the Burrows place, four miles east of the Felding farm. She wondered how he managed to get everything done. Besides milking about sixty head of Holstein cows, farming a sprawling 250 acres and being Bishop, he was also the father of seven very active children between the ages of two and fifteen.

Darcy could not think of a better man to give Todd the support he needed right now than Bishop Olsen, and she was glad. Of course, he would also do anything he could for Shad, if Shad would let him. Maybe he eventually would, Darcy thought hopefully. She feared that if someone was not able to do something for him, he would really louse up his life, and who knows how many others'!

But not hers. She had learned her lesson. She would like to be his friend, but no more than that. She stole a quick glance back at Shad again. His eyes were on the floor, his face dark and brooding. Regret stung her. Why did he have to turn into such a jerk? she wondered with pain in her heart. She really had liked him. Still did...in a way.

Darcy's father stood to conduct the meeting. While he waited for the organist to finish playing, he smiled down at Darcy. What a great dad, she thought. Why couldn't Shad be like him?

# Chapter Five

DARCY MET TODD in the foyer when priesthood meeting and young women's ended. He was smiling and looking at ease. Several of the boys his age were chatting with him. Darcy's friends joined them and soon he was laughing along with the rest of them.

Billy Cleverly pranced up to them and said, "Darcy."

She turned away from the other kids and responded, "Why, hi Billy."

She was shocked at the anger in his bright eyes and the tightness of his features but tried not to show it. He bore a few minor marks of the scrape with Nate but nothing that amounted to much. Billy was a year behind in school and nearly two years older than Nate who was young in his class. Billy was a big, strong kid for his age. As Darcy looked at him, wondering what he was about to say, she was almost overwhelmed that little Nate had shown the courage to stand up to him.

"Slut!" he suddenly said so loudly that all the kids turned in surprise.

Without another word, he tried to make a hurried exit, but he had overlooked one rather formidable obstacle: his mother!

"Billy Cleverly!" she exclaimed, her face burning as she latched onto his arm with a fist of steel. "Whatever made you say such a horrible thing to Darcy? Now you tell her you're sorry," she said, the shock at Billy's behavior betrayed by her trembling voice.

"For what?" Billy asked belligerently. "I just called her what Shad says she is."

Sister Cleverly's face turned still a deeper shade of scarlet, and Darcy's heart went out to her. She was a good woman who had married a very stubborn man. Her eyes filled with pain and her shoulders slumped visibly.

"Darcy," she said, almost in tears, "I am so very sorry. I don't know what has come over Billy. It's Shad's influence, I guess. But there is no excuse for what Billy said to you. I just don't know what I'm going to do." Turning to her youngest son, she said firmly, "Now, Billy, you tell Darcy you're sorry, and you do it right now."

Billy mumbled something that seemed to satisfy his mother, although Darcy had no idea what he said. Then the boy fled. Sister Cleverly, with misty eyes, said, "And please tell Nate that we're sorry. Is he going to be all right?"

"Yes, of course," Darcy said, suddenly aware that all other talk in the entire foyer had ceased, and everyone was watching her and Sister Cleverly.

"Well, if there's anything I can do..." Shad's mother said, but she let the rest of her offer go unstated.

"Oh, no, Sister Cleverly. Nate is fine. He shouldn't have been fighting anyway. But thank you for your concern. How is Shad feeling?" Darcy asked, but then wished she hadn't, for the look of abject misery that clouded Sister Cleverly's face was heart-wrenching.

When she spoke to Darcy again, her voice was breaking. "He feels better, I think. I just wish..." Her voice broke and, without another word, she turned and hurried from the church into the pouring rain outside.

For a long moment the foyer was silent. Darcy and Todd both stared at the closing door, too shocked and upset to speak. Darcy had not seen Shad since sacrament meeting. She wondered if he had gone home. She didn't wonder for long.

Shad hit the door like a runaway train. He swung it open with his good arm and stalked up to Darcy, his face black with anger. "You..." he hissed. "Just can't let things alone, can you?"

Darcy gasped and felt the blood drain from her head. Todd stepped closer and grasped her arm, steadying her. Everyone else moved back nervously.

"I...I...don't know what you mean," she stammered.

"Don't deny it," Shad said, his voice rising. "I don't know exactly what you said to Mom and Billy, but it was so awful that you have them both in tears. I hope you're proud of yourself, you little slut!"

"Shad, I didn't do anything, honest. I only said hi to Billy, and he called me..."

"Liar!" Shad interrupted. "Wow, your true colors are sure coming out. And I thought I knew you. Well, all I can say is, you better leave my family alone," he threatened.

"Shad, you cut it out!" Todd said menacingly. "You've got it all wrong. Darcy didn't say one unkind word..."

"Stay out of this, Todd. You are such a jerk," Shad interrupted hotly.

"Hey, this is the church house, Shad. Why don't you just knock it off?"

"Shut up, Todd."

"Come on, Darcy," Todd said, taking her firmly by the hand. "You don't have to listen to this."

Todd led her away by the route of least resistance which was up the hallway. Shad, rain still dripping from his hair, stood and glared at them as they left. Darcy feared that he would follow, but he did not.

The rain was still pouring outside, and Darcy and Todd were both drenched by the time they reached the Felding's Ford and jumped in. Darcy was in tears, and Todd was boiling mad. "I can't believe it. I just can't believe it!" Todd exclaimed. "I've been a jerk, but this Shad is just too much!"

Darcy sniffled and dug in her purse for a tissue. She wiped her eyes and nose. Todd put a hand on her wet arm. "I'm sorry, Darcy. This is all my fault. I should never have gone to church with you. It was all a big mistake."

Darcy turned her green eyes on him and said firmly, "That's not true, Todd. What's past is past. Please, don't let the way Shad's acting stop you from doing what's right."

"But this is all so unfair to you," he moaned.

"It's okay, Todd," she said solemnly. "I just don't want it to upset you." She hesitated, then she said, "Thanks for coming with me today."

"Well, I don't know if I should of done it. It surely upset Shad."

"Actually, I think Shad is upset with Shad. I don't believe that what either you or I did has much to do with his anger. He's basically a selfish guy, and I think that he's more upset over losing his truck and breaking his throwing arm than anything else."

"I guess, but I could punch his lights out for the way he talked to..."

Darcy cut Todd off with a wave of her hand. "He didn't mean it. Maybe we can help him, Todd," she suggested, fumbling in her purse for the keys to the car.

Todd was silent while Darcy started the engine. She cast a sidelong glance at him. He was staring at her as if dumb-struck. She smiled. "He's our friend, Todd. Surely this thing will blow over. We can't just give up on him, can we?"

Todd slowly shook his head, and Darcy watched the anger fade. Then, without another word, she pulled out of the parking space and away from the church.

When Todd finally spoke, he said, "You are really something, Darcy. Can't you see what a rotten guy Shad is turning into?"

She glanced over at him quickly, then back at the rain-slick road. "He'll get over it, Todd. Part of this is my fault. I probably handled it all wrong. I was so mad that I even said I'd never talk to Shad again, but that's wrong. I've been thinking a lot about it. It's only me it will hurt."

"Darcy, I been a real jerk for a long time. I guess I ran around with jerks, too. I just never saw nobody who could talk good about somebody that hurt them," Todd said in subdued tones.

"So, how about it then? Should we try to be friends with Shad again?" she asked, casting him another sidelong glance and a bright smile.

"Sure. What the heck. I really didn't want to bust his other arm very much, anyway," he said with a grin. "But I ain't drinking with him again."

"And I'm not dating him anymore...I think," Darcy said softly.

After school the next day, Darcy busied herself in the kitchen. Nate, who had stayed home from school that day, entered, his battered eight-year-old face plastered with a king-size grin. "Making cookies, Darcy?" he asked.

"I am, Nate," she responded with an affectionate smile.

"Who they for?" he asked hopefully.

"Well, I suppose if I make a great big batch that there will be enough for several people."

Nate's face grew serious. "Am I one of them?" he asked.

"Of course, Nate. Have you ever known of a batch of cookies being baked in this house without you getting some?"

Nate grinned. "I love cookies," he said. "Thanks Darcy. But who are the rest of 'em for?"

"Well, let's see now. I might want a couple of them myself." He nodded in agreement as she spoke. "And I know Dad will want some, and so will Mom," she went on, wrinkling her brow thoughtfully.

"That all?"

"No."

"Who else then?" he asked, his battered face suddenly showing signs of concern that the cookies were going to be spread far too thin to suit his taste.

"Shad and Billy," Darcy answered softly, without looking at her little brother.

"What!? Darcy, that's dumb! They don't deserve any cookies. If they want some, their mom can make them," he protested.

Darcy did not look up, but she knew from the tone of Nate's voice that he was convinced she was slipping over the edge. "Would you get the salt for me, Nate? If you'll help, I can tell Shad and Billy that they're from both of us," she suggested, ignoring his protest.

"Why would I want to do that?" he asked indignantly.

Darcy finally looked at him again. His face bore a look that told her he was now convinced that she had gone bananas. He stood with his little hands on his hips, and his feet were spread wide apart like he was ready to fight. "Please, Nate," she pleaded.

"I don't wanna do nuthin for Shad or Billy," he said firmly.

"Nate, is that any way to feel? Would Jesus have felt that way?"

Nate did not speak a word, and Darcy let him think for a moment. Then she said, "I'm awful mad at those guys, Nate. But I've done a lot of thinking. We can't hate them. In fact, Jesus said to love those who despitefully use you."

"What's that mean?" he asked in a huff.

"That means that we should do nice things for people who say mean things about us or do things to us that hurt," she explained. "Even if we don't want to."

The scowl Nate had been harboring slowly left his face as he pondered her words. She went back to work, and after a moment he got the salt canister for her. "Here, I wanna help then, but are you sure Jesus meant we had to make cookies for Shad and Billy?" he asked skeptically.

"He meant that we should do something nice for them, and this was the only thing I could think of."

"Well, okay," he said, "but we don't have to give them very many, do we?"

"Would Jesus be stingy?" she asked with a grin.

"Well, no, I guess not."

"That's right, Nate. So how many should we give Billy and Shad?" she asked as she measured the salt.

It took a minute for him to come up with an answer. When he finally spoke, she could tell that it was costing him a lot of mental effort. "Half of em?" he asked tentatively.

"Why, Nate, I think that would be just fine. Will you get two cookie sheets for me, please, and set them on the table? Then you can start putting the salt, sugar and flour away," she suggested.

Nate, with the sticky issue of how many cookies to share with those who had been mean all settled, pitched in cheerfully.

After helping her mother with supper dishes a couple of hours later, Darcy prepared a large plate of the newly baked and cooled cookies. Nate was right there to supervise and seemed satisfied that she hadn't carried her act of charity too far.

"Do you want to come, Nate?" she offered.

"Naw. You take 'em," he said generously, subconsciously touching the badly swollen eye as if remembering how it had come about and at whose hands.

"All right, but I'll tell them you helped me make them."

"Okay. See ya later," he said.

Despite her good intentions, Darcy felt a pang of fear and a weakening of her resolve as she left the farm lane and drove toward town. What if Shad refused the cookies? she wondered anxiously. Then she'd just give them to someone else. Maybe Randy's family...or Todd.

She wished Todd was coming with her to provide moral support. She could use that right now, but he had said that he just couldn't. He was going to have to testify against Shad, so his gestures of goodwill would have to wait a few weeks, he decided. She really couldn't blame him. Maybe she was being foolish and...

The sharp wail of a siren jerked Darcy out of her reverie, and a glance in the rear-view mirror made her jump. A patrol car with its bar of red and blue lights flashing was right behind her. Instinctively, her foot came off the accelerator, and she glanced at the speedometer. It was reading just over forty.

Her eyes darted to the mirror again as the car slowed. She took a longer look this time. Randy's grinning face eased her anxiety, and she pulled over and stopped.

"I wasn't speeding," she protested in mock severity as he approached the car and she stepped out.

"I know. You were going too slow—impeding traffic," he said, trying to look stern but doing a poor job of it.

"Impeding traffic? Yours is the first car I even saw after leaving the house."

"I'm traffic, too," he said with a wide grin. "I saw you and thought I'd see how Nate's doing."

"While everyone who passes thinks I'm getting a ticket?" she said, tossing her head. Then she grinned, too, and said, "Nate's feeling better. The swelling in his eye has gone down enough that he can see a little."

"Good. Is he going to school tomorrow?"

"I doubt it."

"Then maybe the boys and I will swing by and take him a little something to help him forget his troubles."

"He'd like that, Randy."

"I hope. He's a great kid. Hey, where are you headed, anyway? To the store?"

"No," she replied hesitantly.

Randy picked up on her hesitation, grinned, and said, "Must be going to see some lucky young man."

Darcy shifted her feet uncomfortably, then, with downcast eyes, she mumbled, "I was just taking Shad and Billy some cookies." Randy was silent and she looked up. He appeared dumbstruck. Before he was able to think of something to say, she added, "Nate and I baked them. Here, let me get you a couple."

Darcy felt Randy's searching eyes on her back as she moved to the door of the old Ford and reached in. She fumbled for a moment with the thin covering until she was able to retrieve two cookies. She carried them back to Randy who accepted them with a mumbled, "Thanks."

Randy took a bite, then his face lit up. "They'll like these," he said. He took another bite, all the while studying Darcy thoughtfully. Finally, he asked, "Peace offering?"

"Sort of, I guess," she answered. "I just thought maybe I should."

"Be careful, Darcy," he warned. "First thing you know…"

Darcy broke in with a touch of anger. "Don't get this wrong, Randy. I'll never go out with Shad again, but I don't want him to think I hate him. I would like to still be his friend."

Still shaking his head, Randy said, "Sorry. A fellow could learn a lot about living a Christ-like life by hanging around you, kid." Then she found herself in a quick, firm embrace. "I'm right proud to be your uncle," he said as he released her. "Now, off you go on your mission of mercy before someone passes and thinks I'm attacking a good-looking motorist. I'll see you later, Darcy."

"Thanks, Randy," she said. "I'm sorry I got huffy. This hasn't been easy for me."

"You gave me the cookies and taught me a lesson. I should be thanking you, and I do. The cookies are delicious."

"You'd say that even if I mixed up the sugar and salt like I did when I was five. Do you remember that?" she asked with a laugh.

Randy chuckled, "How could I ever forget? I thought you were trying to poison me. They were awful."

"You didn't say that then. Here all these years I thought you liked them despite all the salt," she teased. Then her smile faded. "Thanks for understanding, Randy—about Shad and the cookies, I mean."

Again, her uncle slowly shook his head, and Darcy could have sworn she saw his eyes glisten. But he turned away quickly and headed back to his patrol car. "See you later, kid," he called over his shoulder, his voice husky with emotion.

"Yeah, see you, too," she murmured.

Darcy drove by Shad's house twice before she finally got the nerve to stop and attempt to deliver the cookies. As she walked up the sidewalk in faltering steps, the huge plate in her hands, she saw Billy part a curtain and watch her. His angry scowl almost robbed her of her waning courage, but not quite.

After ringing the bell, she waited for an interminably long time before the door finally swung open. Sister Cleverly stood there looking surprised. Her eyes darted from Darcy's face to the cookies and back.

"Darcy, please come in," she said, swinging the door wide.

"Thank you, Sister Cleverly," Darcy mumbled, wishing her knees would quit trembling. "Are Shad and Billy home?"

Sister Cleverly appeared to feel every bit as uncomfortable as Darcy. And her voice quivered as she spoke. "Yes, I'll get them," she said, hurrying from the room.

As Darcy stood there alone, she wondered where Billy had gone. The curtain was still slightly parted where he had been peering at her a minute earlier. The door still stood open behind her, evidence of Sister Cleverly's shock at seeing Darcy.

Afraid that she might be tempted to set the cookies down and flee through the open door before she got to confront Shad, Darcy turned and eased it closed. With the temptation removed, she stood uneasily, fidgeting with the cookies, passing the plate from hand to hand.

When Sister Cleverly reappeared, she was followed closely by Billy. "Shad will be down in a minute," she said. The brief interlude had given Sister Cleverly time to compose herself, and she appeared more relaxed. "Won't you sit down?" she went on, waving at the sofa.

Darcy took the offered seat, still juggling the cookies self-consciously. "Hello, Billy," she said, trying to sound normal but fearing that she did not.

Billy's face was still hard, but he answered with a civil tongue. "Hi, Darcy. How's Nate?" he asked, and Darcy knew he had been primed by his mother before coming in to face her.

"He's doing all right," she said, not wanting to discuss the extent of his injuries. "He and I baked some cookies for you guys," she went on awkwardly. "Would you like to try one?"

He was silent and appeared baffled. His mother answered for him. "Of course he would."

Billy accepted a cookie. "Thanks," he said very quietly and stepped back, putting it gingerly to his mouth.

A movement caught Darcy's eye, and she glanced past Billy. Shad stepped into the room, stopped, and stared at her. She was glad she was sitting down already, for she feared that if she hadn't been, she might have fainted.

"Hi, Shad. I brought you something," she said softly.

# Chapter Six

TIME WAS SUSPENDED. Not another word was spoken. No one even moved. Shad's eyes flicked to the plate in Darcy's hand, then back to her face. Finally, he broke the spell. "I thought you didn't want anything to do with my family," he hissed.

Darcy rose to her feet. "That's not true, but I'll be leaving now. I brought these cookies for you and your family," she said, fighting off the tears that threatened and forcing her balky legs to propel herself and the cookies toward Shad.

He looked confused. Before she knew what she was doing, Randy's words popped out of her mouth. "Peace offering," she said.

She reached him and held out the plate. For a long time he just stood there staring at it. Then he finally reached for it. "Billy likes cookies," he said.

"Peace?" She said the word as a question and forced a smile.

"Wh...what?" he asked, temporarily disarmed, his face turning red.

"Peace. Can't we at least be civil to each other? Please, Shad."

"Yeah, sure, if you insist. Peace," he agreed reluctantly. "And...and thanks, Darcy."

"Thank you, Shad." She touched his arm. "I'll be going now. See you around," she said, backing awkwardly toward the door.

"Thank you so much, Darcy," Sister Cleverly said when Darcy had retreated to the door. "Do come again."

Darcy merely nodded, opened the door, and left. From the Cleverly home, she drove the three blocks to where Todd lived with his mother and drunken father. The experience at Shad's had turned out better than she had dared hope, and she had to share it with Todd.

She fairly skipped up the walk, but she stopped abruptly when she heard the voice of Mrs. Albright screaming. Then Todd yelled, "Stop it, Dad!"

A drunken bellow of rage followed, shaking the window panes with the force of a small tornado. "You little swine you!" the man shouted at his son, although Todd was not so little. Darcy was sure that he outweighed his father by at least fifty pounds.

The urgent drawing power of the screams proved stronger than the desire to flee, and Darcy continued apprehensively up the walk. The front door stood ajar, and Darcy peered inside, horrified at what she saw. Mr. Albright had one arm around his wife's frail neck, choking her as he pulled her back against his chest. In his other hand was a long kitchen knife which he was waving about in front of her face.

Todd was not in sight, but Darcy only had cause to wonder what he was doing for a moment before Mr. Albright bellowed, "Don't you dare call the cops, you worthless little whelp!"

"So help me, Dad, if you don't drop that knife and let Mom go, I'll see you rot in prison," Todd countered from around a corner somewhere. Then, in a slightly softer voice, but one still highly agitated, he said, "Hurry, my dad's trying to kill my mom!" There was a brief pause, then he said, "Albright residence," and rattled off the address.

It was but a moment before he stepped into Darcy's view. His dad threatened, "So help me, you better a been faking that call, you little..."

Darcy slapped her hands over her tender ears and shut off most of the vile name calling and profanity that followed. Suddenly, she realized that Todd had seen her and was looking past his father's shoulder at her face. For the briefest moment he appeared embarrassed, but the desperation of the situation interceded, and his look changed to one of pleading—an unspoken call for help.

Darcy threw her hands in the air as if to say, "But what can I do?"

Todd's eyes darted back to the struggle between his parents. He spoke to his father, but somehow Darcy knew he was really vocalizing his plea to her for help and even suggesting how she might give it. "If I had that shovel that's on the porch, I'd pop you on the head with it," he shouted.

Todd had no sooner mentioned the shovel than Darcy spotted it. She stepped out of his view a few steps, picked it up, and stepped back to the doorway. Todd continued to berate his father who in turn was cursing his son in a drunken slur.

Todd caught Darcy's eye after staring briefly at the shovel she now held delicately in her hands. She hesitated—did not lift it. He nodded vigorously, still telling his father what a terrible thing he was doing and how he would like to hit him over the head with a shovel.

Darcy's palms were sweating, her legs shaking, and her stomach was doing somersaults. But fear of what was about to happen to Mrs. Albright was enough motivation to make herself slowly advance through the open doorway. She raised the shovel and held it over Mr. Albright's greasy head. Todd nodded desperate encouragement, but she froze in fear of the horrible act she was about to commit.

Just then a siren began wailing in the distance. Mr. Albright quit yelling and his slurred voice was low and deadly. "You just killed your mother, Todd," he declared ominously. "It's all your fault that she's dying, 'cause you called the cops—betrayed your old man."

Darcy was confused for a moment. Mrs. Albright was still very much alive and struggling. Then she realized that the drunken man was making a prediction. Todd understood, too, and he screamed, "Now, Darcy!"

The kitchen knife was slowly descending toward Mrs. Albright's chest. Then, closing her eyes as if to blot out the horror, Darcy brought the shovel down upon Mr. Albright's head with all the strength she could muster. He staggered and Todd lunged toward him, grabbing the knife-hand in a vise-like grip. His father swayed, the knife dropped, and Todd let go. Mr. Albright fell to the floor with a resounding crash and lay there unmoving, his face against the hardwood floor, blood pouring from his smashed nose.

Darcy looked at the shovel in her hand with horror, then she dropped it. It bounced off the limp body of Todd's dad and clanged on the floor. Todd bent and, ignoring the shovel, retrieved the knife and threw it violently across the living room. Then he embraced his sobbing mother and said, "It's over, Mom. Are you all right now?"

She nodded, cried, swayed dangerously, then clung to her son. Darcy fled through the door. When Sarge pulled up and ran to the house a moment later, she was retching miserably in Mrs. Albright's faded flower bed near the porch.

"Darcy, are you hurt?" Sarge shouted.

"No," she gasped between heaves. "Inside!"

Sarge understood and surged through the door. Another siren was wailing its approach. Then it came to an abrupt halt. Darcy was aware of a car door slamming, running footsteps, then a hand on her shoulder.

"Darcy! Darcy!"

She wiped her mouth with the back of her hands, lifted her head, and looked through tear-filled eyes into the alarmed and frightened face of Trooper Randy Hutchins. "Sarge, is everything under control in there?" he shouted while reaching for his niece.

"Yeah, Randy. You better see to Darcy. She's had quite a shock," he responded from just inside the doorway.

Randy helped Darcy to her feet. She fell helplessly into his arms and began to sob. "I killed him! I killed him!" she wailed.

"Killed whom?" Randy asked in alarm.

"Mr. Albright," she cried. "Oh why? Why me? I didn't mean to kill him, just to stop him from hurting Todd's mom." In her tortured state of mind, Darcy firmly believed Mr. Albright was dead, and nothing had ever caused her such terror and anguish. It was to Darcy as though her soul were doomed.

Randy reacted swiftly to the appalling news by loosening her arms from around his neck, scooping her up in his long arms, and rushing inside with her. He laid her gently on the sofa and began smoothing her hair and stroking her perspiring brow. "Darcy," he said. "Listen to me, honey, and you listen good. Mr. Albright is alive."

"He's not...d...dead?" she stammered.

"No. In fact, Sarge is just now putting a set of handcuffs on him. What made you think you had killed him?"

"I hit him with a shovel."

"Boy, did she!" It was Todd's voice. "Darcy, you saved Mom's life and kept Dad from doing something he would have regretted when he got sobered up enough to realize what he had done."

Darcy opened her eyes. Randy was smiling at her, his straight white teeth gleaming. Todd was staring over Randy's shoulder, his face creased with concern. "Thank goodness you came when you did!" he exclaimed.

Several minutes passed before Darcy recovered enough strength to sit up. Randy did not leave her side for a single moment, and he kept her hand in his. She was aware of Sarge as he escorted a struggling, cursing Mr. Albright out of the house. She knew that Todd had taken his mother into her bedroom and stayed there with her.

After Darcy was finally sitting up, Randy left her long enough to call her folks. He explained as simply as he could what had happened and why she had not yet returned home. He suggested that they come for her. Then, while they waited, Randy coaxed the story from her.

When she had finished, she felt better about what she had done. Going over it served to reaffirm how desperate the situation had been. Randy said, "You really did save Mrs. Albright's life, Darcy. It's really lucky you showed up when you did, but why did you come here? I thought you were going to take some cookies to Shad."

Just then Todd came into the room looking haggard and worn. "Mom's asleep," he reported as he slumped down on the badly soiled sofa beside Darcy. "Wow, am I glad you came by tonight," he said. "What did you come for, anyway?"

"That's what I just asked her," Randy said with a fleeting grin.

"Well, let me tell you," Darcy said, and she went on to explain.

After listening attentively to her story, Todd said, "Gee, Darcy, maybe there's a spark of hope left for Shad yet. I thought for sure he would throw you out."

"So did I, especially when he first walked into the living room. But I'm glad now that I went," she said.

Suddenly, Todd sprang to his feet and began to pace in front of the sofa. "Darcy, this is crazy. You shouldn't have anything to do with Shad or me. Look at all the trouble it's caused you."

"It's not your fault, Todd. I just wish your dad would follow your example and leave that awful alcohol alone. How do you stand it when he's drinking?" she asked.

"I'm used to it. I don't ever remember it being very pleasant around here, but tonight was the worst. I was scared spitless when Dad grabbed that knife and took after Mom. In fact, I'm still shaking." He paused for a minute, and when no one else spoke, he stopped pacing and asked, "You know what I need right now?"

"No, what?" Darcy asked innocently.

"A good stiff shot of whisky!"

"Todd!"

"Just kidding, Darcy," he replied, a good-natured grin popping out on his freckled face. Relief flooded over her.

Randy stood and put a hand on Todd's shoulder. "It's good to see you can joke about it. Just don't ever forget your promise."

"I won't. I may be dumb and worthless, but I'll never mess with booze again," he said, the grin fading. He looked very serious for a moment, then asked, "What do you think they'll do with Dad?"

"I don't know, Todd. Not for sure, anyway. But he could be charged with aggravated assault or even attempted murder. In either case, it would be a felony."

"Oh," Todd moaned.

"Maybe this will be the thing that can start your dad on the road to recovery, Todd. The judge can order some real good help for him," Randy explained.

"Really?"

"Yes, and that's what he needs, what your family needs."

"Hey, I have an idea. Will you two help me?"

"Do what, Todd?" Darcy asked, finally beginning to feel like her old self again.

"Empty out all Dad's booze. He usually has some stashed in a dozen different places around the house." He grinned sheepishly. "I know, 'cause I used to get into it all the time."

"That's a good idea, Todd," Randy said hesitantly. "But I think it would be best if you did it yourself. Darcy and I will just watch."

It didn't take long, for Mr. Albright had already consumed most of his stashes of alcohol. When Todd was done, Darcy's folks arrived. She met them outside and climbed in the truck with her father. Her mother and Nate followed them in the car when they pulled away.

❈

Randy left a few minutes later. Todd stood on the porch and watched him drive off. His heart was heavy. He felt like he carried the weight of the whole world on his shoulders. He stood there for a long time after the Crown Victoria had disappeared.

When he finally re-entered the house, darkness had settled in. He dropped wearily on the sofa without flipping on any lights. There all his pent-up emotions erupted, and Todd cried like a frightened child.

An hour later, the light suddenly came on, stinging Todd's eyes. When they had adjusted to the brightness, he spotted his mother standing in the doorway from the hall. Todd stood up and hurried over to her. "Come sit down, Mom. Would you like me to get you a glass of milk or something?"

"No, son, but I do need to discuss something with you."

"Okay," he agreed, and he led her to the sofa.

Once she was comfortably seated, he grabbed a small wooden chair, turned it around backward and plopped down, leaning on the back of it, looking at his mother earnestly.

"I'm sorry, Todd," she began.

"It's not your fault, Mom," he said.

"Todd, after all that's happened, this may surprise you, but I really do love your father," she told him.

Todd nodded. He was not surprised; he had heard the same thing after many beatings administered by his father to both his mother and himself. However, he was not sure that he could say the same, so he said nothing at all.

"I'm so glad you've found someone special. I hope you can have a better life with Darcy than your father and I have had," she said earnestly.

That brought Todd bounding to his feet. "Mom! Darcy is just a friend, and that's all she'll ever be! She's a good friend, but she would die if she heard you say what you just did. Don't go jumping to dumb conclusions."

"But I thought..."

Todd interrupted her. "Let's get one thing straight right now, Mom.

I'm grateful to Darcy for being a friend when I really needed one. She's been a big help to me the past few days, and she is about the best person I ever met. But, I ain't never going to mess up that friendship by expecting or even hoping for more. I ain't going to ruin her life if I can help it. And as you know, I've caused her a bunch of problems already."

"My, I thought that...Oh, Todd, she would be so...so good for you," his mother said earnestly, not willing to give up.

"She is good for me as a friend, not as a girlfriend. The last thing she needs is a boyfriend like me."

"Well, okay, but maybe that will all change someday," Mrs. Albright said, still sounding frustratingly hopeful.

"Mom! Don't you hear me? It ain't never gonna be the way you think. We're just too different. She's so smart and serious, and I ain't either one. She's so good, and I ain't that, either," he said earnestly, believing what he said and not even hoping that it was not true. For him, Todd Albright, just the friendship of a special person like Darcy was enough to last a lifetime.

"Okay, okay. Anyway, we need to discuss your father. He'll be sobered up by morning, and we need to figure some way to get some money together so we can put up his bail," she said. "The house is about paid for, and..."

Todd had just started to sit down on the backward chair again, but he flared at her words and sent the chair reeling across the room. "Oh no we don't, Mom! He's right where he needs to be and that's where we're gonna leave him!" he said with fierce determination.

"But Todd, he's in jail! He's locked up! I can't bear to think of him all cooped up and miserable with a bunch of criminals," she moaned. "He's not like the rest of them."

"Yes he is," Todd said through clenched teeth. "And I say he needs to be locked up. All he's ever done is hurt us, Mom. And if it hadn't been for Darcy, Dad would have stabbed you tonight, and probably killed you."

"Don't be silly, son. He would never have..." she began.

"He almost did! He was trying to! That was only a couple of hours ago. Mom, how can you forget so fast?" Todd demanded angrily.

Mrs. Albright began to cry. "Todd, you don't understand your father. He's a good man, and I need him. I need him here with me. I depend on him. I am nothing without him."

"You were almost nothing because of him!" Todd shouted. "He's the one that depends on you! He doesn't even have a job. I can't remember when he ever did. There ain't another kid in school whose old man don't work."

"Todd, we are going to get him out of jail, and that is final," his mother shouted, angry now herself.

"Not with my help, you ain't. And if I can prevent it, I will," Todd said stubbornly.

The doorbell saved further hot words between mother and son. Grateful for the distraction, Todd hurried over. "Hello, Sarge," he said upon opening the door. "Come in."

"I need to get a little more information from you folks," Sarge said apologetically. "I really hated to bother you, and I know it won't be easy for either of you, but I need to know exactly how things happened tonight."

"Fine by me, but I ain't too sure Mom will be much help," Todd said bitterly as he led Sarge toward the sofa.

"Sergeant Howard," Todd's mother said stiffly after Sarge was seated in the overstuffed chair near the sofa. "I'm glad you came by again. I was just getting ready to call you and see what I needed to do to get Ed out of jail in the morning."

Todd had retrieved his wooden chair and was just sitting down as his mother spoke. "See what I mean?" he said flatly.

"Yes. Well, I'm sorry, but I called Judge Simper and he set the bail at $25,000.00, and because you are the victim, your home as a property bond will not be accepted," Sarge said evenly, looking Mrs. Albright right in the eye as he spoke.

"What! That is the only way. We could never..." she began.

"Good deal," Todd interrupted. "Give a cheer for the judge."

"Todd!" his mother scolded.

Sarge cleared his throat, then he went on, "Please, tell me what started the trouble this evening."

"Sergeant Howard..." Mrs. Albright began.

"Sarge, please," the officer interrupted with a disarming smile.

"Sergeant Howard," she said again, not about to be disarmed. "I have decided not to press charges against my husband. It was Todd that called you in the first place, and it was all a big mistake."

Todd leaned forward on his chair, angry and frustrated, but curious to see how Sarge would go about getting what he wanted from his mother.

"I'm afraid that is not an option, Mrs. Albright. You see, we are charging Ed with aggravated assault. We discussed attempted murder, but because of you and your boy, we decided against that," Sarge said.

"But I refuse to sign a complaint," Todd's mother said stubbornly.

"The charging document is called an information, and the county attorney is the one who signs it. I called him just before I did Judge Simper, and he is going to prepare the information first thing in the morning and affix his signature to it," Sarge explained patiently. He could have been giving directions for a tourist to find the local hardware store if Todd were to judge from his tone of voice.

He went on. "Now, as I mentioned earlier, I came for a little more information. It would be helpful to know a few more details, Mrs. Albright."

"It will do you no good, officer. I refuse to testify against my husband," she said angrily, folding her arms stiffly across her thin chest.

Sarge's face reddened only slightly, and he shot Todd a quick look of exasperation. But when he tried again, his agitation was not apparent in his voice. "We all know that your husband Ed has a serious drinking problem. Would you like to see him overcome it?"

"Of course," Mrs. Albright began cautiously. "But not by making him stay in your smelly old jail."

"The sheriff runs the jail, not the city police, thank goodness. But that is not what I meant. There are avenues of treatment that the court can order in felony cases such as this one. This is the best chance Ed will ever have to get the help he needs. Now, I realize that he would never dream of hurting you when he is sober, Mrs. Albright. But when he is drunk, he is a different person. Drunk, he can be very dangerous, as you witnessed again tonight," Sarge explained. "Now, let's start right at the beginning. What time did he begin drinking today?"

Mrs. Albright gave in, and over the next thirty minutes, the complete story of the tumultuous, almost disastrous, evening unfolded. Sarge took copious notes while directing the interview with skillfully-stated questions.

Finally satisfied, he closed his notebook, pushed his big frame out of the ancient overstuffed chair, and thanked Todd and his mother for their cooperation. As he went through the doorway, the phone began to ring.

# Chapter Seven

"**Y**OU ANSWER THE phone, Todd, and if it's for me, I don't want to talk to anyone else tonight," Mrs. Albright said, rubbing her red eyes.

Todd didn't either, so he took his time walking to the phone. But when he finally reached it, it was still ringing persistently. He finally reached for it, having decided that whomever was calling was prepared to let the phone ring all night long.

"Hello," he said sharply, letting his agitation show.

"Todd? It's me. Darcy."

"Darcy! I'm sorry. I thought you'd had enough of the Albrights for one day."

"Don't be silly," she said. "I just called to see if you and your mother are all right."

"We're fine, thanks. Sarge just left," Todd responded.

"I see. Okay. Well, if there is anything that I can do, you know how to reach me."

"You've done enough, Darcy, and thanks again for popping in when you did and having the guts to do what you did."

"Well, I'm sorry that things happened like...I mean...well, you know," she stammered.

"Yeah, I guess I do. I ain't very proud of it, either. Ain't you glad you got your family. Nothing like this would ever happen at your house."

"No, but your dad is a good man, I'm sure. He just needs some help. He can change. We all need to pray for him and help him however we can," Darcy suggested.

"Yeah, I suppose so. Well, thanks for calling, Darcy," Todd said curtly.

"I just had to, Todd. Please don't be angry. We're friends, remember?" Darcy pleaded.

Todd was angry—not with Darcy, but with himself. Darcy was so decent and so sensitive. He hadn't really meant to be so sharp with her.

"I'm sorry, Darcy. I ain't exactly myself tonight. I'm still mad and upset."

"And you have a right to be. See you in school tomorrow."

"Okay," he agreed. "And thanks for calling."

"Was that Darcy?" Mrs. Albright asked when he had hung up.

"Uh, huh," he responded glumly.

"Only friends you say?"

"Yes, Mom. We are only friends. Darcy cares about people, that's all."

"But she called you, Todd. If she didn't..."

"Mom!" Todd interrupted impatiently. "Darcy took a plate of cookies over to Shad tonight. That's why she came by here. She told me at school that she was gonna do it, and she just wanted to tell me that he accepted them."

"Oh, I see," Mrs. Albright said flatly. "She's after all the boys."

Todd couldn't take anymore. "Darcy's not like that, Mom. Goodnight," he said abruptly as he strode angrily to his bedroom.

❖

Darcy missed Todd at school the next day. So, with Nate's help, out came the flour, salt, sugar, pans, and all the other things needed for another batch of cookies.

"Are they for us this time?" Nate asked.

"Some of them."

"For Shad and Billy?" he groaned.

"No, for Todd and his mother," she replied.

"Why?"

"Never mind that," she said sharply. "I just want to, that's all." But when she looked at Nate and the hurt on his face, she added, "But you may have some, too."

Darcy had a Laurel activity that evening. The cookies sat in the car until it was over. She hurried from the church so that she wouldn't be too late in delivering them to Todd.

"Darcy!" someone shouted.

She turned to see her best friend, Jill, running toward her. "I need a ride home, Darcy. It's too chilly to walk tonight and I forgot to bring a coat," Jill said breathlessly as she approached the old Ford.

Darcy smiled. It was a cool night. She had been so wrapped up in her thoughts that she hadn't even noticed. Now she shivered. "Sure, hop in," she said cheerfully.

"Hey, where'd you get the cookies," Jill asked as she slid in.

"They're for Todd and his mother," Darcy said, feeling a bit uncomfortable. "They had some trouble last night, and I…"

"Yeah, I hear his dad's in jail. That's awful. Hey, mind if I tag along while you deliver them?"

"If you'd like to," Darcy said, glancing at her friend in the semi-darkness of the car's interior. The bluish glow from a street lamp lit Jill's face. She wasn't one who most would call beautiful, but she was attractive and fun. Darcy really enjoyed her. Her red hair was cropped short and the dim light was just enough to allow the freckles on her face to stand out.

"I would," Jill said with excitement in her voice. "Todd's kind of cute, and if we all treat him right, I'll bet he'll get active in the church again."

Darcy glanced at Jill again in surprise. "You're right. He wants to make a change in his life, and with the accident and the problems with his father and all, now's the time to help him."

"I'll help…if it's all right, that is," Jill volunteered softly.

"Of course it's all right, Jill," Darcy responded as she turned into the street.

Darcy parked in front of Todd's house. The terrible events of the night before flooded back, and she shuddered. "What's the matter, Darcy? Are you all right?" Jill asked, looking at her with a worried frown on her freckled face.

"Yeah, I guess."

"Well, you don't look it. You do look a little pale, though. What is it, Darcy?"

"I wasn't going to say anything to you, but if you promise not to mention it to anyone else, I'll tell you something awful."

"What!?" Jill exclaimed, her eyes wide and expectant.

"Promise?"

"Of course."

"Well, I stopped to see Todd last night, and I kind of came at a bad time."

"You mean you saw the fight?" Jill asked, her eyes wide open in wonder.

"Yeah. It was terrible," she said with a shudder. Then, changing her mind, she decided not to say anything more about her part in it. She opened the car door and stepped out, reaching back in for the cookies. "Come on, Jill, let's go."

With a deep breath, Darcy started up the walk. Todd answered the door a minute later. "Darcy!" he said in surprise.

"Hi, Todd. I thought you might like some cookies."

"Great, thanks. Hi, Jill," he said, looking at the short red head who had quietly shouldered her way beside Darcy on the porch.

Darcy glanced at Jill and was surprised at the look on her friend's face. Jill was not known to be shy, but now her eyes were lowered, and a faint touch of red high-lighted her freckles.

"Do you want to come in?" Todd asked, holding the door wide.

"Sure, thanks," Darcy said, stepping past him. She was surprised that after a full day the stale odor of beer was nearly as strong as it had been the night before. It made Darcy feel slightly ill.

"Coming, Jill?" she heard Todd ask, and she turned, surprised to see her friend still standing on the porch in a trance-like state.

"Oh, yeah," she said, shaking her head and stepping through the door into the dingy, smelly interior of the Albrights' home.

Mrs. Albright was planted in front of the television. She scarcely looked up when the girls came in. The volume was turned up quite loud, so Todd invited the girls into the kitchen. The cupboards were piled high with dirty dishes, and it smelled rank, like spoiling food and sour dishrags. Todd cleared a spot at the table, and Darcy sat the plate of cookies down. With a grin, he took one. Then he offered one to Darcy and Jill.

Jill munched happily, but Darcy declined. "I'll take one to your mother," she said and left the kitchen and the cookies under the hungry supervision of Todd and Jill.

Mrs. Albright looked at Darcy through troubled, red-rimmed eyes. "How are you tonight?" Darcy asked awkwardly, holding the cookie out for her.

She accepted it with a fleeting smile, then she said, "I'm okay, I guess. I never did thank you for what you did last night."

"That's okay," Darcy said, and Mrs. Albright must have agreed, for she still did not thank Darcy.

"Can I do anything for you?" Darcy asked, looking about at the disarray in the living room. The television was so loud that she found she was shouting to be heard.

Mrs. Albright had to speak very loudly herself. "No," she answered bluntly.

For a moment Darcy just stood there, trying to think of something else to say. Mrs. Albright needed help, but she was not sure how to get her to accept it. Then she remembered the mess in the kitchen and was determined to do something about it before she went home.

When she entered the kitchen, she was surprised. Jill was on her feet, stacking dishes on the table. "I told Todd we were going to clean the kitchen. Is that okay with you, Darcy?"

Darcy grinned, noted the half-empty cookie plate, then said, "That was just what I had decided. Let me call my folks so they won't be worried and we'll dig in," she said with enthusiasm.

"After last night," Todd said glumly, "they might not let you stay in this house for another minute."

"Don't be silly," Darcy said with a grin as she departed the kitchen once more. She paused at the television and asked, "Mrs. Albright, may I use your phone?"

"Of course," Todd's mother responded without looking up.

Darcy slipped past, made her call, then returned to the kitchen. Todd and Jill stood side by side at the sink, working with a glow on their faces. Darcy pitched in, and in thirty minutes the kitchen was sparkling. Darcy took another cookie to Todd's mother, who seemed surprised that she was still there. Then she returned to the kitchen where Jill and Todd were finishing off the final crumbs.

Jill blushed and hurriedly stood up. "Well, should we go?" she asked.

"I guess, unless there's something more we can do for Todd first," Darcy answered.

"Nope, I'm fine, now that the kitchen's clean. First time in days," he said, "thanks to you two. You know, it ain't been so peaceful around here for as long as I can remember. With the old man gone...I mean with Dad gone, it's quiet, even with the TV blaring," he said with an embarrassed grin.

Jill giggled, blushed, and said, "We better go."

Back in the car a couple of minutes later, Jill appeared ill at ease. They discussed Todd's tough home life until Darcy pulled the old red Ford up in front of Jill's home. Then Jill, after opening the door, turned back to Darcy. "Is Todd going to church with you again on Sunday?"

"We haven't discussed it. I guess I should ask him. He probably won't come alone—at least not yet," Darcy said.

"That's what I thought. Sure is nice of you to bring him," Jill said quietly.

Darcy smiled at her friend, then to herself as inspiration struck her. There was no mistaking the sparkle in Jill's eyes. "Hey, I have an idea, Jill. If you wouldn't mind, would it be too much to ask you to pick up Todd this week. I'm sure he'll want to go," Darcy suggested slyly.

"Gee, Darcy. Do you think I should?" Jill asked hopefully.

"I think you should. Go call him right now, and I'll see you tomorrow at school," she said firmly.

Darcy watched Jill glide up the sidewalk, and a lump came to her throat. Now there is a match for Todd, she thought to herself. Darcy liked Todd, but only as a good friend. Deep down, she knew it would never be any more than that, and she didn't want it to be any more than that. Todd was a nice guy and he was definitely straightening out his life, but he wasn't her type. But Jill? Yes, there was a match for Todd. With a delighted grin, Darcy drove homeward.

*

Shad came late to church on Sunday. The hymn was under way when he sat, as usual, on the back row with his mother and Billy. His dad couldn't make it. He was not sure why, but his dad managed to find an excuse not to go to church at least half the time. Shad felt a little resentment that his dad always insisted that his family go to church, even though it was never all that important for himself.

His arm itched inside the cast, and he felt as obvious as the wart on Brother Snyder's nose. He spotted Darcy and was surprised that Todd wasn't with her. He found that he was more angry with Todd for becoming chummy with Darcy than for blaming the accident on his drinking.

Not that it made any sense, because he was especially angry with Darcy, although he honestly knew he did not have a valid reason. He guessed it was because she tried to be so good. Like the cookies! That had really floored him at the time and he had actually began to hope that she might agree to go out with him again. But thinking about it during the week, he had concluded that she was just rubbing her righteousness in his face.

He was smugly glad that Todd wasn't in church with her today. If he worked it right, he figured he could get Todd to tip a can with him again—maybe after he'd beaten the drunk driving rap that the super-cop pinned on him.

The hymn ended, and Brother Snyder, huge purple wart and all, offered the opening prayer. Shad watched him as he left the stand, thinking how easy it would be to just slice the grotesque thing off with a sharp pocket knife. He didn't hear a word of the prayer, and it was when Brother Snyder began to excuse his way to where his family sat about five or six rows from the front in the center section that he recognized Todd Albright's thick, unruly hair. It was combed more neatly than he had ever seen it before.

His former friend was sitting beside Jill Steelan, Darcy's red headed friend. Inwardly, Shad gloated. Now that serves Darcy right, he thought, and snickered.

"What's funny?" Billy asked as Bishop Olsen stood at the pulpit again.

"Nothing," he whispered, looking about to see who else might have heard him. Only his mother, he decided, ignoring her stern glare of disapproval.

Shad spent the entire meeting waiting for Darcy to spot Todd with her best friend. But the meeting, for his purpose, was a complete flop, for not once did she seem to notice Todd and Jill. After the meeting, Shad slipped into the hallway and slumped down in a soft chair near the main entrance. From there, he would make his usual escape from Sunday School.

To his surprise and consternation, who should stroll up, chatting amiably with Todd and Jill? Darcy! Then, to make matters worse, Darcy said, "Hi, Shad." And Todd did the same!

Even Jill grinned at him and said, "How's your arm, Shad? Better, I hope."

He lurched to his feet, preparing to bolt out the door, but Darcy, misinterpreting his movement, said, "Hey, great. Come with us to class, Shad."

And so, to his disgust, Shad found himself in Brother Wartnose Snyder's Sunday School class, sandwiched between a girl he was trying his best to dislike and a former friend who had betrayed him. For the first time in his life, Shad Cleverly sat through an entire class without speaking a single word!

Instead, determined not to listen to the lesson which Brother Snyder had so diligently prepared, he spent the entire forty minutes thinking of different ways that the wart on Brother Snyder's nose could be removed.

He considered everything from a hot iron to thin piano wire and from sulfuric acid to course sandpaper. After class, Darcy said with a broad smile on her unforgivably pretty face, "Thanks for coming with us to class, Shad. Wasn't that a good lesson?"

Shad had no response concerning the lesson, for he hadn't really heard it, but he did realize, as her warm smile lit the stuffy classroom, that Darcy Felding was a difficult person to dislike. She was so pretty. If only...

"So how's the arm?" Todd asked as they crowded out the door and into the busy hallway.

"It doesn't hurt," he said, not truthfully, for he was much too proud to admit anything else.

"How long do you have to wear the cast?" Jill enquired from her position beside Todd—very close position, Shad noted with interest.

"I dunno. Two months the doctor says, but I'll probably take it off before that," he said in an attempt to demonstrate his toughness and to impress the girls.

"Ooh, don't do that!" Jill exclaimed in horror.

Just then, Brother Snyder appeared between them, smiling his betterthan-thou smile of superiority—as Shad interpreted it. "It was nice to have you in class today," he said.

Shad's ears burned and, forgetting the other kids, he headed for the nearest exit. Old Wartnose never would realize that Shad was not a kid. He fumed. Well, never again, he vowed, would Darcy or anyone else put him through the misery of sitting through that man's Sunday school class.

Twenty minutes later, Shad was home changing his clothes, still in a sour mood. After making three phone calls, he located a six-pack of beer. By mid-afternoon, in company with one Dwight Arnot, a twenty-four year old loser, Shad was feeling mellow, the memory of a miserable Sunday school class fading in the fumes of his beer.

❋

A heated argument was in the making at the Cleverly house. Shad's dad was glaring at his wife. "Why do you ask me? Shad went to church with you! Why didn't he come home with you?" he demanded.

"Because I couldn't find him there, Bill," Paula Cleverly said for the third time in the past minute.

"Couldn't find him? Paula, you must not have looked very hard. His truck is demolished. You had your car and I had my truck. He hasn't got the Trans Am running yet. Now, how do you suppose he went anywhere?" Bill asked flippantly.

"Walked?"

"Walked!" Bill exclaimed. "Shad hates to walk. Anyway, supposing he did, then where did he go?"

"Home."

"But he's not here, remember?"

"His church clothes are. He changed his clothes and went somewhere."

"With whom?"

"I don't know, Bill, and that's what worries me. I'm afraid he's gone drinking with someone," Paula said, her voice breaking.

"There you go again. Why is it that anytime he goes somewhere, you have to conclude that he's out drinking. Give the poor kid a break, Paula," Bill said in disgust.

"Bill, Shad hasn't exactly been doing the kinds of things to earn our trust lately. The kids he should be with were still at church, so whomever he's with now is not likely to be a good influence," Paula argued.

"Good grief, woman! You don't give the poor kid a chance. Anyway, what if he is drinking a little? It's just a phase. He'll grow out of it. You're getting all worked up over nothing."

"Nothing? His broken arm and wrecked truck are nothing?" she shouted.

"Now calm down. That wreck was not Shad's fault. Old Man Burrows' cow caused that wreck, not Shad. You're as bad as that hot-shot Hutchins, Paula," Bill said, his face burning with anger.

"You don't really believe that, do you? You're just making excuses for Shad. My word, Bill, wake up. He could have killed someone! Blaming someone else is not going to help Shad," Paula said, her temper flaring and tears streaming down her cheeks.

"You'll see," Bill said in an even voice. "I have hired a good attorney, well worth the money he costs. He'll get Shad off that rap."

"And if he does, what will you have accomplished? You will have told Shad that you condone his drinking and driving. I shudder to think what that will lead to. You're certainly not helping Shad. The best thing that can happen is for him to take his punishment and maybe learn something," Paula reasoned desperately. "And I still think he's out there drinking right now."

"He is not! Give the kid a break. He'll be home in a bit, and he'll be stone sober when he gets here," Bill argued.

"I'll bet he will have beer on his breath," Paula insisted stubbornly.

"I'll tell you what. I still trust Shad. I don't believe he's drinking today. If he is, then I'll make him wish he hadn't."

"How?"

"I don't know. I'll think of something if I have to," Bill shouted lamely.

"Okay, so think of some thing," Paula challenged.

"All right. I'll show you how sure I am. If Shad's been drinking when he comes home, then I'll make him take the drunk driving rap, even if it is Burrows' fault. How's that?" he said, puffing out his chest and wiping perspiration from his brow.

"Fine. And if he comes home sober, I'll get off your back about the expense of your attorney friend," Paula offered in fairness.

"Sounds fine by me, Paula," Bill said, starting to cool off.

"So what do we do now?" Paula asked meekly.

"Wait.

# Chapter Eight

WHILE SHAD'S DISTRAUGHT mother and stubborn father waited, he was trying to demonstrate his superior drinking skills to Dwight Arnot. That was a tall order for a novice guzzler like Shad.

Tall, lanky, and lazy, Dwight had been known to put away a lot of beer and still keep his feet beneath him. No one knew for sure where Dwight got the money to drink like he did, but gossip had it that most of it was not obtained honestly. One thing was certain, Dwight seldom held any job for more than three or four months.

Shad knew where some of Dwight's money came from. Him! Shad had just paid double for the six-pack he was drinking. But, since he and other underage drinkers like him were breaking the law by drinking, they were not about to turn Dwight in to the cops and dry up a sure source of illegal booze.

They were in a hard-to-reach spot beside the lake, relaxed on a couple of old lawn chairs that Dwight always kept for this purpose in the back of his battered old Dodge pickup. Dwight was busy extolling the virtues of beer drinking to Shad, who in turn was so blitzed that he did not realize that Dwight was only making an effort at converting Shad from a new to a permanent customer.

Dwight's thin face supported a scraggly beard. His left eye constantly drifted outward as if on assignment to watch for cops, a constant fear in Dwight's less than upstanding life. The lazy eye gave the twenty-four-year-old hoodlum a sinister look which he took a great deal of pride in.

Shad eventually polished off his six-pack of Coors. Dwight quickly offered him another can, at his single-can rate, he told Shad, of triple the retail price. Shad forked over and popped the top, sipping the cool foam that bubbled out. And so went the rest of the afternoon. The evening was more of the same. Shad was too drunk to realize that he was not having a good time. He was also too drunk to realize that he was out-drinking his shrewd new friend two cans to one, and that the price went up outrageously on each can.

Finally, Shad's pockets and billfold were empty. That was when Dwight loaded him up and headed for town, informing him that it was late and the party was over. Dwight pulled over at the edge of town. "You'll have to walk from here, Shad," Dwight said. "And remember, one word about who got you your beer and I'll bust your head open and then make sure no one lets you have a drink in this town again."

"Oh, that's no problem, buddy," Shad said in a slurred voice. He belched and then went on, "My slips are...I mean, by lips are sh...sh..."

"Sealed," Dwight interrupted helpfully. "You have my number, Shad. When you need some booze, just call."

"Sure thing, Dright..."

"Dwight."

"Yeah, right," Shad agreed, crawling carefully from the truck to the undulating pavement in the moonlight outside. Shad promptly sat down on the edge of the road, waiting for the asphalt tide to go out so he could walk home. Dwight drove off, totally unconcerned about Shad's precarious condition. He had accomplished what he had set out to do; Shad's money was in his pocket, and Shad was now a firm and loyal source of more.

Dwight had not told Shad that he made it a policy never to drink with a young customer after the first night. He only did that as a pretense of friendship. He would sell them every drop he could after that, but only under carefully concealed terms. His risk was limited to the first sale. Or so he thought. Leaving Shad as he had just done was, at the best, poor judgment on Dwight's part, for Shad could easily be picked up or turned in to the cops before ever making it home. Dwight, even though he had not consumed half the beer his recruit had, was certainly long past the point of impaired judgment. The beer he had consumed replaced what little good judgment he normally had with the confidence of the untouchable.

Several minutes passed before Shad was able to get to his feet and stagger toward home. Several cars passed, but they just swung wide around him and went on their way.

All but one, that is. After darkness had settled over the town, and Shad had still not come home, Paula Cleverly finally convinced Bill to go out and look for him. The staggering figure he finally spotted after two hours of fruitless driving angered even Bill.

Once his dad had him loaded in the car, Shad was only vaguely aware of the chewing out he was receiving. "You fool, Shad! If you're going to drink, you could at least have the good sense to stop before you get drunk! Your mother will never let me live this one down."

Shad missed school the next day. He threw up more times than he could count. And when his stomach did finally settle down sometime after noon, he was too weak to crawl out of bed. Despite her anger and disappointment, Paula tried to make her wayward son comfortable. "I hope you learn something from this, Shad. You're sick only because of the beer you drank. Surely this will be the last time."

"Sure thing, Mom," he lied. He was too sick to argue with her right now. "I was just feeling sorry for myself. I won't let it happen again."

That promise brought a sigh of relief from his mother. Shad smirked inwardly and thought to himself that his promise was true, only not the way she understood it. He really did not plan to allow himself to get caught drunk again. The key, in his mind, was not getting caught, not in giving up drinking altogether.

Bill Cleverly sat with Shad and faced the juvenile court judge on Wednesday afternoon. Shad had argued with his dad for all he was worth when informed the day before that the attorney had been dismissed.

"But you promised you'd get me off," he had protested.

"And you let me down, Shad. After I stood up to your mother and bragged about how you had the sense not to be drinking Sunday night, what do you do? You get so slobbering drunk that you can't even talk," reinforcing the notion that the sin was not in drinking, but in getting caught.

Shad was learning, but he was not ready to throw in the towel just yet. "What about Old Man Burrows' cow?" he had reasoned. "You gotta have a lawyer to prove it was his fault."

His father had an answer to that, too. "Saw the police report, Shad. Seems the cow wasn't branded, and Hutchins and the state brand inspector are claiming they can't prove whose it was."

So now, here he sat, staring at the table while his broken arm throbbed and itched miserably. He was wracking his brain, hoping he could remember all the advice his father had given him as they waited outside the courtroom. If he was smart, he could still get out of the worst of this, he hoped. Finally, the judge called him by name and ordered him to stand up. Meekly, Shad obeyed.

The judge read the charges of driving under the influence and illegal possession of alcohol by a minor that had been brought against him by Trooper Hutchins and the prosecuting attorney. When asked if he admitted to or denied the charges, he heard himself reluctantly admitting to them.

"Young man," the judge said sternly, "the biggest concern I have is whether or not you have learned something from this experience."

Now was Shad's chance to shine. His dad's advice had included how to act if the judge asked if he was a changed person. He was prepared to follow that advice now.

"I have, Your Honor," he said, forcing himself to look the judge in the eye.

So far, so good, he thought.

It got better. "Have you had any alcohol to drink since the wreck?" the judge asked.

"Oh, no," he lied. "I've learned my lesson." From the corner of his eye, he saw his dad nodding in agreement to his deception. Thus bolstered, he went on, "I hadn't drank much beer the day of the wreck, but I shouldn't have had any."

The judge beamed at him, and Shad decided to add a little more. "I probably could have stopped in time to miss the cow that caused my wreck. For sure I could have slowed down enough that it would not have been a bad wreck, and my arm wouldn't have got busted," he said, waving the offended appendage in its bulky cast for the judge to get a good look at while he screwed his face up to give the impression that he was in worse pain than he actually was.

The old judge seemed to be buying his act. "So you will commit to this court that you will never drink and drive again, or even drink until you are of age, Shad?"

"Oh, yes, I promise," Shad said with a false air of sincerity painted on his face over the one of excruciating pain. "This was the first time I'd ever drank. So the next time my buddy, Todd Albright, or anyone else, tries to get me to drink, I'll have the guts to tell them to get lost."

The judge seemed very interested in that. "Todd, is that the boy that was with you in the accident?"

"Yes. He was hardly scratched. He was so drunk that nothing could have hurt him," Shad exaggerated.

Finally, after a few more questions, the judge said, "Shad, I am pleased with your attitude. I am convinced that you have learned a valuable lesson from this experience. I know you have suffered much already, and it is not my purpose to cause you further hurt. So, I will make your punishment as light as I can. Of course, you cannot drive for three months, and there is nothing I can do about that. In that time your arm should about be healed. It would not be safe to drive until you have both arms in good shape, anyway."

"Of course, Your Honor," Shad said in feigned humility.

The judge went on to inform him of the legally mandated DUI course he would have to take and explained how to make arrangements for it. Then he said, "Finally, it will be a two hundred dollar fine. You have three months in which to pay it. If you need more time, just let me know. I do expect you to pay the fine yourself. It is your responsibility, not your father's."

Shad glanced at his father who seemed to be giving a sigh of relief similar to Shad's own. They had both expected the punishment to be much worse at best. He really had beaten the rap! Furthermore, his dad had already promised to pay his fine if he conducted himself like a gentleman in court. From the smile on his dad's face, he believed he had done it.

As Shad and his father left the court room, Shad spotted Todd, sitting alone on the bench in the hallway. Todd's mother was getting a drink of water. Shad slipped quickly over and said, "Hi, Todd."

"Hi, Shad," Todd said as he arose stiffly from his seat. "So when's your trial?"

"Won't be one. I changed my mind."

"Really? Great!" Todd exclaimed with obvious relief. "So was it hard in there?"

"Naw. Piece of cake. The judge is a real softy. He only hit me two hundred bucks on both charges. Said I'd suffered enough and learned my lesson," Shad gloated.

"I'm glad," Todd said, feeling much better about his own prospects. "I think I'm next."

"Good luck," Shad said. "Let me know how it goes." With that, Shad strutted confidently from the courthouse.

✻

Todd's mother was not a lot of support. She was far more concerned about her husband, who was still in jail and would be for awhile, than she was about Todd. On the advice of a court-appointed attorney, Todd's dad had waived his right to a preliminary hearing and pled guilty in District Court to aggravated assault. Now, he was being held for another month while the judge had both a mental evaluation and a pre-sentence report prepared.

So, when the bailiff called Todd's name, he had to wait while his mother dragged herself reluctantly after him. Once seated in the courtroom, the judge looked at Todd very sternly. He felt a quiver of apprehension. The man in the black robe didn't look like a piece of cake to Todd. Then he remembered Shad's much more serious charges and the light sentence he had received. That made him feel a lot better.

At the appropriate time, Todd admitted to the charge of illegal consumption of alcohol on the evening of the accident. "Are you the Todd Albright who furnished the beer for Shad Cleverly?" the judge asked.

"Yes. It was my father's," Todd admitted truthfully.

"Why isn't your father with you today? Where is he?" the judge asked.

Todd hesitated, embarrassed about his father being in jail.

"Young man, I asked you a question," the judge said sternly.

"Yes, sir. He's in jail, sir," Todd admitted with downcast eyes. He was aware of his mother fidgeting nervously beside him.

"For what?" he demanded.

"He got drunk and threatened my mother."

"How?"

"Todd, please," his mother whispered.

That action did not go unnoticed by the judge, and he said, "Mrs. Albright, perhaps you would be kind enough to explain to the court why your husband is in jail."

Todd was relieved, even though his mother's account was a very watered down version of what actually happened. He was grateful to her for not mentioning Darcy's involvement.

When his mother finished, the judge addressed Todd again. "Todd, it sounds to me like your father has a drinking problem."

"Yes, sir."

"Is there always alcohol somewhere in the house?" the judge asked.

"Usually, until I..." he began.

The judge cut him off. "Did you ever get into it?" he inquired sharply.

"A few times, sir."

"Have you touched any of it since the accident?"

"No. I ain't had a drink of beer or nothing since the night Shad and me was in the wreck."

"Do you expect me to believe that you haven't so much as touched a single can?" the judge asked skeptically.

"Yes, sir. Er, well, I did touch some, but only so I..."

"So you admit that you lied to me a moment ago?" the judge asked, his face growing hard and cold.

Todd was feeling desperate, but he was telling the truth, and there was nothing else he could do. So he said, "No, sir. I just dumped it all out so there wouldn't be none when my father came home."

"You dumped all his alcohol out?" the judge asked, obviously not believing a word Todd was saying.

"Yes, sir. After he went to jail."

"Mrs. Albright," the judge said, making Todd's mother jump.

"Yes, Your Honor," she said timidly.

"Did you see Todd dump your husband's alcohol out?"

"No, but then..."

"Did he ask your permission?"

"No, but..."

"Did he tell you he had done it?"

"No, but if he says..." she tried again.

"That will be enough," the judge interrupted once more. "I believe I have the picture now. Todd, I am ordering you to pay a fine of five hundred dollars," he barked.

"But, sir..." Todd began to protest.

"I will expect it to be paid in full to the clerk of this court within ninety days. Is that clear?"

"Yes, sir."

"Do you have a job?"

"I am in school. I don't have..."

"You had better get one, and real soon. If you stay busy, then maybe you won't have so much time on your hands to get into your father's alcohol. You are to report to me right here in this courtroom in two weeks. If you are not working after school by then, I will put you in a community service program, and you may not enjoy the work you have to do there. One way or the other, you will pay your fine," the judge said emphatically.

"Yes, sir," Todd answered, tempted to say something about Shad's light fine but wisely avoiding the temptation. He was in enough trouble already, and he had told nothing but the truth. It would be best if he did not stir the judge up any worse.

"Now, Todd," His Honor went on, "I sincerely hope this will teach you a lesson about the dangers of drinking. I would have thought that with a father like yours, you would have already learned, but apparently you haven't. What I am doing is for your good. I hope you understand that."

"I know, sir," Todd responded meekly. "I don't ever want to be like my father."

"So, I am getting through to you already. I hope you also will see the importance of always telling the truth."

"Sir, I have been!" Todd blurted. I even promised Trooper..."

"That will be all, Todd. You may be excused now. I still have other cases to attend to."

Todd glared angrily at the judge. His mother touched his arm. "Come on, Todd. You've already said far too much."

Todd walked glumly from the courtroom. "So much for being honest. It's not fair, Mom," he complained. "He didn't hardly do nothing to Shad, and I'll bet he lied through his teeth. He ain't about to quit drinking."

"I know, son, but you better go look for a job, starting tomorrow after school. I certainly can't pay your fine, and with the worries of your father in jail, I just can't worry about this, too," his mother said sadly.

"Yeah," Todd replied bitterly. He just could not believe the injustice of it all. Right now he needed a friend, and he thought of Jill and Darcy. If left on his own, he was not sure he was strong enough now to keep from drowning his frustrations in a can of beer. He glanced at his watch. School would be out in a few minutes. Maybe he'd just call Jill.

❖

Jill walked Darcy to the bus. "I wonder how it went for Todd today in court," she said.

"I've been thinking about that, too," Darcy replied. "I think Shad had to go in, too, but he has an attorney, and all he was going to do was set up a trial. Today will be easy for Todd compared to testifying against Shad when he goes to court with his attorney and all."

"Hey, do you think your mom would let you come to town after you get home? We could go see Todd," Jill suggested.

"We do have a Laurel activity tonight, but if I promise not to be too long, I'll bet she'll let me. I'll give you a call as soon as I get home," Darcy decided as she turned toward the bus. "I better get on or I'll be walking home."

Later, as Darcy and Nate strolled up the lane in the cool October air, Nate said, "I talked to Billy today."

"You did?" Darcy said, glancing with surprise at her little brother. His eye was back to normal and his broken nose looked pretty good. It was amazing how quickly he'd healed.

"Yup. I guess he's not mad at me anymore."

"What did you two talk about?"

"Lots 'a stuff. He even told me that Shad got in trouble with his mom and dad Sunday night," Nate said importantly.

"He did?"

"Yup."

"What did he do to make them angry?"

"Drinking."

"Again?" she said, a painful knot gripping her stomach.

"Yup. Billy says his dad and mom both hollered at him. He says he was supposed to be in bed, but he snuck out and seen Shad when he come home. He says he couldn't hardly walk. He kept bumping into the walls and stuff."

"Oh, Nate, that's awful, isn't it?" She wanted to cry out. Why couldn't Shad just do what he had been taught?

"Yup," Nate continued. "So Billy says his dad told Shad he was in a lot of trouble."

"What kind of trouble, Nate?" Darcy asked. Wondering what could be worse than facing a trial for drunk driving.

"Dunno."

"That's all he told you, Nate?"

"Yup," Nate concluded. "Race ya, Darcy," he said after they'd walked in silence for a moment, and he was off like a jack rabbit.

Darcy followed, but her heart was not in the race. Somehow, she had tried to make herself believe that Shad wouldn't really keep drinking. They had been such good friends. Maybe it was just hope, she decided. She so wanted him to be the kind of young man she liked to be with. It saddened her terribly to learn that he had been drunk again.

Her mother said it would be fine for her to take the car to town, but not to be long. Before she could call Jill, though, her friend called her.

"We better hurry, Darcy," Jill said as soon as Darcy answered. Her voice was agitated, and she sounded on the verge of tears.

"What's the matter, Jill?" Darcy asked, feeling a cold chill in the room.

"Todd called. He's really upset. He thinks he got a raw deal today."

"Did you tell him we'd come over?"

"Yes, so please hurry. I'm afraid of what he might do if we don't get there pretty quick," Jill said, the alarm she was feeling clear in her voice.

Darcy was on her way a minute later. What could have happened to upset Todd so badly? she wondered. He had, as recently as this morning in school, told both her and Jill that he would accept whatever the judge did.

She recognized Sister Cleverly's car approaching and was surprised when the horn began blaring. As it passed, Darcy was shocked to see Shad's grinning face behind the wheel. Now she was worried about Todd. Something was definitely fishy.

# Chapter Nine

"HI, JILL. HI, DARCY. Come in," Todd said glumly.

Darcy had never seen Todd so depressed. She wanted to just throw her arms around him and say it was okay. But Jill beat her to it.

Todd wanted to talk, and Darcy and Jill let him. Darcy worried about the bitterness he displayed as he recounted in detail his experience in court that afternoon. And the look on Jill's usually bright face was one of dark and brooding anger.

Finally, Todd finished and asked gloomily, "So what am I going to do, girls?"

Jill spoke up quickly, as she was wont to do when agitated. "I can't believe it, Todd. I just can't believe it. This makes me so mad I could chew nails. You got punished the worst out of you and Shad just because of your dad's problems. I think someone should go talk to the judge and tell him what a mistake he's made. It's just awful!"

"That wouldn't help," Todd moaned. "It would only make him mad, and that would make it worse for me, not better."

"But something's got to be done," Jill said with fire in her eyes.

"Yeah, like maybe I just oughta go get drunk," Todd suggested with downcast eyes.

Jill's eyes popped and her face went blank. "Oh, no! Please don't do that, Todd."

Darcy spoke up, her voice choked with emotion. "Todd, you promised, remember?"

"I know I did, Darcy," he said bitterly. "But look where it's got me so far. I haven't had a taste of beer since the wreck, and I get hammered while Shad gets practically nothing. And he's been drinking like a fish and bragging about it all over the school. So give me one good reason why I should even try anymore."

"Because it's right, Todd. But if that isn't enough, here's another one; you'll be a stronger and far better person when it's all over. It seems to me like getting off easy hurts a person in the long run, not helps them. Do you really think Shad is getting a break?"

"Yeah, I'll say. It's pretty obvious!" Todd stormed.

"I mean in the long run, Todd. I don't think his DUI arrest means a thing to him now. Let me tell you something. I saw Shad driving his mother's car on the way to town a few minutes ago, and he was grinning like he owned the world. Does that tell you anything?"

"Yeah, that he got a break," Todd answered stubbornly.

"No, not that, Todd," Darcy reasoned patiently. "He doesn't have a license anymore, but he's driving anyway. It tells me that he thinks he can get away with anything when all..."

"That's right! He got a great big break, like I said," Todd interrupted fiercely.

"No, that's not completely right, Todd. He may get away with it for awhile, but he'll get caught again, and then..."

"Another slap on the hands," Todd interrupted again.

"Maybe. Shad will be eighteen in a couple of weeks. Then he has to see Judge Simper if he is arrested for anything, because he'll be too old to go to juvenile court," Darcy revealed.

"Oh, oh. I hear Simper's tough on underage drinkers and murder on drunk drivers," Todd said, his face lighting up with understanding.

So did Jill's, and she echoed Todd's sentiment. "Shad'll be in trouble for sure."

"Probably," Darcy agreed. "Randy did tell me that Judge Simper is a whole lot stricter on drunk drivers than juvenile court. To tell the truth, Todd, I feel sorry for Shad."

"You do?" Todd and Jill asked in mystified unison.

"Yes, I do, because now he probably thinks that he can do what he wants whenever it pleases him, and that nothing will be done about it. Well, I'm afraid that with that attitude, he'll really end up in big trouble some day. And that makes me feel bad. Really bad," Darcy reasoned.

"Well, maybe so, but I'm the one in big trouble now, and that makes me feel real bad!" Todd said.

"Oh, come on Todd. It isn't that bad," Darcy said lightly.

"Yeah it is. I gotta' have a job in two weeks or I have to do community service. And the judge told me it would be miserable, and that I would hate it," Todd complained.

Darcy sat thoughtfully for a moment while Jill suggested several businesses in town where Todd might apply. Then Darcy said, "I have an idea. Can I get back with you tomorrow? I know just the job for you, but Jill and

I will need to put in a good word first. We'll do it tonight, won't we Jill?"

Jill nodded. "Of course, but what…"

Darcy interrupted. "It'll work out, you'll see."

"Gee, Darcy, would you do that for me?"

"We will. We're friends, Todd." She paused, then grinned and winked at Jill. "There is one condition, of course."

"What?" Todd asked cautiously.

"Can't you guess?"

Todd gave a long sigh. At length a smile flirted with the corners of his mouth. "I can't get drunk."

"That's right, or even sniff the stuff. You have to promise both of us, huh, Jill?"

"Yes, and if you don't, I'll…" Jill began.

"You'll what?"Todd asked, leaning toward the pert red head with wide eyes and the beginning of a smile.

"I…I won't…I won't go to the homecoming pageant or the dance with you!" Jill finally blurted.

"Hey, you guys didn't tell me you were going on a date!" Darcy exploded in mock anger.

"Oh…well…ah…you ain't mad, are you, Darcy?" Todd stammered, his face turning a deep shade of red.

Jill looked worried for a moment, but when Darcy grinned, she relaxed. "Of course not," Darcy said. "I'm just kidding. I think it's great. So, Todd, if you want to go out with my best friend…my other best friend, I mean, then you better get to promising."

"I do, I do," he said with a chuckle. "And you better win queen, Darcy Felding," he went on sternly.

Darcy had been nominated as one of the candidates for Homecoming Queen. She frankly did not want to do it. In their school, it was a regular pageant, with formals, talent competition, judges, tricky interviews, and the works. She had given in to pressure from the senior class, but only half-heartedly. "I don't have a chance of winning, and it doesn't matter anyway," she said with a slight frown.

"Of course you have a chance, Darcy, and all your friends will be rooting for you," Jill said. "What will you do for your talent number, play the piano or sing?" Todd asked.

Darcy could do both very well, although she was very modest about her talents. "I don't know, you guys," she said self-consciously. "I'll probably muff whatever I try. But, Mom thinks I should sing and accompany myself on the piano."

"Hey, great!" Todd shouted.

"She'll win for sure, Todd," Jill said with a grin. "You'll see."

"I bet she will," Todd agreed enthusiastically. "Gee, you know, I feel good now. What is it about you two? I was feeling so rotten I could of slit my wrists before you came. Or worse, I might a got drunk!" A tear wet his eye and he brushed it away self-consciously. "I'm really lucky. Thanks for coming by. You two really cheered me up. I'll be fine now."

In the old family car a few minutes later, Jill was still concerned about Todd. She turned to Darcy and asked, "Do you really think we can help him get a job, or were you just trying to make him feel better?"

"You know me better than that, Jill," Darcy scolded mildly. "Dad said today that Bishop Olsen needs a fellow to help milk in the evenings. He'll be at the church tonight. I thought maybe we could talk to him then and let Todd know in the morning."

Jill brightened up instantly. "Hey, that would be great!" she exclaimed.

And it was.

Bishop Olsen did not hesitate for a moment when the girls explained Todd's dilemma. "It'll give me more of a chance to get close to him. I've got a few minutes right now. Maybe I could just run over to his house and talk to him tonight," he suggested enthusiastically.

Darcy thanked Bishop Olsen and said, "I know he'll work hard."

Jill cried.

Not long after Darcy got home that evening, Todd called. The appreciation he expressed in his less-than-correct grammar was genuine, and it brought tears to Darcy's eyes. Deep down, she felt that Todd would be all right now. She just wished she could feel the same about Shad.

❉

Over the next two weeks, Darcy saw less of Todd, but Jill saw more. Jill found a hundred and one excuses to drop by and help his mother. At school, Todd was all she talked about. At times it annoyed Darcy, but she bit her tongue and tried to be glad for both of them.

Bishop Olsen ordained Todd a priest the very next Sunday, and he began to speak in terms of going on a mission after he had turned nineteen.

Todd's mother even came to church for the first time in years to see Todd approved to be advanced in the Aaronic Priesthood and to watch him be ordained. His father, a district court judge had decreed, would not be allowed to come home until he had completed an inpatient program of several weeks at an alcohol rehabilitation facility. His family was told that they would not be allowed to see him until he was a month along in the program, and then only if he was making satisfactory progress.

Mrs. Albright had been upset, but several long talks with Todd and one with Bishop Olsen had set her mind at ease. The prospect of having a sober, productive, and loving husband when Todd's dad was eventually allowed to return home made the days more bearable for her.

�֍

While Todd and his family were doing much better, Shad was running wild. Four nights before Darcy was to compete in the Homecoming pageant, Randy's family invited the Feldings for dinner and a family home evening activity. After an exquisite meal, prepared as only Sandy Hutchins could do, they all pitched in and helped clean up. As they were finishing, Randy said, "Next we will all go into the living room and listen to Darcy play and sing her number for the queen pageant."

Darcy resisted, but Nate and the Randy Hutchins look-a-likes begged her to. She finally gave in and performed quite well. "You'd put the heavenly choir and orchestra to shame," her uncle raved when she finished.

"Oh, Randy, you're just saying that. Didn't you hear the mistakes I made?" Darcy said, blushing.

"If you made them, I didn't hear them. Seriously, I mean it. You are really something special, and not just in how well you sing and play the piano. I know how much effort it has required to learn to play and sing like you do. But, you are also special in other ways. Anyone who could do what you did and turn a kid like Todd Albright around has to be something else again," Randy said sincerely.

"I didn't do much. And Jill did as much as me. Anyway, Todd was wanting…"

Randy held up his hand, stopping Darcy mid-sentence. "Whoa now, girl. Others pitched in and helped, I know, but only because of you."

"Todd wanted to change. He was ready," Darcy was quick to point out.

"Yes, he was at that. I only wish Shad was ready, too." Randy grew somber and thoughtful.

Alarmed, Darcy asked, "He's not in trouble again, is he?"

"I'm afraid so. He's just going from bad to worse."

"Billy says he's been driving and the cops can't stop him," Nate chipped in from his position on the floor beside Randy's boys.

"That's not quite true. He's gotten away with it for several days now, I know, but it caught up with him today. Things just got very complicated for Shad, I'm afraid," Randy said, looking at Nate, but really talking more to Darcy.

She squirmed on the hard piano bench, fearing the answer to the question she had framed in her mind. Finally, she asked, "What happened today?"

"I picked him up this morning when he should have been in school," Randy revealed.

"Oh, no," Darcy moaned, feeling both let down and depressed.

"You did?" Nate echoed, sounding and looking anything but depressed.

"I'm so sorry for Paula Cleverly," Sharon said, wringing her hands and then placing one of them on her husband's arm.

"I was afraid it would have to be you again," Kerry said, putting a calloused hand over the small, soft one of his wife.

"What did you stop him for?" Darcy asked, almost sure of what she'd hear. "Was he drunk again?"

Randy surprised her. "No, thank goodness for that. He was driving just over eighty when he came into my radar about ten miles east of town. He should have been in school. Of course, after I got him stopped, I arrested him for driving while his license was revoked as well as for speeding. Judge Simper was in, so I took him straight to court," Randy explained.

"I thought he had to go to Juvenile Court," Sharon said.

"Not anymore. Shad turned eighteen a few days ago. He must have thought he was back in front of the same judge, though. He acted like he thought it was no big deal and that if he gave the judge a sob-story that it would end there."

"Did it?" Kerry asked.

"Not hardly. Shad entered a guilty plea. Wouldn't even try to get hold of his parents first. Of course, since he's eighteen, he didn't have to, although I had to call them later since I had the car towed in."

"Oh, no, that's awful," Darcy moaned. She was feeling worse again, after the brief relief she felt when she learned that he had not been drinking.

"So what happened?" Kerry pressed.

"Well, he told the judge some wild story about having to run an urgent errand for his mother. He never did make it clear what the errand was, but I guess he figured after his experience with the juvenile court that it didn't matter much," Randy explained. "Anyway, when he got finished talking, the judge slapped him with a $580.00 fine and gave him five days in jail which..."

"You mean he's in jail now?" Darcy asked Randy in alarm. It hurt her more than she cared to admit to think of him locked in jail like a common criminal.

"No, but he will be if he gets picked up again. Judge Simper gave him six months to pay the fine, and he put Shad on probation for one year. Any more violations and he will be serving the five days and probably more to boot." Randy paused and smiled at Darcy. "I'm just glad he wasn't drinking today," he added.

"Me too," she said in a quiet voice. She dropped her eyes and turned to face the piano. She absently played a few notes, then turned back and asked, "What will happen to Shad?"

"Nobody knows that, Darcy, anymore than we can predict our own futures. However, it is fairly safe to assume that Shad's troubles with the law have only just begun unless, of course, he changes his attitude," Randy said, shaking his head sadly.

Darcy watched him for a moment. Randy had a far-away look in his eyes, but a brief smile flashed across his face, and he said, "At least you have made a favorable impression on him, Darcy."

"On Shad?" she asked in surprise. "He's mad at me."

"Not as mad as you think. He was ranting at me after Judge Simper fined him. Among other things that I won't repeat, Shad said, 'The only decent thing I can think of about you, Hutchins, is that Darcy is your niece.'"

"Yes, Darcy, I'd say you have made an impression on that wild young man. I just wish," Randy said sadly, "that I could believe that would be enough to soften his attitude, but I'm afraid he's determined to show the law that he can't be tamed."

Darcy wiped a tear away. Then another. Nate stood, moved to the piano bench and sat beside her, putting a slender arm around her almost equally slender waist. Darcy smiled down at his upturned, concerned face and felt an almost overwhelming surge of affection for him.

"What's the matter, Darcy?" he asked in an emotion choked little voice. "Is Shad still your boyfriend after all?"

"Nate!" she said with a sudden burst of anger. "Don't you ever say that again!"

Nate looked shocked. "What's the matter, Darcy?" her mother asked. "You have no right to talk to Nate in that tone of voice."

A tense silence prevailed in the Hutchins' house and Darcy was shamefully aware of every eye in the place on her. Even Randy's little boys stopped their noisy play and gazed at her burning face. Finally, with a heaviness of heart that she could not explain, Darcy said, "It's just Shad, I guess. I have this horrible feeling that he's going to do something terrible. I just know it. And I can't stand it."

"Now, Darcy," Randy spoke up quickly. "Don't let him get to you. He's not your responsibility."

"Randy, please be careful," Darcy interrupted, looking at him with concern. "It would just kill me if Shad hurt you." She paused to wipe away her tears again before saying, "Or any of you. Nate, don't you go playing too close to the highway anymore, please. You know how crazily Shad drives."

"Darcy! You're scaring me!" her mother said with wide eyes as a cold chill descended on the room. "Shad won't hurt any of us. And Randy is always cautious, aren't you, Randy?"

"Of course," the young trooper said.

"You are just upset and nervous," her mother went on. "Maybe you're under too much pressure over the pageant," she suggested.

Darcy untangled Nate's arms from around her waist and rose to her feet. "Maybe. I wish I hadn't told them I'd be in it. I don't even care if I win or not." Everyone nodded and she went on, "The trouble is, everybody but one will lose. It's awful, when you think about it."

"Well, don't worry about that. Just do it and have fun," her father said.

"Oh, I will, but I just wish there didn't have to be losers. No, Mom," she said, turning to face Sharon, "I don't think it's the pageant that's making me so cranky. It's just Shad that's upsetting me. I get these awful feelings lately. I'm sorry, I didn't mean to upset everyone," she blurted, and, sobbing, she fled toward the back yard.

❊

Kerry watched as Sharon stood with one hand over her mouth, watching her daughter's rich chestnut hair bouncing gaily as Darcy fled. Turning to her husband, she said, "Kerry, do something. Go talk to her."

"No, Sharon, I think she just needs a few minutes to herself, then she'll be fine."

"I'm sorry," Randy said. "I wouldn't have said a thing about Shad if I'd had any idea it would upset her so much."

"It's not your fault, Randy," Kerry said shivering. "I just wish she'd forget about him. I'm a little afraid that she likes him more than she cares to admit, and that frightens me." He paused, then said, "Hey, is it just me, or is it cold in here? I feel like someone just turned on the air conditioning."

"Kerry, it is not cold in here. I think Darcy has just upset us all. Whatever has gotten into her?" Sharon said, reaching again for the support of her husband's arm.

Nate stepped beside them, his eyes wide with fright. Kerry put an arm around him, then he noticed Randy, who was just pulling his little boys to him. Sandy stepped close to them and encircled all three with her arms. Kerry felt his wife shiver as the two families huddled and faced the door where Darcy had just exited the room.

"I want to repeat what Darcy just said," Kerry suddenly announced ominously, and every head turned toward him. "Maybe it's just a mood, but all of us need to be careful. Darcy isn't very often given to irrational statements. She felt something, and I feel it, too. Nate, you stay away from that highway. And Randy, you be extra careful."

Randy said, "All right." Then he broke the somber mood. "Okay, now let's play some games. That's why we invited you folks over. Darcy can join us as soon as she is ready, which won't be long, or I miss my guess. Now, on the count of three, everyone cheer up. One...two...three."

As if by magic, the somber mood faded, and Randy pulled out a stack of table games. Ten minutes later, Darcy came back in. "I'm sorry," she said, brushing her long, wavy hair over her shoulder. "Am I too late to join in the fun?"

"Of course not, there's always a place for Darcy," Randy said fondly.

Kerry Felding watched his daughter with affection. Their eyes met briefly and in the depths of brilliant green, he was sure some terrible foreboding still lurked. He felt a pang of fear clutch his heart.

❄

The days were flying by. It was Friday evening, and Todd was herding his mother's rusty Chevrolet out to Bishop Olsen's farm as he did each evening. As he walked into the barn to begin the milking, Bishop Olsen greeted him with a smile and firm handshake. He had come to admire Bishop Olsen and thoroughly enjoyed working with him and his two oldest boys, both of whom were younger than Todd.

A flighty heifer kicked and sent one of the boys flying a few minutes later. Todd moved over and, with a few soothing words and a gentle hand on the young cow's back, soon had her calmed down, and the younger boy took over without further problems.

The bishop witnessed the scene and said to Todd a moment later, "You must speak Bovine, Todd. I've never seen anyone who could settle one of these heifers down the way you do. I'm surely glad to have your help."

"Thanks," Todd responded. "I enjoy it."

He settled into the evening's routine and thought of how much happier he was now than he had ever been. He thought of his father and realized that he missed him. He wished he could be here and work alongside him. That was something Todd had never experienced, and he craved it as he watched the bishop and his sons. What fun they had working together. Todd silently promised himself that when his father was allowed to come home, he would try to build the relationship they had never had.

Todd worked quickly this evening, for he had a date with Jill, their first formal one. The more he was around her, the better he liked her. And for her friendship, he had Darcy to thank. He thought of Darcy with affection. It was not the same kind of affection that drew him to Jill, but something more like he thought he might have felt for a sister.

Darcy was special to Todd in a unique sort of way, and nobody wanted her to win the queen contest tonight more than Todd did, unless maybe it was Jill. He whistled as he turned out the last of the cows and helped Bishop Olsen clean the milking parlor. They were done in record time.

"Gee, Todd, what's the hurry tonight?" Bishop Olsen asked.

"The queen contest is tonight. Jill and I are going to go root for Darcy Felding," he answered with enthusiasm.

"I hope she wins," Bishop Olsen said with a smile. "She's a good gal. Of course, so is Jill," he added with a twinkle in his eye.

"Yes, she is," Todd agreed as he pulled the rubber boots from his feet and replaced them with his worn tennis shoes.

At six-forty-five sharp, Todd was at Jill's door, brushing his unruly shock of hair nervously with one hand while rapping with vigor on the door with the other. Jill answered his bold knock, and her pretty, freckled face lit up. "You're right on time, Todd Albright," she said with a giggle.

"Of course, it's my first date with you. Anyway, we can't be late. After all, we're the leaders, you know," he said, grinning as he helped Jill wiggle into her sweater. He tingled at the way she wiggled.

"Leaders? Of what?" Jill asked, taking his offered arm and heading out the door.

"The Darcy Felding for Queen Fan Club, what else?"

"Of course," she agreed gleefully, and together, they skipped toward the rusty Chevy, the closest thing to a limo that Todd could produce for his important first date with Jill Steelan, the girl of his dreams.

# Chapter Ten

EVERY GIRL IN THE contest looked pretty that night, but none of them were as radiant as Darcy Felding. At least, that was Jill Steelan's opinion, and when she whispered as much in Todd's ear, he agreed.

With faith and enthusiasm unwavering, they watched the girl with the rich chestnut hair and startling green eyes take her moment in the lights. In a dark green formal made by her mother, Darcy was not only the most gorgeous girl on the stage, but she was also one of the two most modest. The only other one who was dressed as nicely as Darcy was another of her friends, tall and pretty Stacy Seltz.

When Darcy performed her talent number, she brought the house down. No one did as well, and Jill just knew Darcy was going to win. Waiting was difficult for Jill, and she fidgeted like a kid in a candy store as they prepared to announce the winners. Todd held her hand so tightly she had to ask him not to crush it. "Sorry," he said, "I'm nervous."

"Me, too, but she's going to win," Jill squealed. "Darcy is going to win."

Darcy did not win.

Darcy was first attendant.

Jill was heartbroken. Todd was gloomy. Darcy glowed and hugged Stacy Seltz, the new queen, and appeared to be as happy as if she had won herself. Stacy was one of their friends. The only reason Darcy and Jill hadn't been closer with Stacy was because she lived in a different ward. Darcy was truly glad for Stacy.

Todd and Jill worked their way forward to where the new Queen and her court were receiving congratulations and offered their own rather unenthusiastic good wishes. As they moved away in the throng of people who were trying to reach the royalty, Jill spotted Darcy's parents. They were both smiling and excited, but little Nate looked thoroughly disgusted. Jill turned and looked back at Darcy. A pang of guilt swept over her as she caught a glimpse of Darcy's radiantly happy face. How could she be so unhappy and disappointed when Darcy was not?

Holding tightly to Todd's hand, she followed him toward the west exit. She was surprised and came to a stop when she noticed Shad standing near the next exit. He was looking directly at Mr. Truman, the school principal, who appeared to be in an intense conversation with the three pageant judges.

When Shad looked away, his handsome face was dark with anger, and Jill winced. Shad shouldered his way past several milling students and strode close to Mr. Truman. There he paused a moment, listening, then he said something that caused the principal to look at him in alarm. Then Shad was gone.

"Did you see that?" Todd whispered urgently in Jill's ear.

"Yeah. I wonder what's going on," Jill said, her attention still drawn to the principal and the three judges, all of whom appeared to be upset. Mr. Truman repeatedly threw his hands in the air.

"Whatever's wrong, Mr. Truman doesn't know what to do about it," Todd suggested with a chuckle. "Must have something to do with Shad."

"They all keep looking toward the stage where Stacy and Darcy and the others are. That one judge is getting real mad," Jill said, referring to a slender middle-aged woman whose face, even from this distance, appeared distorted and red.

Suddenly, the woman slapped a paper in the principal's hand, whirled, and stalked out. The other two followed a moment later. Mr. Truman faced the front of the auditorium. He took a step forward, faltered, and stopped.

Jill and Todd were both fascinated as they watched him. Suddenly, Shad reappeared, stalked right up to Mr. Truman and said something. Mr. Truman turned pasty white, and Shad pointed to the stage and said something else. Mr. Truman appeared to have nothing to say, but whatever Shad had told him had an effect on him, for he started toward the stage again.

Jill and Todd watched him advance. Shad did not move until the principal had worked his way through the gradually dwindling crowd and spoke briefly to Darcy. At that point, Shad departed.

Mr. Truman led Darcy out of sight behind the huge black curtains at the far side of the stage. "Well, that's why Shad was mad," Todd guessed. "It must have something to do with Darcy. You know, Jill, I don't think Shad hates her anymore. He just hates me."

"He never hated her, but I wonder what happened," Jill murmured.

❊

Darcy listened in shock. Mr. Truman had just informed her that a very serious mistake had been made. "I don't know exactly how it happened, but someone got your name and Stacy's mixed up. Maybe because they're similar. Anyway, when the judges' points were totaled, you were the clear winner, Darcy. The judges were out in the hallway when Stacy was announced as the winner instead of you. They didn't realize what had occurred until several minutes later when they overheard several kids talking about how surprised they were that Stacy won and you got first attendant. That was when they came and found me."

"Oh, no," Darcy moaned in misery.

"So, anyway, Darcy, I must go break the news to Stacy that she's really only first attendant and you are queen. Most of the people are..." he was saying.

"No, Mr. Truman, don't," Darcy said urgently.

"Don't what?"

"Don't tell her."

"But I must. You won, Darcy. It was a mistake, and it would not be right, and anyway..."

"Please, Mr. Truman, don't do it," Darcy interrupted tearfully. "She's my friend and it would hurt her badly. She is so happy, and I don't even want to be queen. Please."

"But..."

"No, I mean it," Darcy said, genuinely alarmed at the prospect of having Stacy's moment of glory jerked cruelly away.

"Darcy, listen, please," Mr. Truman begged.

She listened, her heart pounding fiercely, wishing she had followed her instincts and not become involved in the pageant in the first place.

"Shad Cleverly overheard the judges in the hall and followed them when they came to inform me. That complicates things, for had he not heard, I might have been able to do as you suggest. Now, do you see why we must straighten it out?" Mr. Truman asked.

Darcy studied his face for a moment. She, as was the case with most of the students, was fond of Mr. Truman. He was kind, gentle, and fair, and had earned the respect of the whole community in the five years he had been here. That this problem was a difficult one for a man of such tender feelings was clearly visible in the form of unusually deep lines on his forehead.

Finally, she answered him. "No, Mr. Truman, I don't see why Stacy has to know. Shad surely won't..."

"Shad will!" Mr. Truman exclaimed. "He threatened to tell everyone if I didn't make it right."

"Then I'll just have to talk to him," Darcy said decisively.

"It won't help, Darcy. He was so angry, and..." The principal stopped.

"And what, Mr. Truman?" Darcy pressed, afraid to hear what he had to say, but knowing she must.

"Shad has been drinking. He smelled like a brewery, and..." he was saying until he was interrupted by a short, slender little boy with bright green eyes that were so like Darcy's. He had been standing in the shadows in a fold of the long black curtains that encircled the stage.

"Shad has to go to jail if he's drunk," Nate announced.

"Nate!" Darcy exclaimed. "How long have you been standing there?"

"Not very long," he said in a timid voice, a look of shame on his face.

"Nate," Mr. Truman said, the lines on his forehead turning a sickly shade of grey. "Did you hear what your sister and I were discussing?"

"Uh, huh," he said in an even smaller voice. "Darcy won, didn't she?"

"No, Nate, I did not win! Stacy Seltz won," Darcy said sternly.

"Darcy, you shouldn't lie," he said a little bolder.

"I'm not. Maybe the judges thought I should have won, but I didn't, and it is a secret what they thought. You are to tell no one, because..." She stopped abruptly as Nate turned and scampered through the curtains.

"Oh, no, he'll say something," Darcy groaned, and she started after him.

"No, Darcy. Let him go," Mr. Truman ordered brusquely, stopping her. "We just as well face it."

"I can't. I just can't. Stacy will be crushed. Oh, please, no," Darcy cried, tears washing down her face.

The curtains parted, and Nate reappeared, dragging his mother. His father followed a step behind. "Tell em," Nate said, looking Darcy squarely in the eye. "I promise I won't say nothing to nobody else if you tell Mom and Dad."

"Darcy," Sharon said, pulling her unhappy daughter into her arms. "What is the matter?"

Darcy choked up and couldn't force out a single word. Mr. Truman came to her rescue. While he explained, Sharon and Kerry listened in stunned silence.

"Darcy insists that I not correct the wrong that has been done to her," he concluded.

"And we concur with that," Kerry said as his wife nodded her agreement. "Stacy is so radiant and happy, it would be devastating to her. It just would not be right."

"Shad knows!" Nate interjected.

"About the mistake!?" Kerry exclaimed.

"It's true, I'm afraid, and that makes this very difficult," Mr. Truman said, shaking his head sadly.

"Someone must speak with Shad at once," Kerry said.

"That's what Darcy suggested, but it's too late, I'm afraid," Mr. Truman said wearily.

"Shad's drunk!" Nate added, proud to impart his accidentally gained knowledge.

Darcy had regained her composure and spoke up. "I'll talk to him. I think I can make him listen."

"I think you oughta' be queen, Darcy," Nate quipped.

"You made a promise, little brother, and I trust you not to forget."

"I know I did, Darcy, and I won't tell, but Mr. Truman can."

Darcy dropped to one knee in her long green formal and looked at Nate earnestly from his level. "Nate, what if Stacy had really won, but I had been the one who was accidentally named the winner in front of all those people, would you want them to tell me I wasn't the winner anymore?" she asked.

"No, you'd feel bad, Darcy," he answered without hesitation. "And you'd be embarrassed, too."

"Exactly, and that's why we can't tell anyone, because Stacy would feel badly and be embarrassed, and we don't want that, do we?"

"Nope. But I still feel sad for you, Darcy," he said with a tight little voice.

"Thank you, Nate. I would be hurt if you didn't, but it really is not important who the queen is. Not to me, anyway."

"It's not, Darcy?"

"It's not, Nate."

❉

Todd was so curious that he was chewing his fingernails, and he hadn't done that for years. "Darcy is gonna' have to come back on the stage pretty soon," he said anxiously. "They're getting ready to take some pictures."

"Oh, Todd, something bad has happened. I just know it has," Jill said, absently brushing at her fiery hair.

"There she comes! And she's smiling!" Todd said with relief.

"But she's been crying," Jill said with a sudden intake of air.

"How can you tell from back here, Jill?"

"I just know Darcy, that's all."

Todd jumped involuntarily when a deep, very slurred voice said from behind them, "Looks like old Truman's gonna' make an announcement."

Todd whirled to find Shad, bleary-eyed and reeking of beer, smiling smugly and waving toward the stage with his good arm.

"What do you mean?" Todd demanded, trying to cover his disgust and surprise.

"Truman was gonna' let Stacy be the queen when Darcy was the winner."

"What are you talking about?" Jill demanded.

"Yeah, I told him I'd make it hot for him if he didn't straighten things out." Shad belched, and Jill covered her nose and glared at him in disgust.

"Explain yourself, man," Todd ordered, also glaring at Shad.

"Hey, they're taking pictures, and Darcy ain't wearing her crown yet!" Shad exclaimed loudly, waving his cast in the air like a saber.

"Shad, Stacy won," Todd hissed angrily. "Quit making a fool out of yourself."

"She did not! She lost to Darcy and some fool messed things up. I tell ya', I heard the judges talking about it. They was mad, too," Shad shouted.

Suddenly, Todd understood, and from the sick look on Jill's freckled face, he knew she did, too. "Shut up, Shad. Even if it's true, Darcy ain't gonna let nobody tell Stacy," he said, and he grabbed Shad by the casted arm as Shad opened his mouth to shout again. "So don't you say nothing, man."

Sober, Shad may have listened to Todd, but he was plastered, and he tore away from Todd and ran up the aisle. "Hey, here comes Darcy now," he yelled. "Congratulations, beautiful queen. I knew you would win, even if some jerk tried to rob 'ya!"

"No, Shad! Please!" Darcy cried in alarm, running as fast as possible in high heels and a long formal.

The small crowd remaining on the stage was watching Darcy with gaping mouths. The photographer was shouting at her to come back. But she was intent on stopping Shad before they heard what he was saying!

Todd lunged after Shad, who was now dragging Darcy toward the stage, loudly proclaiming her the winner. Todd freed her, and she fell in a heap, overcome with grief and embarrassment.

Shad swung his cast in an angry, powerful arc. Todd saw it coming and ducked, and then he threw all his weight behind a punch that connected with Shad's face. Blood spurted from Shad's nose, and fire shot from his eyes.

The cast-clad arm came around again. Todd tried to duck again but was too slow this time. Pain exploded in his head, and his legs turned to rubber and folded beneath him. As he slipped into unconsciousness, he was vaguely aware of Jill alternately shouting his name and then Darcy's.

✳

The Homecoming celebration had turned into a rather sad affair. Between the royal thumping the football team had suffered that afternoon, the embarrassment of the mix-up over the queen, and Shad's drunken scene, the kids were all grumpy and upset.

Shad did not create any more trouble, though, for Sarge appeared on the scene a few minutes after Todd was knocked out. Shad was removed from the crowd that had gathered again in the auditorium and hustled off to jail.

Darcy was unhurt from her little tussle with Shad—other than her already damaged feelings. Those he had shattered. But she gallantly picked up the tiny pieces, pasted them back together, and then helped Jill wash Todd's bloody face. A nasty cut over his left eye needed stitches, so Mr. Truman assigned a teacher to run him over to the emergency room. Jill, of course, went with him.

After they were gone, Mr. Truman called the girls and their parents together and explained what had happened. "So, here we are, folks" he said awkwardly. "I'm terribly sorry about the mix-up tonight, but what's done is done. Now we need to decide what to do about it."

"There is nothing to do," Darcy said quickly, and tugging at the white satin sash she wore that announced that she was first attendant, she continued. "This is mine, and I'm going to keep it." She smiled and concluded with, "Stacy is the queen, and that is the way it stays."

Stacy had trouble talking when everyone looked at her. "No. I can't be queen. I didn't win," she managed to sob while attempting to hand the crown to Darcy.

"No, please Stacy. You keep it," Darcy insisted.

And so it went, with Darcy finally prevailing and Stacy reluctantly replacing the coveted and despised crown over her straight blonde hair.

Darcy's appearance at the dance a few minutes later was brief. Todd and Jill did not show up, and Stacy only stayed a few minutes before leaving in tears. Darcy followed her out, spoke a few words of comfort, hugged her, and trekked to the old Ford.

She leaned against the door, clad now in a loose red blouse, light blue jacket, and slim white slacks. The cold of the evening was refreshing, and she breathed in the clean air, savoring its freshness while she reflected on the turbulent events of the evening. There was nothing she could do to change what had occurred, but she firmly committed herself to never enter another queen pageant as long as she lived.

From the school, Darcy drove to the Albright house. As she suspected, Jill was there, comforting Todd who was stretched out on the sofa with a huge ice-pack over the left side of his face. "Okay, pal, let's see your battle scars," Darcy said jokingly.

Jill removed the ice-pack to reveal an eye that was nearly as swollen as Nate's had been after his fight with Shad's brother. Above the purple eye, Todd sported a shiny white bandage. "Five stitches," Jill announced with a grin.

"I'm sorry, Todd. It was all my fault," Darcy said seriously.

"Your fault? How do you figure that?" Todd asked.

"I should never have been in that stupid contest," she answered.

"Hey, that's crazy," Todd exclaimed. "You won it, just like we said you would. What's a little old crown anyway. You did the best. You were really great, and as leaders of your fan club, we congratulate you, huh, Jill?"

"Yes, we sure do. You were stunning, Darcy," Jill agreed.

"Stacy won," Darcy said quietly.

"Not really," Todd protested.

"Yes, really. She won, and that's final. I don't want to hear anyone say any different than that again. Okay guys?" Darcy said. She was firm. Enough damage had been done that night, and she was not about to be a party to more. She wanted this night to be over once and for all.

"That jerk Shad," Todd then said with anger in his voice.

"It's okay, Todd. Don't be mad at Shad. I feel badly that he's in jail tonight, and so do you, I'll bet," Darcy said.

"But he ruined everything," Jill said. "Do you mean to tell me that you can forgive him again, after what he did tonight?

"What should I do? What should we do?" Darcy countered.

"Well, I don't know," Jill said, managing a feeble grin. "Be mad, I guess."

"Wrong," Darcy scolded mildly. "We could be mad. I could be really angry, in fact, but who would that help? I can only forgive him and feel badly about him. Yeah, I admit, he scares me, but I don't hate him. No matter what he does, I will never hate him."

"It's hard not to hate him, Darcy, but if you don't, then neither do I, and that's too bad," Todd said with a weak grin that was partially covered by the bulky ice-pack.

"Why is it too bad?" Darcy asked.

"Because I was gonna' break his other arm, but now I can't. That's twice you've saved his arm." He grinned, then he became serious. "Why does he scare you, Darcy?"

"I am just afraid that someday he'll really hurt someone close to me. You know, like Randy, or Nate, or my parents, or even one of you guys," she said.

"He already hurt me, twice!" Todd said, grinning again.

But the grin faded when Darcy said, "No, I mean really hurt someone badly."

She shivered and pulled her jacket tight.

# Chapter Eleven

RANDY DROPPED BY the Felding house on Sunday evening. He was on duty and in uniform. "I've got a message for one Darcy Felding from an inmate at the county jail," he said with a grin.

"Shad?" Darcy asked, puzzled.

"Who else do you know that's in jail?"

"I don't know that she wants to hear from Shad, Randy," Sharon said firmly.

"I think she needs to hear this," Randy countered.

"What is it about?" Darcy asked, more than mildly curious.

"He specifically asked the jailer to have me come by the jail and talk to him. I did and he said he had a message for you, and would I please deliver it tonight? I said I would. Then he said, and I quote, 'The only decent person in this town is Darcy.'"

Sharon shook her head, but Darcy nodded and said, "What else did he say?"

"He said, 'Tell her I'm sorry I hurt her and that I will stay out of her life. She will never be hurt by Shad Cleverly again, and that's a promise.' Then he said to tell you that he was sober when he said that."

"That was it?" Sharon asked.

"Yeah, that was all," Randy said.

"Tell Shad Cleverly that Darcy Felding has already forgiven him and that his apology is accepted. Would you do that for me, tonight, Randy?" Darcy said softly.

"Of course. Anything else?"

"No...well...yeah. Tell him I'm not mad."

"You aren't, not even a little bit?" Randy asked, raising a questioning eyebrow.

"No, not a bit. Oh, I admit, I was at first, but then I wondered what good would it do for me to be mad."

Before Randy could find a response to that profound statement, the phone rang, and Darcy jumped up and ran for it. When she returned, Sharon asked, "Who was on the phone, Darcy?"

"Bishop Billow of the Third Ward."

"What did he want?" Randy asked.

"He asked me to sing in his ward next Sunday."

"How nice. Are you going to?" Sharon asked.

"I guess."

"Hey, isn't that the day Quin Seltz will be reporting his mission? I know he will be returning from Russia on Thursday," Randy said.

"Yeah, that's what Bishop Billow said," Darcy agreed, less than enthusiastically. "Mom, if I'm going to sing, I need an accompanist. Will you be able to go with me and do that?"

"Of course, Darcy. I'd love to, but you don't seem very happy about this."

"I'm not."

"Why not?"

"Mom, Quin Seltz is Stacy's big brother. I feel like such a heel."

"Darcy, you are not a heel. You are a very loving and forgiving person who cares more for the feelings of others than for her own. There are not many girls who would have done what you did for Stacy, let alone what you would have done had Shad not interfered," Sharon said with deep emotion.

"That's right, kid," Randy agreed. "Many would have jumped at the chance to be queen, no matter who suffers."

"But Stacy is so hurt. She'll probably avoid me at school, and I don't blame her. I just feel awful. She might hate to see me in her ward—and at her own brother's homecoming!"

"Darcy, Stacy is a sweet girl. You have been her friend for years. It isn't you she's upset with. It's the terrible embarrassment of the mistake that was made, and especially the way Shad blew it all up," Sharon pointed out.

Randy nodded. "You just do your best. Everyone loves to listen to you sing, Darcy. You can stop worrying about Stacy and try to be her friend again. I'm sure that's all she wants," He advised. "I'll bet that you two will soon be even better friends than you were before."

At school the next day, Darcy's fears proved true. Stacy avoided her, and their common group of friends was split, some giving their loyalty to Stacy, others to Darcy.

It hurt Darcy deeply to see the division. That evening she made several phone calls. Those girls who had stuck by her that day were the recipients. Darcy begged each of them not to shun Stacy but to help by being especially good to her.

On Tuesday, Darcy was apprehensive as she stepped from the bus. She was not at all sure that the other girls would respond as she had requested. But her fears were wasted. Stacy was the most popular girl in school that day, and Darcy found herself alone much of the time. The same was true the following day, and Darcy began to wonder if her actions had cost her most of her friends. Not that she would have changed what she had done, but she was lonely and depressed.

Jill and Todd were all that saved her from total depression. They were there for her, and their friendship alone carried Darcy through the difficult hours. It was at lunch on Thursday that Todd mentioned Shad, an otherwise absent personality to Darcy, both in person and in conversation, if not in thought.

"I hear Shad has been expelled," Todd said, fidgeting nervously with his empty lunch tray.

"How did you find that out?" Darcy asked, pushing her own almost untouched one away.

"Hey, Darcy. You gotta eat! You ain't had enough to sustain a teeny little old mouse this week," Todd said as he watched her through sad, worried eyes.

"You're already so slender it makes me jealous," Jill added.

"I'm just not hungry, and you didn't answer my question, Todd. How did you find out about Shad being expelled?"

"Okay, it's your health, Darcy. Shad told me that Mr. Truman went to the jail and informed him he was out of school! Told him he wouldn't be getting back in, neither."

"Oh, did Shad get out of jail?" Darcy asked, feeling both encouraged and discouraged at the same time.

"No, he's still in jail," he began, and the part of Darcy that was encouraged plummeted. "He said Judge Simper was madder than an old hen," Todd finished.

"So, how did you..." Darcy began, but Todd cut her off.

"How did I see him? I done like Mr. Truman. I went to the jail last night."

"Hey, Todd. That was great of you!" Darcy exclaimed.

"It was darn hard, that's what it was."

"I'll bet Shad was glad you came."

"Yeah, matter-of-fact I do think he was at that. He's sure gone and messed himself up. At least he ain't as mad at me as he was. He even said he was sorry about this," Todd said, indicating the discolored eye and the cut above it.

"He apologized to me, too—through Randy," Darcy said gloomily. "So what's he going to do?"

"Get a job, he says. I just wish he'd quit drinking. I asked him if he was going to now, but he wouldn't say. Darcy, what's the matter!?" Todd suddenly asked in alarm.

She felt faint—the haunting feeling was back. Why wouldn't, or couldn't, Shad quit drinking? she wondered sadly.

"Darcy!" It was Jill this time.

"I'm okay, guys—just thinking," Darcy mumbled, struggling to shrug off the cloud of gloom that had settled over her.

"You scare me when you do that, Darcy," Jill said with frightened eyes that punctuated her words.

"I'm sorry, guys. It's just Shad. He...Oh, never mind. Should we go?"

Her friends did not pry any deeper, and Darcy tried to tuck her fears away where none could see them. But she still felt them.

Only one thing brightened Darcy's week. On Friday, Stacy spoke to her in the hallway. Darcy could see that it took a great deal of effort. Their conversation was brief but friendly. Stacy seemed much better now, and that cheered Darcy up. With a little more time, maybe things could sort of be normal again, Darcy hoped.

On Sunday, Darcy's mother and little brother accompanied her to the Third Ward which met in the old chapel across town. They sat on the front row. Darcy attempted to sit there with them, but Bishop Billow insisted that she sit on the stand behind the bishopric.

Her heart thumped when Stacy's blonde head and willowy figure appeared in the doorway at the back of the chapel. Then, a moment later, Stacy's brother, Quin, came in, and Darcy's heart nearly stopped!

Tall, blond, serious, and very, very handsome, Quin Seltz had changed in the two years he had been gone. Darcy had never really paid much attention to him before his mission. Of course, she had been a couple of months shy of sixteen when he left for Russia, and he had been several months beyond twenty. Quin had gone to two years of college before his mission call, and she had hardly seem him after he graduated from high school—not that she had wanted to, or even thought about it. There had always been Shad.

Darcy noticed Quin now.

She could scarcely pull her eyes away as he walked up the aisle beside his mother, just a step behind Stacy and her dad. Two younger sisters, almost as blonde as Stacy, trailed behind. Near the front of the chapel they all found seats but Quin. Nodding soberly at this person and that, he made his way to the stand.

How sober and serious he is, Darcy thought as he approached. He stopped in front of the bishopric, shook each of their hands and started to sit beside the second counselor. Darcy's heart was in her throat—Quin moved with such muscular grace and poise.

Then he looked up and his eyes met hers.

She almost choked! Quin's eyes were the bluest blue she had ever seen. And when his sober face lit up in a smile, it was the broadest smile a man could have. And the sparkle in his eyes that accompanied that smile was like raindrops striking the calm blue of the sea.

He moved toward her, extended a hand, and spoke. "This can't be Darcy Felding, can it?"

It was, but words failed Darcy Felding! Quin's eyes sparkled a little more, and he asked, "Mind if I sit beside you?"

He had been maneuvering into just such a position as he spoke to her. She looked at the empty seat beside her, and he asked, "This okay?"

Was it! How could any girl not want to sit beside Quin Seltz? Quin reached for her hand. She gave him a wet rag, but he seemed not to notice and pumped vigorously before releasing her hand, dropping his eyes and sitting down.

Leaning toward her as soon as he was seated, his broad shoulders touched hers, sending shivers through her, and he asked, "Are you on the program with me today?"

Darcy found her missing whisper muscles. "Yes," she managed to say.

"Singing?" His eyes had hers in their grasp again, and she felt like someone had bashed the breath out of her with the trunk of a cottonwood tree.

"Yes," she gasped.

"Great! Stacy's been telling me all about you. She says you sing beautifully. It'll be a treat to hear you, I'm sure," he said, and he leaned away, releasing her eyes.

It took Darcy a couple of minutes to catch her breath and calm her wild heart. But even then she could not shake the silly thrill that sitting next to Quin Seltz produced in her usually serious and mature self. Her eyes drifted to the congregation. Her mother smiled and Nate grinned. Then her eyes met Stacy's. She was smiling nervously. Darcy smiled back, then looked away self-consciously, painfully aware of the young man at her side who was calmly thumbing through his scriptures.

Darcy's eyes roved nervously through the chapel as the meeting began. She was surprised to see Todd and Jill. They were sitting near the back, almost hidden from her view by the podium. Both were grinning like the cat who had just found the cheese. Jill made eyes at her. Darcy read the message clearly and felt her face redden. Jill had not missed Darcy's reaction to Quin Seltz.

Darcy glanced at Quin nervously as he opened a hymn book and held it so she could see. Darcy failed to hear even one other voice in the whole congregation as she tried to make hers blend inconspicuously with the clear, strong baritone of Quin. Now she was really nervous. She had no idea he could sing like that! In fact, she realized, she had no idea what kind of things he could do, except make her poor heart flutter. But, to sing a solo in front of him—the thought made her shrink in terror.

During the sacrament service, Darcy closed her eyes and forced her thoughts to the Savior. How unworthy she felt as she considered the sacrifice He had made for her. For a few brief minutes, her nervousness vanished as her love for her Savior filled her soul, bringing tears to her eyes. She even briefly forgot the magnificent presence of Quin Seltz beside her as she pondered the deep significance of the atonement of Christ.

Then, her nervousness came rushing back as her name was announced to precede Quin's missionary report. She had to force herself to stand on two legs with badly trembling knees. She was grateful for the long dress she wore, for it hid the embarrassing situation that threatened to send her sprawling to the floor in front of Quin and the whole Third Ward if she didn't gain control, and quickly.

Darcy's mother moved gracefully to the piano, seemingly unaware of the fright and plight of her daughter who found the podium and leaned against it to steady herself just in the nick of time. Sharon began to play, forcing Darcy, at the appropriate time, to begin her song. As the notes flowed from her throat, the nervousness again vanished and her knees quit knocking. Darcy became caught up in the spirit of her song of Christ.

Darcy felt the influence of the Holy Ghost, and strength flowed from her in the form of beautiful music, although she, in all honesty, did not realize how touched the audience was. As her last note faded and the accompaniment died out, the chapel was plunged into sacred stillness. Darcy waited as her mother silently left the piano and, on cat's feet, returned to her seat.

Quin stood and stepped back to make room for Darcy to take her seat, but before she slipped past him, he grasped her hand firmly and turned those incredibly blue eyes on her. They were misty, and his cheeks were wet.

"Beautiful," he whispered so only she could hear. Then, only after she was in her seat, he moved to the podium. His deep voice was the first to break the reverent stillness inspired by Darcy's number. "Beautiful," he said for all to hear, and heads nodded. "Thank you, Darcy, for setting the tone for what I hope to say this morning." He had turned toward her as he spoke and for a moment his eyes again searched hers with piercing intensity, and she felt faint.

As Quin spoke that morning, Darcy discovered that he was a deeply spiritual person. And as strongly as his eyes, his rare smile, and his masculine good looks had affected her, his testimony and love for the Lord touched her even more deeply.

Near the end of Quin's address, Darcy glanced at Stacy, and their eyes met. Stacy again smiled—more easily this time. Darcy smiled back once more, and when she did, a feeling of profound peace and love came over her. She knew then, and somehow she knew that Stacy knew, that the stigma, the embarrassment, and the hurt feelings were behind them. Darcy had witnessed the powerful comfort of the Comforter, and she closed her eyes and silently gave thanks.

"That was great," she whispered to Quin when he returned to his seat after completing his talk.

His look of gratitude and whispered words of thanks left her heart beating wildly again. Never had Darcy met anyone who stirred her in the way that Quin Seltz did! Not even Shad.

One of the first to the stand after the benediction was Stacy. She hugged her brother, then faced Darcy. "Wow, that was great, Darcy. You're great," she said in a choking voice, and the two rivals, who were rivals no more, fell into one another's arms. A moment later, with tears in her eyes, Stacy said, "We're having a meal at our house following the rest of the meetings for our family that is here. Would you go with me to the rest of our meetings and then come to our house for dinner?"

Darcy was touched but taken back. "Oh, Stacy, thank you, but I would be intruding."

"You would not. Quin?" Stacy said, turning to the tall blond who was her brother.

"What can I do for you, sis?" he said with a serious face.

"I just invited Darcy over for dinner. She thinks she'd be intruding," Stacy said.

"Intruding!" he exclaimed as his face exploded into a grin and those clear blue eyes showered Darcy with sparkles. "Please come!" he said.

Darcy went.

Quin drove her home afterward.

"How did it go?" Sharon asked with a smile when Darcy floated into the house.

"Fine," Darcy answered.

"Just fine? You come in here with your face all aglow and tell me it was fine?"

"It was wonderful," Darcy admitted with a smile. She was really thinking about the ride home, not the dinner, but she wasn't about to say so.

"Tell me about it," Sharon said, patting the sofa beside her.

Darcy sat next to her mother and said, "Everything's all right again with Stacy. In fact, it's better than it used to be. We are closer than we've ever been. The kids in her ward acted like nothing had ever happened. And Stacy and her family all treated me just like family at their dinner. It wasn't even awkward."

"I'm glad for you, Darcy," Sharon said, her look telling Darcy she wanted some particulars.

"Thanks, Mom. It's been a rough week, but the whole family made me feel so good. Sister Seltz is so sweet. She hugged me and said how glad she was that I could come. And Brother Seltz was really nice, too. He kept saying how much he likes to hear me sing." Darcy paused at that and pulled a face. "He was just being nice. I was so scared today. I must have sounded just awful."

"You sang beautifully, Darcy," her mother corrected.

"It didn't feel like it to me."

"Well, it was."

"Thanks. Anyway, I got to know a lot of Stacy's cousins. They seem really nice."

"Did Stacy bring you home? I planned to come for you if you'd have called."

"I know, Mom. No, Stacy didn't bring me home."

"Then who did?" Sharon asked with a raised eyebrow and a twinkle in her eye.

"Stacy was going to, but Quin said he wanted to," Darcy answered, and she felt the beginning of a blush as she remembered how easily Stacy had been persuaded.

"Quin's a nice young man," Sharon said.

"Nice! Mom, he's super!" Darcy said with more vigor than she had intended. "I...I...well, I mean...I sure do...Mom, I have a date with him!" she blurted after stammering embarrassingly, and the blush deepened.

"He seems quite taken by you, Darcy. But remember, he's been on a mission, and he was older before he went. You're still young—not quite eighteen, and he'll be looking for a wife," Sharon cautioned seriously.

"Mom!" Darcy exclaimed, but words failed her after that, for she knew her mother was right, and it made her heart sing.

"Well, sweetheart, I just don't want you to get hurt. I've never seen you quite like this over a young man, and he'll be off to school again soon where there are a lot of very pretty older girls So, you just..." Sharon cut herself off abruptly and exclaimed, "Darcy, what's wrong!?"

Darcy had struggled to keep it from showing, but that fear, that persistent, unwelcome foreboding centered around Shad had suddenly returned. "Mom, it's Shad. I keep..."

"You need to quit thinking about Shad," Sharon cut in sternly.

"Mom, you don't understand. I can't. I keep trying, but I just can't. What if he hurts someone...like Quin? Mom, I'm frightened."

"Stop it, Darcy!" Sharon ordered curtly. "You have got to stop torturing yourself this way. Shad is hurting himself and his family. You go on your date with Quin and quit thinking about Shad and his troubles. You tried to help him. There is nothing more you can do for him, so quit thinking about him and scaring yourself this way."

"I can't, Mom," she repeated, and she began to sob.

❋

Shad was at that very moment sitting on his bunk in a drab cell in the county jail. In his left hand was a small photograph. He was staring at it sadly.

"Who's the broad in the picture?" his cell-mate asked.

"Watch your mouth, Buster! She's no broad!" Shad retorted angrily, half rising from the bunk.

Buster Maheeny, a small framed, small-time burglar, a definite non-violent type, retreated quickly across the little cell. "Sorry, man. Didn't know it was your woman."

"She's not my woman. And if you were from around here, you'd know who she is. Everybody does!" he thundered at Buster. Then, dropping his eyes back to the photo in his hand, he said, almost reverently, "Her name is Darcy Felding. She is the most beautiful, smartest, and sweetest girl I have ever met."

Buster's courage began to return as Shad relaxed. "She's not your girl, then?" he asked.

"Not anymore," Shad said wistfully.

He was silent for a moment, thinking about Darcy and the fun times he had shared with her. Those startling green eyes, long chestnut hair, and perfect figure—oh, how he regretted the hurt he had brought to Darcy. Finally, he lifted his eyes from her picture. "Not anymore," he repeated.

"She think she's too good for you, man, just because you got yourself throwed into jail?" Buster suggested, his foolhardy courage nearly restored.

Shad came to his feet with a roar and smashed Buster's narrow face a wicked blow with his cast. As the smaller man slumped to the floor with a whimper, Shad looked at the now crumpled photograph in his left hand, the face of Darcy distorted and unrecognizable. A rage filled him. He kicked Buster in the face viciously, then in the stomach, shouting, "Too good for me! You bet she's too good for me, but she's too much of a lady to ever admit it." He kicked again and went on, "If I hadn't a been such a big shot, I wouldn't be here and she wouldn't have been hurt so much. I'm the one that ain't no good. She's an angel!" He stopped his violent actions and stared at the unconscious man on the floor, realization of what he had done slowly coming over him.

Then the door slid open and two husky jailers jumped him. "Isolation for you, buddy!" one of them shouted as Shad struggled in vain to free himself.

"But he spoke bad about Darcy," Shad retorted, kicking his feet as they cuffed his hands.

"Poor Shad," one of them taunted. He was a new jailer, a local fellow only three years older than Shad. "Don't you know she's too good for you, Shad? She thinks she's hot stuff, and you're just..." His mouth flew shut with the aid of Shad's bare foot.

"Shut up!" Shad screamed. "Don't you say nothing more. You don't even know her."

For another minute, the three men struggled, then finally Shad's feet were in leg-irons. As the jailers dragged him off to the isolation cell, he cried, "I love her. Don't you ever say nothing bad about Darcy. I love her!"

# Chapter Twelve

THE NEXT WEEK, EVEN though things were back to normal at school, was a roller-coaster-ride for Darcy. She alternated between ecstacy, as she thought of her upcoming date with Quin, and deep depression when haunted by thoughts and fears of Shad and worry over what would eventually become of him if he didn't change.

It was Todd who reported Shad's latest troubles to Darcy. She had asked Todd on Friday during the lunch break if he'd seen Shad lately. "I tried to yesterday, but they wouldn't let me," he said. "Shad's not getting any visitors for awhile."

"Why not? They can't do that to him," she said with genuine concern.

"He got in some trouble," Todd said evasively.

"What did he do, Todd?" she demanded with a sharp stamp of her foot.

"It doesn't matter what he did. Let's just forget it. Did I mention that my dad's doing really good? Mom and I get to see him pretty soon," Todd said.

"I'm happy for you, Todd. But you told me about it yesterday. I want to hear about him, but you're evading my question. What did Shad do to get himself in trouble? You know I'll find out anyway. Randy will tell me," she said slyly.

"Oh, all right, but if you weren't my friend I wouldn't tell you, and after I do you might not be anyway. It might spoil your date with Quin tonight, and I'd feel just awful if it did," Todd said, still not coming to the point.

"Todd! Tell me, please!"

"I was getting to it, Darcy. I was just thinking about you and Quin, that's all," Todd said as Darcy stamped her foot again. "Okay, okay. He got in a fight with another prisoner."

"Is that all?" Darcy asked with relief.

"Is that all! Darcy, he's in lots of trouble now."

"But maybe he was just defending himself," she said, sincerely hoping that might be the case, but doubting it from the troubled look on her friend's face.

"Not hardly that, Darcy. They told me that the other guy said something that made him mad," Todd explained. "They said he knocked the guy down with his cast. Don't I know how that feels! Then he kicked him several times."

"Ohh," Darcy moaned. "So now does he have to do more time in jail?"

"I'd say. But that ain't the worst of it, Darcy. He kicked a jailer in the mouth and broke a tooth. He's really in trouble for that. He has to go to court again. Only this time..."

"Judge Simper doesn't like him, does he?" Darcy interrupted.

"Not so you'd notice it, but it don't matter anyway. He has to go to District Court. They've stuck him with two felonies. That means he could go to prison," Todd said. Then, almost as an afterthought, he added, "And he hadn't even had a can a beer."

Darcy moaned. "What can we do, Todd? He was...is our friend, you know."

"Nothing. Not a darn thing. We've done our best for him, but it's beyond us now. Has been all along, I suppose," he said with a shrug.

"I wonder what that other prisoner said that made Shad angry," Darcy mused, quite sure that Todd at least had some idea.

Todd turned away, but not before the look of guilty knowledge confirmed Darcy's suspicions. "Todd! You know! Make him tell me, Jill," she appealed to her friend who had endured the entire conversation in uncharacteristic silence.

Jill turned helplessly to Todd. "You just as well tell her."

"You know, too!" Darcy broke in. "And you weren't even going to tell me. Some friends you guys are."

"Okay, okay, you win. But we are your friends, Darcy. We're just sick of seeing you hurt. You ain't a gonna like this. Why can't you just forget all about Shad?"

"Because...because...I don't know! Just tell me."

"It was over a picture of you, Darcy. The guy said something bad about you. At least Shad thought it was bad. That was all it took."

"Why did he kick the jailer?" she asked, her voice all but failing her.

"I guess he said something about you thinking you were too good for everybody. He just don't know you, that's all. I'm proof of that!" Todd said with sudden feeling.

"Is that all?"

"Yeah, that's about it. And I don't blame him! Nobody that knows you would ever…"

"It's okay, Todd. Thanks for telling me. But there's more, isn't there?"

"Not that had anything much to do with anything," Todd said with a red face.

"Tell me, please," she begged, close to tears and trying to hide it.

"Well, I guess he told them he done it cause he…he…"

"He what, Todd?"

"He loves you," Todd blurted, turning three shades darker.

"Ohh!" Darcy moaned and turned away as the tears began to flow. That was just too much. She really had been fond of him, and now, the more trouble he got in, the more she was haunted by a feeling that somehow, somewhere, someone close to her was going to suffer because of Shad. This sudden revelation of his feelings for her only made that feeling stronger. She left Todd and Jill standing alone, both of them silently grieving for her.

The noon hour was almost over, and she hurried toward her class, trying to compose herself as she went, oblivious to the other kids rushing about her, some going this way and others that. But she could not shake the thought of Shad's words. She was suddenly interrupted by Stacy who called out from behind her.

"Hey, Darcy. Wait up."

She dabbed at her eyes and then, with a forced smile, turned to face Stacy. "Hi, Stacy," she said flatly.

"How's it going? Hey! What's the matter, Darcy?" Stacy asked with concern. Darcy had been unable to hide her red eyes or streaked mascara.

"Nothing much," Darcy tried to say lightly.

"Something much!" Stacy insisted, and she proceeded successfully to pry from Darcy what had happened to Shad.

But Darcy left out the bit about love.

"Forget him," Stacy said when Darcy had finished her abbreviated account. "Aren't you excited about your date with my big brother tonight?"

"I'll say! And I'm scared half to death," Darcy answered, grateful for the change of subject.

"So's he," Stacy revealed.

"Quin? Scared?" Darcy asked in astonishment.

"Yeah, I'll say he is," Stacy said as the bell began its ear-shattering clamor. "Oh, oh. Better run. Have fun tonight. And Darcy—play it right and you and I could be sisters-in-law!" she said with a giggle as she darted away, leaving Darcy with her heart in her throat and her spine tingling.

After the first thirty minutes with Quin that night, the nervousness Darcy had felt was gone. Never had she felt so good with a guy. By the time he left her at the door with a polite handshake and invitation for another date in less than a week, Darcy was in love. At least she guessed that's what it was—hoped that's what it was.

Lying in bed that night she could not fall asleep. Over and over she shivered with delight as she remembered the feel of Quin's long arms around her waist, and of his big hand holding her small one. And she thought with longing of the piercing intensity of his sparkling blue eyes.

Then her mother's warning came back and left her trembling. In January, a week before she turned eighteen and just two months from now, he would be leaving for the university to begin his studies to become a doctor. She thought about all those pretty coeds her mother had mentioned and felt an emotion that was new to her.

Jealousy!

Darcy scolded herself. She had no claim on Quin; she'd only had one date with him! But, she admitted, and not reluctantly, that she had felt something this night—something wonderful. Then, for the first time in several hours, she thought of Shad, and she felt something she was becoming only too familiar with of late.

Fear!

✳

Bill Cleverly came into the small jail visiting room wearing a frown. As Shad peered at his father through the bullet-proof glass, he tried to think of a way to convince him that it was not his fault that he was in more trouble. But, deep down, Shad knew it really was.

"Son, they tell me you caused quite a scene here a couple of weeks ago. I had quite a time getting them to let me see you. Fact of the matter is, I forked out quite a bit of cash before Mac, that is, Roger MacArthur, would persuade the sheriff to give me a few minutes with you today," Bill said, the frown deepening. "Want to tell me about it?"

"Sure, Dad. It wasn't my fault. Well...I mean...it wasn't all my fault. They put me in a cell with this con named Buster. Buster Maheeny, that is." From there, Shad told the story fairly close to how it actually happened, only making it favor himself more than it really did in the most crucial places.

When he had finished, his father's frown wasn't quite so pronounced, but he moved the phone to his lap and was silent for a long moment. Then he leaned toward the glass, pressed the phone back to his ear and said, "Okay, Shad. That's a bit different than the jailers told the sheriff. I'll have Mac in here to see you sometime tomorrow. I think we can beat this rap if…" Bill paused, leaned still closer to the small window that separated father and son, and finished with, "…if you keep your cool and don't let anybody goad you into more trouble."

"I've learned my lesson, Dad. I'll just keep my mouth shut and let them make fun of…let them say whatever they want," he said lamely.

"And Shad, forget about Darcy. She's history anyway," Bill advised shrewdly.

"What do you mean, Dad?" Shad asked sharply.

"I hear that Seltz kid's back. He seems pretty interested in Darcy, they say," Bill revealed. "So forget her, son. She's nothing but trouble."

Shad tensed. "Dad, don't you…" he began, then forced his mouth shut. This was no time to make his father angry. He desperately needed his father's ample supply of money to retain Mac, the attorney, if he was going to stay out of prison. But, he could not help but feel a hot, burning anger swell in his breast at the thought of Darcy, the girl he loved, and Quin Seltz!

Roger (Mac) MacArthur spent two hours with Shad the next morning without any glass between them. They sat at a desk in the jail office area. After listening to Shad's version of the altercation with Buster and the jailers, Mac said, "First thing I'll do is subpoena every other prisoner that was on the block with you that night. I won't have much trouble establishing just cause for your actions. If I know prisoners, and you can rest assured that I do, they'll come through with flying colors for you. Any that don't choose to cooperate I will simply weed out before we ever get into court."

"I heard a couple of them yelling at the guards to lay off me when they drug me out of my cell," Shad added helpfully.

"Good. Now, to add a little pressure on the sheriff and the jailers who manhandled you, I think I'll slap a lawsuit on them for use of unnecessary force," Mac added with a shrewd and experienced smile.

"But I was kicking and…"

Mac leaned forward, his face suddenly angry and dark. "No more of that kind of talk, Shad. You let me handle things. That's what your dad is paying me for. Anyway, it's just for leverage. Anything we can do to put pressure on the county attorney to consider not prosecuting is certainly worth our time. Do you understand?" Mac asked, looking at Shad through tinted, horn-rimmed glasses with his piercing grey eyes.

"Yes, sir," Shad said meekly, having just made the decision to trust this man, even if he didn't particularly like him.

"All right then. The sentence you received from Judge Simper will be served in full by next Wednesday. Your dad has already arranged bail on these new charges, so you'll soon be out. And when you are, I would strongly advise you to be a model citizen—at least until we get the current charges resolved," Mac said as he gathered his papers together and began stuffing them into his sleek leather briefcase.

Shad thought, but did not say, that when this case was over, Mac would probably welcome it if he got himself into more trouble. After all, his dad's money was as good as the next guy's, and that was all Shad believed his attorney really cared about.

A week later, Shad sat beside his father and again looked into the cold grey eyes of Roger MacArthur. They were across the dining room table from him. "We're making progress," Mac reported. "I trust you are enjoying your freedom and behaving yourself, Shad."

"Yes, sir," Shad responded as Mac stroked his ridiculously long mustache.

"What progress?" Bill demanded.

"Well, the sheriff and his jailers were served with our suit, the one charging them with excessive use of force. Let's see, that was on Monday. The constable who served it for me said the sheriff looked quite ill. I suspect he looked worse after he read the entire document. I emphasized the fact that it does not require two large men to remove a single inmate with a badly broken arm from a cell. Ha, ha. Yes, I do believe we're making progress."

✳

Thanksgiving morning was clear and cold. A thin layer of snow from a fast moving storm the previous evening had left the Felding farm looking like a photograph from *Country* magazine. The bright sun and blue sky of mid-morning was a striking contradiction to the forecast of more snow by late afternoon.

Darcy, in a warm coat and insulated boots, tramped through the glistening snow to find her father in the barn. He was just finishing the chores. "Grandma Felding is on the phone, Dad," she announced. "She wants to talk to you."

Kerry shrugged. "They should have been on the road an hour ago."

"I don't think they're coming, Dad," Darcy said. She was disappointed, too, for she dearly loved her grandparents and had been looking forward to their visit.

"Flip off that light for me, would you, sweetheart?" Kerry said, pointing to a switch on the far wall. "I was afraid of this when it snowed. That means they'll be alone for Thanksgiving again. I should have insisted that we go there."

"You did, Dad," Darcy corrected him. "But she said the weather could not be bad on Thanksgiving day two years in a row."

"Yes, and it's not that bad, at least if I were driving. The roads are cleared off good. But your grandpa doesn't drive as well as he used to, and the least skiff puts your grandmother into mortal fear these days," he said as he shut the barn door behind Darcy and then led the way toward the house.

Darcy followed him partway, then lingered behind, enjoying the sweet, clean scent of the cold air and the serenity imposed by the soft blanket of fresh snow.

"Coming, Darcy?" he called from the back door.

"In a bit. I'll be in the back yard."

She brushed the snow from the wooden swing that hung from a high branch of an ancient apple tree behind the house.

She sat down and began to slowly swing back and forth. A smile brushed her lips as she entertained sweet thoughts of Quin Seltz. They had been spending quite a bit of time together the past few days, and the difference in their ages had faded in significance. Darcy no longer wondered if it was love she was feeling—she was sure of it. And though Quin had not said so directly, she felt strongly that he loved her as well.

That he respected her, there was no doubt. She felt safe with him, safe and protected. He had not forced himself on her in any way, and when he kissed her, which he had finally done at the end of their fourth date, it had been sweet and wonderful.

She no longer worried about all those coeds at the university, but she did wonder what she would ever do with herself when he was over one hundred miles away. Yes, in her mind, Darcy was beginning to envision a sweet future with Quin Seltz, and she shivered in delight.

Then, that dreaded, haunted mood intruded, and she shivered again, violently this time. Nothing could ever happen to Quin! She just couldn't bear to ever see him hurt. With the gloom came visions of Shad Cleverly. Though she had not seen him since the night of the Homecoming pageant, she still kept up on his activities.

Todd spoke of him regularly. Shad had a job in a neighboring town. He was staying with an aunt and uncle there. But he would be back, for he had a trial scheduled for the middle of December. Billy also kept Nate up to date. If Nate had gotten it straight, Billy was claiming that Shad's attorney, a guy her father called a shyster, had some tricks up his sleeve that would get Shad off for sure.

Darcy actually found that she hoped so. But her hope was conditional; it contained a clause that had Shad straightening out his life. Billy also claimed that Shad didn't drink anymore, but Randy refuted that. He knew the cops all across the county, and even though Shad had not been caught, reports had come in, and Randy believed them.

The blare of a horn pierced the cold air, and Darcy looked up. But whomever it was stopped in front. She continued to swing. Randy and his family were expected, but not for another hour. Idly, she wondered who it might be, then she forgot all about it as she shut off the gloom and expelled Shad from her mind. That was a practice she was getting better at. She closed her eyes, pictured the handsome, sober face of Quin and coaxed the swing higher.

Footsteps crunched in the snow behind her, and she grinned. "I can hear you, Nate," she called out.

Nate did not answer, but the soft crunching continued.

"Nate?" she called again.

"Forget my name already?" a deep, laughter-filled voice boomed.

"Quin!" Darcy shouted in delight as she tumbled from the swing. "What are you doing here? You're supposed to be with your family for dinner."

"I couldn't stay away," he confessed soberly as their cold hands touched and their warm eyes met. "You are like a giant magnet, Darcy, and I am but a tiny fleck of iron. I felt your pull...and here I am."

Darcy laughed. "Thanks for coming, Quin," she whispered as his eyes looked deep into hers. "How did you know I was out here?"

"The magnet, remember? No one has to tell the fleck of iron where the magnet is. It is just drawn to it."

She laughed again and his arms encircled her slender waist. That was good enough for her. He was here!

"Aren't you cold, Darcy?" he asked as he gently pulled her close to him.

"I'm fine. Isn't it pretty today?" she said, laying her head with its pillow of long chestnut hair against his broad chest.

"Very. I haven't got long, but would you mind if we went for a short drive?" he asked.

"I'd love to," she answered, and together they walked through the fairyland that was the Feldings' back yard on this unusually cold Thanksgiving day.

Before they left, Darcy turned, intending to run to the door and let her folks know where she was going. "They already know," Quin said, surprising her with his ability to read her mind. He spun her gently around again. "How do you think I really knew where to find you?"

Darcy looked up at his face. He was sober, only a hint of a smile on his lips, but the sparkle in his eyes he could not disguise. "So much for the magnet thing," she said with a laugh.

"You drive," he suggested as he opened the driver's door to his faded blue Oldsmobile.

"Why?" she asked, looking at him in surprise.

"So I can gaze at your angel face and put my arm around you," he said boldly.

She blushed and climbed in. "Where to?" she asked as she pulled to a stop a minute later at the highway.

"You're driving. Just don't run me out of gas," he teased.

She instinctively glanced at the fuel gage. It was full. She chuckled and turned his car toward town. She had only gone two miles when she spotted a fiery red Trans Am coming toward them. She felt the blood drain from her face, and she hoped Quin didn't notice.

As the Trans Am sped by, she caught a glimpse of Shad. He was looking right at her, and the anger and jealousy etched in his dark face shocked her. Had he forgotten the promise he had commissioned Randy to deliver? she wondered. He was past before she realized the cast was gone. Both hands had been on the wheel, plainly visible. That shouldn't have surprised her, she knew, because it had been over two months since the accident.

"Who was that?" Quin asked in an uncharacteristically cold voice.

"Shad Cleverly," Darcy managed to say as that haunting, familiar fear pricked her heart.

"Looked like he'd prefer it if I'd drop dead," Quin observed. Then he said, "Darcy, are you all right? You're face is as white as that snow out there."

"Don't say that! It scares me!" she blurted as tears blurred her vision and she let up on the gas.

Quin's strong arm tightened around her shoulder, but Darcy was shaking so badly that she had to pull over and stop. "I'm sorry. Darcy?" Quin said, his voice full of an emotion that she had not heard from him before. Fear? Maybe.

"Hold me, Quin," she sobbed.

He did, and to a small degree he managed to soothe her troubled mind, and Darcy's young heart ached with love for Quin Seltz.

# Chapter Thirteen

"SHARON," RANDY SAID with a contented sigh, "I do believe you are as good a cook as Mom was."

"Now that is a compliment, Randy. Thank you. Are you sure you wouldn't care to have more pie?"

"I'd love to—tomorrow. Right now I'm so full my eyeballs think they're an extension of my stomach. I best let it settle some so I can see." As Randy spoke, his eyes drifted to Darcy. Something was bothering her. Maybe if he could get her alone…

"Randy, can Scotty and Jeremy help me make a snowman?" Nate asked.

"They may try, but I think the snow's too cold and dry," he answered.

Darcy started to clear the table as the boys scampered off. Sandy came to her aid and began to carry the dirty plates to the kitchen. Then Sharon pitched in, speaking to Randy as she did so. "What time do you go on duty?"

"Four," he said, rising to his feet. "I'll help and we'll get these dishes done in no time."

"No, you relax, Randy. You have a full day's work ahead of you. Why don't you and Kerry watch a game on TV or something while we girls clear up this mess? We'll hurry so we'll have a chance to visit before you have to go," Sharon said firmly.

"I'll help," he said, even more firmly than his sister.

It was two o'clock by the time the kitchen was sparkling to Sharon's satisfaction. The boys had joyfully failed in their snowman construction project and came in wet and cold but with rosy cheeks and happy laughter. Sandy dried her sons off, beginning with little Jeremy. Nate scampered to his room to see after himself.

Randy glanced again at Darcy and their eyes met briefly, but she ducked her head. Something was troubling her. She hadn't spoken ten words while the dishes were being done. He searched for an excuse to speak with her alone.

Jeremy soon provided one. By the time Sandy had finished cleaning Scotty up, Jeremy was fast asleep on the carpet. Randy glanced at his watch. "I better be going. I need to get ready for work pretty soon," he said to nobody in particular.

His wife responded. "I'll wake Jeremy, and…"

"No, let him sleep, dear. If I can get Darcy to run me home, then you and the boys can stay longer," he said, turning his head toward his niece.

"Sure, Randy," she said, seeming glad for an excuse to leave the house for a few minutes.

They were no sooner in the Felding's old Ford than Randy broached the subject that was on his mind. "You and Quin have a little tiff, Darcy?" he asked. "Nate said he took you for a ride just before we came."

Darcy glanced at Randy in surprise, and he knew he had guessed wrong. "Oh, no," she said. "What made you think that?"

"You're a bit glum, kid. I'd have thought you'd have been bubbling all over. Just doesn't fit," he said, watching her intently as she started down the lane.

"I know."

"So, what is wrong, Darcy? Maybe I can help."

"Does Shad have his license back?" she asked abruptly.

"No. He won't be driving for over a year. Does this…this mood of yours have something to do with him?" Randy asked.

She glanced at him. Her green eyes were clouded, even haunted, he thought, and Randy experienced a fierce tremor of apprehension. She turned her eyes back to the road. "He was driving this morning," she said softly. "I guess he finished rebuilding his Trans Am. He was in it."

Randy shook his head. "Looks like I got my work cut out."

"No, I didn't mean you had to go after him. I don't want to get him in trouble, or…" Darcy's voice trembled and she did not complete her thought.

Randy waited a moment, then asked, "Or what, Darcy?"

"Or hurt you!" she cried in anguish.

"He won't hurt me!" Randy said, suddenly angry with Shad. More angry than he had ever been. "But I won't let him just thumb his nose at the law, either. Oh how I wish he would just straighten up his act."

"Me, too," Darcy said in a plaintiff little whimper.

"Hey, cheer up, kid," Randy said, trying to sound cheerful himself, even though he felt anything but that. "Tell me about you and Quin Seltz.

He seems mighty interested in my favorite niece."

He watched Darcy closely. A gradual smile grew on her profile. "Ah, ha!" he said. "Quin is part of the gloom."

"No!" Darcy protested. "He makes me very happy."

"Exactly, my dear girl. And in five or six weeks he'll be off to the university, right?"

"Uh, huh."

"You will miss him, won't you?"

"Terribly," she agreed with a sigh.

"Darcy, give it to your old uncle straight."

"Young uncle," she corrected, smiling at last.

"Thanks, kid. So give it to me straight about this young Seltz fellow. I know your mother is concerned that he'll get to school and find some other gal, and..."

"No," Darcy interrupted firmly. "I'm not letting him get away."

"Ah, now that's straight. Kind of like him, do you?"

Darcy glanced at Randy again and blushed as she nodded.

"Don't tell me it's more than like," he persisted.

Again she nodded, and when she looked over at him, the clouds were gone from her eyes and they were filled with bright green stars.

"I thought so, and I think it is just great. He's a fine person. Plans to be a doctor, your mother tells me," he said.

"He'll be a good one, too," she said with conviction.

Randy sighed with relief. The glow was back. Darcy was radiant. What a lucky fellow Quin was. He hoped that the young man appreciated what a pure gem Darcy was.

Randy looked out of the car and was surprised at the massive bank of black clouds in the east. It could be a long shift tonight, he thought, but he said nothing to Darcy, pleased at the smile that now accented her pretty face.

Quin was smiling at that very moment. He had not been a hundred percent sure of his feelings for Darcy until she had begged him to hold her that morning. As she had fallen into his arms sobbing, his heart had been wrenched, and he had known then that an eternity with her would not be long enough for him.

"What's the smile about, oh sober brother of mine?" Stacy quipped.

Quin had not heard her enter the room, so wrapped up in his thoughts of Darcy he had become. "Darcy, my sweet and beautiful little sister," he answered honestly.

"So I thought," she said with a bright smile, and with a toss of her head, her golden hair flew over her shoulder and she sat down. "She's really something, isn't she, Quin?"

"She is that, and more. You do pick good friends, Stacy."

"Thanks. I was lucky when it came to Darcy. I almost blew our friendship," Stacy confessed. "But never again. I learned a lesson in humility and love. I plan to take a chapter from her book. I really admire her."

"She's an easy one to admire," Quin agreed.

"I think she's in love with you, Quin," Stacy said abruptly.

"Think so?"

"Yeah, I really do. Question is, how do you feel about her—other than that she's a great person, that is?"

"Promise not to give me away?" he asked, favoring his sister with one of his rare smiles.

"Cross my heart," she said.

"I wasn't positive until today. Now I am. I love her, Stacy. Can you believe that? Just a few weeks back from Russia and I'm in love with one of my little sister's best friends. Crazy, isn't it?" he said, shaking his head in wonder.

"Have you told Darcy how you feel?"

"Not yet."

"Going to pretty soon?"

"I imagine. When the time is right, I'll let her know."

"When are you two going out again?" Stacy asked next.

"Good question," he said, looking out of the living room window at the dark clouds that were rapidly moving closer. "Looks like we're in for some more early snow. If it clears up by morning, maybe I could take her to see her grandparents. She was terribly disappointed when they didn't dare come today for Thanksgiving dinner with her family."

"She'd love that!" Stacy exclaimed. "Better call her right now."

"I will," he said, getting to his feet and crossing the room to the phone.

He dialed and the phone rang. "Hi, Nate," he said brightly when the unmistakable voice of Darcy's little brother responded to his call. "Is your big sis there?"

"Who is this?" Nate demanded in a business-like tone.

"Just a guy who wants to talk to your pretty sister really badly," he answered without cracking a smile but winking at Stacy.

"Who?" Nate demanded again.

"Quin Seltz," he said. "Will you get her for me please?"

"Can't."

"Why not?"

"She ain't here," the little voice said, not nearly as business-like now.

"She isn't here," Quin corrected.

"I know she's not at your place, else you wouldn't be calling. But she ain't here either."

"When will she be back, Nate?" he asked, smiling to himself.

"Dunno."

"You have no idea at all?"

"Nope."

"Where did she go?" Quin asked, hoping a little different approach would get him some useful information. It worked.

"Took my uncle home so's he can get to work tonight."

"Thanks, I'll call back in a little while."

"Quin, are you Darcy's boyfriend?" Nate suddenly asked.

Surprised, Quin stammered, "Gee...well...I hope so. Why do you ask?"

"Cause Darcy's my sister and I love her and I don't want nobody making her feel sad like Shad done," Nate said, surprising Quin even more.

"You don't want anybody to, you mean," he corrected again.

"Yup, nobody," he replied, totally unaware of the English lesson he had just received.

"Well, I surely won't do that, Nate," Quin promised, suddenly feeling an almost overwhelming fondness for the little guy.

"Good, cause I like you, Quin, and I'd be real mad if you made her sad." Then, he must have said all he had to say, because he said, "Goodbye," and hung up the phone before Quin could say another word.

"What was that all about?" Stacy asked.

"I just got the third degree from Nate Felding, eight-year-old private-eye," Quin said with a chuckle.

"What do you mean?"

"He was just making sure I was good enough for his sister, I think."

"Are you?" Stacy asked, shaking her head and smiling.

"I think so. Yes, I think I passed his test."

Quin waited twenty minutes before calling again. "Hello," the same little voice said.

"Hi, Nate. Quin again. Darcy home yet?"

"Yup," he said.

"Would you..."

Quin stopped when he heard Nate shout, "Darcy, it's your boyfriend."

"Nate!" she scolded, then she said, "Hi Quin, sorry..."

"Gee, I'm glad you knew who he meant," Quin interrupted with a chuckle.

"I'm sorry, Quin. I don't know why he said that. Kids assume a lot, I guess."

"Don't be sorry, Darcy. I told him I was your boyfriend. I hope I didn't tell a fib," he teased.

"Oh, Quin! That makes me want to c..." She stopped and he could tell she was doing what he thought she was about to tell him she felt like doing.

"Hey, Darcy, the real reason I called was to see if you would mind riding out to your grandparents' place tomorrow. If the storm isn't too bad by then, that is. I'd like to meet them."

"Quin! I'd love to, but you're not fooling me. You are so sweet. You knew how disappointed I was today when they couldn't come, didn't you?" She said, still crying a little as she talked.

Quin dragged the phone over to the sofa and sat down, winking at Stacy who politely excused herself and dragged two rather unwilling little sisters along to give him some privacy. He waved at them and settled himself comfortably. He felt like talking, and he could sense that Darcy did too.

❊

Shad Cleverly had called Dwight Arnot early that evening. Supplied with a couple of very expensive six-packs of beer, he proceeded to drink away his frustrations. Even though he knew Darcy was dating Quin Seltz, actually seeing them together had infuriated him. And as was increasingly the case when something went the least bit against his grain, Shad turned to alcohol.

He was proud of the fact that he had managed to evade the cops since he got out of jail, and he was getting increasingly bolder about driving his very fast Trans Am. He had it souped up until he was convinced that there wasn't a cop car in the state that could keep up with him.

Shad had promised himself one thing; he was not going back to jail.

Mac was going to keep him out on the charges stemming from his fight in the cell-block, and no one else would put him back in!

He drifted around, mixing briefly with several groups of kids who were just hanging out. They admired his car and fed his hungry ego. Then, about eleven o'clock, having polished off the first six-pack and part of the second, he decided to head out. He had to work the next morning and his suitcase was packed and in the trunk. It was snowing now and starting to stick to the road, and he didn't want to wait until it got too bad; that might slow him down. So Shad headed east, easing the speedometer up to eighty, no effort at all for this car, and then he held it there.

Randy was grateful that the traffic was light, almost non-existent this stormy November night. But the hours were dragging by, and he was more tired than usual. Light flakes of snow swirled about in his head-lights, and the road started to become a little slick. He was twenty miles east of town, nearly to the town where Shad worked and lived with his uncle. He pulled over, got out and walked around his car a couple of times, brushed the snow off his uniform jacket and got back in the car. He headed back to town, anxious for his shift to end.

The dash clock glowed bright green, announcing to Randy's inquiring glance that it was eleven o'clock. One hour to go. He concentrated on the road ahead. Randy met only a couple of cars and one semi over the next few miles. Like himself, those drivers were traveling a reasonable forty-five to fifty miles per hour.

Suddenly, a pair of headlights came into view, and he knew in an instant that he had a fast one coming at him. As it came closer, he estimated its speed at close to eighty. He switched the radar on and it immediately flashed a red "79" on the screen. He locked the speed in and slowed down to turn. As the speeder passed, he identified the car as a red Trans Am and thought with a quickening pulse of Shad Cleverly's newly overhauled car. He activated the overheads and turned to make his stop. He half expected brake lights to come on, but they did not. He had been unable to see the license plates or the driver because of the swirling snow which severely curtailed the visibility.

Randy eased his foot down on the accelerator so he would not go into a spin as he increased his speed. The big car responded with a low growl, and after a minute he glanced at the speedometer. He was up to a treacherous eighty-five, and losing ground! The Trans Am was steadily pulling away. Randy reached for his mike, never losing his concentration on the slick roadway, and advised the dispatcher of his situation.

"I am eastbound in pursuit of a red Trans Am. At least, I think that's what it is. I have no plate number. He's running on me at an extreme rate of speed," he said and gave his location before slipping the mike back in place.

With both hands firmly on the wheel, Randy listened to the dispatcher attempt to locate other officers. He maintained a steady eighty-five miles per hour on the slick road, determined not to lose Shad Cleverly, for that was who he was sure he was chasing, although he knew he could never prove it unless he caught him tonight. A roadblock was the only chance, too, and he knew that, but he was determined to keep the pressure on.

He felt his patrol car slip a little on a gentle curve, eased up a bit on the speed, and watched the fading taillights through the lightly falling snow. Suddenly, Darcy's warning of just a few hours ago rang in his ears. He felt a tremor of anxiety. Or was it fear?

With fierce determination, he pushed on. It was time to put a stop to Shad's lawlessness!

He could still make out the taillights of the Trans Am. The snow was falling a little heavier, he thought. Then a set of headlights appeared, coming toward the fleeing car. As it reached the racing Trans Am, it veered, and for a heart-stopping moment, Randy thought it had been forced off the highway. Shad, or whomever, was taking his share of the road right out of the middle of the treacherous two lane highway, leaving little more than the shoulder for approaching traffic to pass. But the veering headlights straightened out as it safely passed the Trans Am. Only a split second later, though, they started swinging back and forth like a lamp in the wind.

"My gosh!" Randy exclaimed aloud. "The guy's out of control." And Randy backed off on his speed.

For a moment he thought the approaching driver was going to regain control, but when Randy was almost to him, the car swerved wildly and went into a spin. Randy made a split-second decision, then drove his Crown Victoria off the shoulder of the road to avoid a collision with the out-of-control car. His was an act of selfless mercy to save the lives of anyone who was in the spinning vehicle.

For several seconds Randy clung desperately to the steering wheel as the car bounced; then it hit a deep depression and flipped end over end. The last thing Trooper Randy Hutchins was consciously aware of was Darcy's repeated warnings of impending disaster at the hands of Shad Cleverly, and he bitterly regretted pursuing the fleeing Trans Am. Then he was totally engulfed in an ebony sea.

❖

Shad caught a glimpse of the flashing lights of the pursuing patrol car as it began its flip, and he felt an alcohol-induced thrill of victory. "Gotcha!" he screamed in glee.

After another mile, he realized that he could slow down now, and he did. Then, fear of what he had done caught up with him, and he started looking for a place to hide. He found a snow-covered back road and pulled just a few feet into a grove of trees, not far from the highway, and killed his lights.

There he sat for the next fifteen minutes, content to polish off another beer or two as he waited. Finally, a cop car went screaming by with wailing siren and flashing lights, and Shad felt safe. Twenty minutes later, he was creeping into his uncle's dark house where he slipped, undetected, into bed.

Lying there fully dressed, he was soon asleep, unconcerned about the cop, whomever he was, that he had seen crash. Any feelings he may have had were swallowed up in two six-packs of Coors!

# Chapter Fourteen

Darcy AWOKE TO THE persistent ringing of the phone. When it finally stopped, she guessed her dad or mom must have answered it. She looked groggily at her alarm clock. It read 12:10 in luminous orange.

With a start, she sat up. Who would be calling at this time of night? She broke into a cold sweat. "Randy!" she cried aloud as she lunged out of bed and into the dark hallway.

A light was on in her parents' bedroom, and she rushed in. Her mother was sitting on the edge of the bed, her face pale and drawn, one hand over her mouth. Kerry was on the phone, listening intently. Sharon looked up, caught Darcy's eye and silently signaled for her to sit beside her.

Darcy's heart was pounding as she sat down. Sharon reached over and grasped her hand. "What is..." she began, but Sharon shook her head, so Darcy listened as her dad spoke into the phone.

"Where is he now?" Kerry asked and paused.

"How badly is he hurt?" He listened again, then he said, "Okay, we'll meet you at the hospital, Sandy." He grimly hung up the phone.

Sharon was trembling so hard the bed shook. Darcy felt like throwing up. Both of them looked at Kerry with dread. Even though she expected something horrible, her father's words hit her like a hammer.

"Randy's had an accident. Sandy has no idea how bad it is, but the officer who called her sounded pretty shook up. He asked her to come to the hospital right away. She is leaving the twins with a neighbor and wants us to meet her at the hospital."

"Are we taking Nate?" Darcy asked with an effort. "Or do I need to stay home with him?"

"What do you want to do?" Kerry asked.

"I want to go. Please, can we take Nate?" Darcy pleaded tearfully.

"Sure, we'll take him. Randy would want you there, Darcy. Now, everyone hurry and get dressed. I'll get Nate," her father said.

Darcy was scarcely even conscious of the moderately falling snow outside the car as they rode to the hospital. Nate sat beside her, wrapped in his own tumultuous little thoughts. In all Darcy's life, she had never experienced a terrible tragedy like she was right now. She remembered well the death of her Grandpa Hutchins, and then a year later the death of her Grandma Hutchins. That had only been a few years ago, but it was different. They were both elderly and had been suffering from poor health. And even though she had loved them both dearly, this with Randy was...well, different.

Darcy prayed like she'd never prayed before. Nate was still as a mouse. Sharon was crying softly in the front seat. Kerry was concentrating on the snowy road, driving slowly but steadily. It seemed like it was taking forever. Never had town been so far away!

Apprehension filled Darcy's soul when they did finally drive into the parking area at the county hospital. The brown brick building loomed large and foreboding in the gentle snowstorm. At the door, as her father held it open for the rest of them to enter, the antiseptic smelling warm air assaulted her, and she turned back and gulped just one more breath of clear, cold air, as if it would sustain her for the entire ordeal in the hospital.

"Go to the emergency room. It's that way," they were told by a receptionist.

Darcy was the first to spot Sandy. She was sitting on a hard blue sofa just outside the emergency room door, staring blankly across the hallway. Sarge, out of uniform but with his revolver strapped on, sat beside her. His hair was mussed, and he looked like he'd dressed in a hurry, like she had, Darcy thought to herself. Sarge was talking softly to Sandy, but she made no move indicating she could hear a word.

"There's Sandy," Darcy said, knowing that everyone else already saw her. But they all walked more quickly down the long hallway.

Sarge rose to his feet and reached instinctively for Kerry's hand. "They called me out. I'm afraid I don't know much," he said.

Sharon and Darcy dropped on the couch, one on either side of Randy's wife as Sarge went on, "Haven't heard a thing since I got here, which was just as Sandy did."

"Surely you know something...how it happened...anything," Kerry pleaded, holding tightly to little Nate's hand.

"All I know was that he turned on a red Trans Am, and..."

Darcy interrupted with a gasp. "Shad!" she cried.

"We don't know that, Darcy," Sarge said gently but firmly. "Randy told the dispatcher that he didn't see the driver or the license number.

Anyway, the Trans Am took off like a shot when Randy turned on his overhead lights."

Darcy leaned back on the sofa, fighting the urge to faint. "He got away?" she asked.

"Well, yes, but Randy did go after him."

"In all this snow?" Darcy asked faintly.

"It wasn't actually that bad then, but it was pretty slick, I suppose. Anyway, the Trans Am was driving right up the center of the highway, and when a car came from the opposite direction it barely made it past, then it went into a spin. Randy took to the borrow pit to avoid a collision, from what I understand," Sarge explained.

"He saved our lives," a voice said and Darcy looked up. Brother Snyder, her Sunday School teacher, had walked up unobserved. "Randy did it for us, for my family and me," he said in a sorrowful voice. His face was white and his eyes downcast, but Darcy was sure he'd been crying.

"Anyone in your car hurt badly?" Sarge asked.

"No. We never even left the highway. The kids and Madge and I are awful shook up, but that's all. Randy saved us—saved us all."

"Did you see how badly Randy was hurt?" Sandy asked. She came to her feet and faced him, pleading with her eyes.

"Yes. I helped as best I could. I backed up and then ran to his car. It ended up on its wheels but was smashed terribly. Air bags were exploded, but I thought he was...dead!" he blurted, and tears rolled down his ruddy cheeks.

"How seriously is he hurt?" Kerry pressed urgently.

"I don't know. The air bags saved him, but the car was sure smashed up. The ambulance people took over and I didn't see him after they got him out of the car."

"Did he say anything that you heard?" Sarge inquired.

"Oh, no. He was unconscious. It was terrible. Just terrible. I'm so sorry. So very sorry. There was nothing I could do. The road was so slick. I wish we'd come back earlier," he said in anguish.

"It was not your fault," Sarge said firmly. "I'll go find out how he is. You folks can't wait here like this forever." He backed up his words by barging through the emergency room door as Kerry helped Sandy sit down again.

Sarge was back in less than five minutes with a young doctor in tow. "Doctor, this is the trooper's wife, Sandy, and his sister, Sharon, and her family," he said.

"Hello, folks. I'm Doctor Smyth. I'm filling in here for a couple of weeks," he said with a smile. "The trooper is tough. He's going to be all right. You may come in now if you'd like. I just finished cleaning him up and doing a little stitching here and there. He's presentable now."

Sarge held the door open, and they all filed fearfully after the doctor. Darcy had the impulse to dash ahead, she was so anxious to see Randy, for at last they knew that he was at least alive! But she restrained herself.

Sandy reached her husband first. Randy was lying on a hard bed with the side rails up. He smiled painfully as he accepted a tender kiss. "I hope I didn't frighten anyone," he said.

"You folks mustn't be too long. The trooper took some hard knocks on the head and as a result, he has a moderate concussion. He's only been conscious for a few minutes," the doctor explained.

"Other than that and a few bruises and scrapes, I think I'm fine," Randy explained with a grimace.

"Not even so much as a broken finger," the doctor agreed. "We will need to keep him here for a day or two, but just for observation. He'll have a bad headache for awhile and could black out again for short spells."

The visit was short, but as they all filed out everyone was visibly relieved. Darcy started through the door, but Randy called her name weakly. She returned to his bedside. "I can't prove it, but you were right, kid. I should have been more careful. I just can't imagine who else it could have been but Shad."

Darcy nodded. "I'm just glad you are going to be okay. You can't imagine the thoughts that I was having before I finally got to see you."

"Well, it's over now. You can quit worrying," Randy replied with the best grin he could muster. "You worried, and rightfully so, because you were right, but there is no need to go on worrying. I'll be just fine."

"Uh, huh," Darcy said with a little relief, but her smile to Randy did not tell the story of foreboding that still overshadowed her. She hurried out before he sensed it.

The snow quit before Darcy awoke later that morning. She hadn't been up long when Quin called. "Hi, sunshine," he greeted her. "The sun is bright and the weather is clear this morning. The snow is nearly melted off the roads, too. What time do you want to leave?"

"Well, I don't know. I'd like to see how Randy is first," she said in guarded tones, aware of the emotion she was feeling, but trying to conceal it from Quin.

"Randy. What's the matter with him?" Quin asked in concern.

Darcy recounted the events of the horrible night she had experienced, and Quin listened with sympathy. When she had finished, he said, "I'll be there whenever you say and we will go to the hospital first."

"Oh, Quin, thank you," she said, and her love for him grew. He was so thoughtful of her.

An hour later, Darcy and Quin stood at Randy's bedside. "I'm fine," her uncle insisted to Darcy's repeated inquiries. "Oh, my head aches something awful, and I can't focus my eyes very well, but I really am okay. I shouldn't have been, they tell me, but I was lucky, I guess—or blessed."

"He looks okay to me," Quin insisted after they had left, but she was still worrying.

"Maybe, but what if there's something terribly wrong that the doctors have missed?" she asked in fear.

"He really is going to be just fine, Darcy. Now quit worrying. We'll check on him when we get home tonight, if you like.

She liked, but as hard as she tried, Darcy was unable to dispel the feeling of impending disaster, even though she told herself it was silly. If anything, Randy's crash served only to heighten her fear for him, or someone else she loved. For Quin's sake she put on a happy face for the rest of the day, but inside she was being torn apart with grief and worry. What if Randy's accident was only a grim warning of what was yet to come if Shad didn't straighten up? she wondered a hundred times that day.

❋

On Monday morning, Shad showed up at the garage to work a few minutes late. He was hung over from the drinking he'd done the night before. It was becoming a nightly thing with Shad. His boss was waiting for him at the door. "Shad, into my office," he said curtly.

Surprised, Shad followed him. The boss did not even invite him to take a seat in the cluttered little room. His face was dark and he turned a pair of angry eyes on Shad. "I'm hearing some nasty rumors, and I don't like them," the boss said.

Shad paled, but he stood his ground. "I guess I don't know what you're talking about," he responded, trying to look the boss in the eye bravely.

Hal Casper, in his late thirties, was usually an easygoing man, but his face turned dark and ugly, and he said, "Randy Hutchins is a friend of mine. And he's a darn good cop."

"Yeah, I know," Shad said, determined not to feel or look guilty. He had heard the news on the radio and was aware that Randy was in the county hospital. "My old girl friend is a niece of his," Shad added when Hal didn't look convinced with Shad's sincerity.

"He's lucky to be alive, they say. No thanks to some hot-shot with a souped-up red Trans Am," Hal fumed.

"What happened?" Shad asked, pretending total ignorance and acting shocked.

"Don't play games with me, Shad. There's only one red Trans Am around here, and I doubt if one just happened to be passing through at eleven o'clock on a stormy night. I don't know what your hang-up is, but..."

Shad cut him off belligerently. "You accusing me of something, Hal?"

"Not directly, but I'm firing you. If you were any kind of a man, you'd admit what you did and..."

Shad interrupted again with a snarl. "Yeah, you are accusing me. I got a lawyer, you know, and a good one."

"Figures. Probably Roger MacArthur, and that's not saying much for you. I should have checked you out better before I ever gave you a job."

"Yup, and Mac'll make you wish you never accused me of nothing," Shad threatened.

"Get this straight, Shad. I have no use for MacArthur, and it makes no difference to me if he is your lawyer. You are still fired," Hal said in a low and angry voice. "Now get out of here. I have work to do."

Shad was angry—and worried. He needed this job to pay off his fines and keep in beer and gas. It would also look good in court. He glared at Hal Casper with malice, then he blurted, "You'll be hearing from Mac. You can't prove nothing, and neither can that hot-shot Randy Hutchins."

"Get out, Shad, before I throw you out! Your check will come in the mail. And I never want to see you in this place again," Hal shouted, lunging to his feet.

Shad left in a hurry. He'd pushed the wrong man too far. Well, he'd show him. He really would call Mac. Shad did just that from a pay phone outside the Maverick station.

Mac's reaction was not what he expected. "You darn fool kid!" the attorney thundered. "I thought I told you to behave yourself until after we got your case settled. Running on a cop and causing a serious accident is not the way to do that!"

"Are you saying I ran on Hutchins? Nobody can prove that!" Shad shouted into the phone. "You gonna' call the garage and get me my job back or not?"

"Don't be a still bigger fool, Shad. The last thing we need now is to draw attention to what you did."

"You're assuming I did it!" Shad shouted.

"Well, you did, didn't you?"

"No way, man."

"Don't lie to me, Shad! You did it, and we both know it. You better come clean with me right now or there's no way I will continue to defend you," Mac said sternly.

"But Dad's paid you and you have to," Shad countered.

"You little whelp you! All your dad has given me is a small retainer. I can drop your case any second if I happen to feel like it. You have a lot to learn, young man. Now, you get busy and tell me exactly what happened out there Thursday night."

"No. I can't. I'm in enough trouble as it is," Shad protested.

"Shad, anything you say to me is privileged. I don't have to repeat a word of it to anyone, not even a judge. Fact is, I'm really the only one you can tell."

Shad looked around to see if anyone was listening. When he was sure he would not be overheard, he spoke again, giving his attorney his version of the events of Thanksgiving night. He did tell most of the facts, but not all of them. He just couldn't bring himself to admit that he'd been drinking, and he strongly denied it when Mac pressed him on that point.

"I don't drink anymore," he shouted when Mac asked for the third time. "I've quit that."

"Okay, okay. Shad, I have some advice, and you better listen this time. You leave that Trans Am of yours parked. Another stunt like this one and I'm off the case. So, no drinking and no driving. Is that clear?" Mac asked.

"Yes, sir," Shad said meekly.

"Good. I am making progress on your case. If you can manage to keep your nose clean, we'll win this thing. I'll see you in a couple of weeks," Mac said and hung up.

Shad did the same. Then he impulsively dropped another quarter in the phone, thumbed through the tattered phone book, and dialed. "County Hospital," a clear, business-like female voice answered.

"Hello. I...ah...I need to know about a patient—his condition, I mean."

"The name of the patient," she said.

"Hutchins. Randy Hutchins," Shad said nervously.

"May I have your name please?"

"No. I mean, I just need to know how he is. You know, his condition. I don't need to talk to him right now," Shad stammered.

"I'm sorry, but unless you can identify yourself, I cannot give out any information on Mr. Hutchins," The woman said formally.

"Ah, Chad. Chad Larsen," he lied. "I'm a friend of H...Randy's."

"Did you say Chad, or was that Shad?" the receptionist asked.

Shad gasped and slammed down the receiver. He broke into a cold sweat as he turned from the phone. The cops were trying to trap him! They had nothing on him—or did they? He better be very careful.

He went inside the Maverick. Everyone in there turned to look at him. At least he thought they did. Did everyone suspect him? he wondered. He had to have a drink fast, just to steady his nerves.

Shad walked rapidly to the red Trans Am, climbed in, and roared off. It took him an hour, but he finally got his hands on a six-pack of cold beer.

❉

Sarge strolled into the hospital about eleven that morning. He stopped and talked to the woman receiving incoming calls. "Anything suspicious?" he asked with a good-natured smile, refering to earlier instruction to the hospital to be alert for a call from Shad.

"More than suspicious," she said. "A young man called in—sounded young, anyway. He asked to talk to Mr. Hutchins."

"Ah ha," Sarge said, suddenly very interested.

The receptionist went on without further urging. "I did exactly as you instructed." She waved the typed sheet of instructions which Sarge had delivered on Saturday at the request of Randy's lieutenant. "He gave his name as Chad Larsen. When I asked him if he meant Chad or Shad, he hung up on me."

"Thank you, ma'am," Sarge said. "We'll keep in touch in case he tries again."

Sarge left and slipped down to Randy's room. "So, how's the bump on the noggin?" he asked as Randy laid aside the book he was reading and scowled.

"I don't know why I'm still here," Randy complained. "My niece thinks it's because there is something wrong with me that they're not saying. Poor kid. She worries far too much. Anyway, I feel fine, and I haven't blacked out since yesterday. I can even read a little, although it is a bit blurry yet. Nothing I couldn't handle at home, though."

Sarge chuckled. "Just don't know when you're well off, do you? Wait till you get my age; you'll be looking for an excuse to be pampered and fed like a baby." Randy shook his head, and Sarge went on. "When do they plan to release you?"

"Tomorrow, maybe. If I had as hard a time making up my mind as these doctors do, I'd never get a ticket written," Randy said with a snort of disgust.

Sarge smiled again, then he said, "Randy, our boy called here this morning, I think."

Randy perked up. "Shad?"

"Probably," Sarge said and explained. "It still doesn't prove anything, though."

"No, but at least it removes some of the doubt in our minds," Randy reasoned. "You know, we're not the only ones who suspect Shad. I got a call a few minutes ago from a friend of mine. You know him. Hal Casper. Runs his own garage over in the east end of the county."

"Yeah, best darn mechanic in the area," Sarge said. "Did he figure it out?"

"I'd say. Seems Shad's been working for him since just a few days after he got out of jail. Hal said the kid shows real promise as a mechanic, but he fired him anyway," Randy said.

"Why?" Sarge asked, wrinkling his brow.

"He called Shad in and confronted him over the red Trans Am he drives. Hal told Shad that he figured it was him. He said when he did that, that he could read guilt all over the kid's face. Shad threatened to call his attorney. Hal figured that was the clincher. He knew it for sure, then, especially when he even guessed who his attorney was."

Sarge just shook his head. "Too bad. Too darn bad. Kid's about beyond help, I'm afraid. Saw his mother in the store this morning. She looks like she's about to the end of her rope. Sure makes a guy feel bad." Sarge paused and scratched his nose. Then he frowned thoughtfully and said, "Red Trans Am. Darn. Wish we could nail Shad and impound that car of his. He's a menace—a real danger."

As he talked, he became more angry. "After what he did to you, we've just got to stop him, Randy. That's all there is to it."

"He won't be easy to stop now, especially without his father's support, and I'm sure we don't have that. He's a stubborn and proud man. And that car of Shad's can really get on down the road. Yes, sir, that's one fast car," Randy mused. "One mean machine."

# Chapter Fifteen

WHILE THE ROMANCE OF Quin and Darcy moved smoothly ahead, despite Darcy's worries, Shad Cleverly's attitude and behavior continued to deteriorate. After losing his job, he moved back home. He gave his parents a skewed account of Hal Casper firing him, proclaiming his innocence and making the garage owner appear to be a crook. Shad's father believed him and loudly threatened to intervene, but when Shad told him that he had already talked to Mac MacArthur about it, he backed off. Paula Cleverly, however, viewed her wayward son with suspicion, cried a lot, and withdrew into a shell, trying in vain to blot out the pain and worry he caused her.

As the day for Shad's trial approached, he looked without success for another job. To avoid his mother's incriminations, he stayed out late, hanging around with a variety of young men and women with habits similar to his own. More and more of Bill Cleverly's money wound up in the pockets of Dwight Arnot as Shad paid his ever increasing price for beer and even some hard liquor.

The morning his trial was scheduled to begin, Shad was hung over and bleary-eyed from drinking heavily the night before, but Mac MacArthur seemed not to notice as he led Shad and Bill into a small conference room in the courthouse. There he smiled and announced, "Well, Shad, I think I have matters well in hand. I've met several times over the past few days with the prosecutor. He has agreed to a settlement in your case. All that is required of you now is to enter a guilty plea to one count of simple assault."

"What! I thought you were going to get me off," Shad barked.

"And so did I, Mac!" Bill added angrily. "I'm not paying you to..."

Mac cut him off with a wave of his hand and a sudden frown of anger. "You are paying me to do the best I can to keep a very guilty young man out of prison," he said in a voice that was low and menacing. "You have made that very difficult, Shad. By ignoring every warning I have given you about drinking and about driving that Trans Am of yours, you have thrown away any chance for a complete acquittal."

Mac leaned forward, punctuating his disgust by lowering his thick eyebrows. Bill started to speak again, but Mac stopped him curtly. "You two best listen to me now. The trial is scheduled to begin in thirty minutes. At that time you better accept the prosecutor's offer and plead guilty to simple assault. Believe me, Shad, it was not easy to get him to make it. If you don't agree, then I'll try your case, but I will almost certainly lose, and you may well go to prison."

"But..." Bill began angrily, rising to his feet.

"Settle down, Bill, and hear me out," Mac ordered in a tone of voice that brought instant compliance. He went on. "The most, and I do repeat, the most Shad can get for a simple assault is six months in the county jail and a fine..."

"Six months!" It was Shad who interrupted angrily this time, and he was alarmed. The thought of actually going to jail again drove fear like a rusty spike into his heart. His chest tightened and his palms sweated.

"Shut up and listen until I'm through, Shad," Mac ordered curtly. "The prosecutor has agreed not to argue for a tough sentence. Nor will he argue for leniency. I'll do my best to get the judge to treat you well, but whatever he does, it will certainly beat two terms of up to five years in prison. That, young man, is what I am helping you avoid."

Shad glanced at his father. The anger was gone from Bill's face, and he was white—shaken. "All right, Mac, I take it the evidence is pretty strong against Shad."

"Almost airtight, I'm afraid," Mac said as Shad's eyes left his father's face for the table top before him, and the fear in his heart grew. "I interviewed the men who were on the block with Shad the night of the altercation. There were six. They all told me that it sounded like Shad started the fight. In fact, he was the only one that even threw a punch."

"But Buster..." Shad interrupted in frustration.

His father cut him off with a curt, "You just listen, Shad. I want to hear this."

Shad forced his lips together, but they quivered as Mac went on. "Four still agreed to testify for Shad, but upon close examination of their records and background, I could see that they would probably not stand up to an intense cross examination, and they could even have their testimony impeached. In fact, the prosecutor made it clear that he would attempt to do just that."

"Do you mean they would have lied for Shad?" Bill asked, shaking his head.

"Well, for me," Mac corrected.

"But why?"

"Never mind that," Mac said, lowering his intimidating eyebrows again. "At any rate, that leaves us on rather shaky ground. The only things in our favor are the fact that one jailer did in fact say something degrading about this girl friend of Shad's, and..."

Shad winced at the mention of Darcy. Mac noticed and stopped, nodded his head, then said, "The other thing is the law suit we brought against the sheriff and his jailers. I had to agree to drop the suit as part of the plea arrangement."

"But..." Bill started to protest.

Again Mac stopped him. "That is the very reason I brought the suit in the first place, Bill. It was to give me additional bargaining power. It worked," he said smugly. "You surely don't think we could have actually won the suit, do you?" The way Mac asked the question was in itself an answer. He obviously knew he could never win—despite Shad's broken arm.

The other two prisoners' testimonies would have hurt him in the lawsuit, Shad thought grimly as Mac frowned and addressed him. "Shad, the sheriff has two men in jail right now who have agreed to testify that you have been drinking heavily lately. They are prepared to name dates, times, and places. One of them was just brought in yesterday. He's out to save his own skin. Fellow by the name of Dwight Arnot."

Shad felt the blood drain from his face. Mac obviously noticed his reaction, for he then said, "I see you know Mr. Arnot."

Shad nodded meekly.

"The sheriff and prosecutor both agreed to drop the charges of contributing that have been brought against Arnot if he agrees to testify that you bought beer from him," Mac said. Before Shad could stammer anything to this disconcerting news, Mac spoke to Bill. "Seems this Arnot fellow has been supplying quite a bit of beer and even some hard stuff to some of the kids in town. He got careless, and one of the deputies and..." he said and paused, glancing at Shad with a frown before finishing with, "...Trooper Randy Hutchins set him up with a controlled buy."

Shad felt like a blown tire. All the air in his lungs left in a gust. The news that Randy, whom his actions had nearly caused the death of, had helped nail Dwight and turn him against Shad was too much. He began to cry.

That brought an angry response from his father. "You can knock off the bawling baby routine, Shad. I'd advise you to take the plea offer."

Shad rubbed his eyes in shame, but not over what he had done in breaking the law. He was almost proud of that. Rather, it was over his own weak emotional response to the news that Randy, Darcy's uncle, had actually helped to bring about his defeat in this case. And Shad did view anything short of acquittal as defeat.

"Well, what about it, Shad?" Mac asked.

Slowly and reluctantly, Shad nodded, even as fear of the clanging doors, hard bunk and dreary gloom of a jail cell filled his mind.

"Good, then I'll run let the prosecutor know. Then all we'll have to do is beg for mercy from the judge," Mac said, starting to rise.

Bill Cleverly stopped him. "This Hutchins," he said through clenched teeth. "He's out to get my boy it sounds like. Isn't there anything we can do to get him off the poor kid's case?"

Mac sank onto his chair and put both hands palm down on the table that separated him from Shad and his father and leaned forward. "I would not advise it," he said sternly.

"But he's the one who got the story of a red Trans Am going around. That has caused Shad a lot of hurt. He can't even get a job because of Randy's story," Bill protested. "And this Arnot guy, why everyone in town knows what a worm he is. He'd lie about anybody to save his own skin. All it would take is a little suggestion from some hot-shot like Hutchins."

Mac looked Bill in the eye, lowered his eyebrows again, and said in a low voice, "Do you really think Arnot's lying?" Before Bill could reply, Mac turned to Shad, and his eyes glared at the young man steadily through his ridiculous, horn-rim glasses. "Shad, did you buy beer from Dwight Arnot?" he asked in a voice that had successfully pried the truth from Shad in the past.

Fighting back his cowardly tears, Shad nodded. Bill roared, "Shad, what in the world did you do that for?"

"Where did you think I got the stuff," he said defensively. "I'm not old enough to just walk into the store and grab a six-pack, you know."

Mac wasn't through. "Shad, do you recall what I said about me not having to reveal anything you told me in confidence to anyone?"

Shad nodded, but he lowered his head. "Well, it is true, Shad. Anything you've told me today or in the past, is considered privileged information. I am leaving for a few minutes to speak to the prosecutor. While I am gone, I would strongly urge you to level with your dad about what we talked about the other day. I have a feeling you will be needing my services again, and unless your father knows everything I do about your actions, I will not represent you when that time comes," Mac said ominously.

"Do I understand that you will do nothing to stop Randy from harassing my son?" Bill demanded.

"It sure does. In fact, Bill, I would advise you to say or do nothing to or about Randy Hutchins, or you could well find yourself on the wrong end of a defamation of character suit," Mac said, rising to his feet. This time, Bill made no move to stop him, and Mac stepped to the door. "Wait here," he ordered. "We'll go into the courtroom together."

After Mac was gone, Bill turned to Shad. "All right, son, level with me. Did you lie to your mother and me about where you were the night Randy Hutchins piled up his patrol car?"

Shad avoided eye contact with his father, but he mumbled, "Just a little."

"Just a little!?" Bill thundered, coming to his feet and towering over Shad. "What does that mean? Was it you that Randy was chasing that night?"

Shad nodded. Bill sank into his chair with a simple, "Oh."

Silence prevailed between father and son until their attorney returned. "I take it he leveled with you?" Mac said after looking at them both briefly.

Bill nodded and said, "I guess you could call it that. It seems he did run on that cocky trooper."

"And almost caused his death," Mac added ominously.

"Still, Randy has no right to harass. Shad's just a kid, and..." Bill began again.

Mac cut him off curtly. "Forget it, Bill. Let's get into the courtroom."

Shad, as he pushed his chair back and forced himself to stand, felt some relief at his father's last words. At least, he thought grimly, he still had his father's support. That, he decided, he would continue to nurture, for he needed Bill Cleverly's money to support his habits of drinking and driving his hot Trans Am.

A couple of days after Shad's court appearance, Todd Albright and Jill Steelan stood in front of Jill's locker just before their first classes were due to start. Jill's clear blue eyes gazed at Todd with concern over what Todd had just told her. "Should we tell Darcy?" she asked.

Todd fidgeted. He knew she had to be told whether she viewed the news as good or bad, because she would eventually hear anyway. But it hurt Todd to say anything to Darcy about Shad, because it always made her so sad. And he hated seeing her sad, because she was largely responsible for the two best things in his life; his newfound activity in the church and the pert red head who was gazing at him so earnestly now.

Finally, he nodded and said, "I suppose we should. But it ain't something

I want to do. Darcy and Quin are so right for each other, and she is so doggone happy. But any mention of Shad makes her worry and I just hate it."

"I know, Todd," Jill said sympathetically. "She's so...good. But I know she'll ask sometime. And it'll probably be soon."

Todd agreed, and at noon, he had to fight the urge to run when Darcy, smiling and radiant, called their names. "Jill, Todd, there you guys are. Let's go to lunch."

"Hi, Darcy," they chimed in unison.

Jill cast Todd an inquiring glance. "After lunch," he said softly.

"After lunch what?" Darcy asked, a shadow crossing her radiant face.

"Oh, nothing," Todd answered, and he was relieved when Darcy did not press him for an explanation.

Todd didn't mind sharing news about things other than Shad with Darcy over lunch, and he was glad when she asked, "How's your dad, Todd?"

He knew she really cared, and he was proud to be able to report, "Great! His case worker called yesterday. He'll be home in time for Christmas." Todd choked up, and Darcy reached across the table and gently touched his arm.

"I'm glad," she said with a bright smile, and Todd knew she really was.

For the rest of their meal, at Darcy's urging, Todd talked about his father. He told of the counseling sessions he and his mother had attended, and of the commitments his father had made. Darcy glowed, and her green eyes glistened as Todd spoke.

After they had finished eating, as the three of them strolled down the main hallway of the school amidst a throng of laughing and talking young people, Jill said, "Todd, it's after lunch."

"I know," he said lightly, hoping Darcy would not suspect anything was amiss, but it was not easy to deceive Darcy Felding.

She stopped, put her hands on her hips, and asked, "Okay, guys, what's up? You know something you think I might not like, don't you? It's about Shad, isn't it? Well, tell me now, please."

"What about Shad?" a crisp voice asked from behind Todd.

"Hi, Stacy," Darcy said lightly, but her face betrayed the worry that Todd knew she felt at the very thought of Shad Cleverly. "These guys were about to tell me how Shad's trial went," she said to Stacy. Then to Todd and Jill, she said, with what Todd recognized as a forced smile, "You hoped I'd forgotten when his trial was, didn't you? I wish I could, but I'm not that lucky."

Stacy put a protective hand on Darcy's arm and said, "I haven't heard, either. I hope it's not bad. I'll be sick if he has to go to prison."

Todd glanced at Jill, mildly surprised. In the few weeks since he had become friends with Stacy, he had seen her change. But she had just spoken as Darcy would have done had it been her speaking. Stacy was becoming a lot like Darcy, and Todd was glad.

"Well," Todd began, "I guess I got good news. Shad's not going to prison."

"Oh, good!" Stacy said, and the relief on her face was genuine as she swept away a lock of long blonde hair.

"So what happened?" Darcy asked, more with apprehension than relief.

Todd was afraid of that, but despite his misgivings, he plunged in. "I talked to him last night."

"Where?" Darcy asked perceptively.

"At the jail," Todd said slowly, knowing she must have guessed.

"Oh," Darcy and Stacy moaned simultaneously.

Again, Todd was impressed at how, like Darcy, Stacy was becoming. Shrugging his thoughts aside, he plunged on. "Shad said his attorney made him plead guilty to assault—not aggravated assault, just simple assault. That's a misdemeanor."

Stacy and Darcy nodded that they understood the significance of the lesser charge. "He got all the other charges dropped. Sort of a trade, he told me. I asked him what about the law suit he had against the sheriff and them jailers. He seemed awful mad about that, but his lawyer made that part of the trade, he told me. Anyway, he ain't going to prison. He has to pay a fine. Five hundred dollars, he says. And he has to give the prisoner he beat up that much money, too. Oh, and he has to pay to fix the jailer's teeth," Todd summed up.

"And jail," Jill added, nudging Todd.

"Yeah, and he'll be in jail for a couple weeks," Todd agreed.

"Is that all?" Darcy asked, finally showing some relief.

"Yup, that's about it. He got off pretty easy, I'd say," Todd added.

"I still hate to think of him sitting in jail," Darcy said. "But, maybe this time he'll learn something."

"I hope," Stacy agreed.

"So, how's your uncle doing?"

"Fine," Darcy said, and as she did, that same familiar haunting look of fear crossed her flawless face, and despite her smile, Todd could see it lurking deep in those startling green eyes, and he felt a chill.

❉

That evening, Darcy was sitting at the dining room table pouring over a Trigonometry assignment when the doorbell rang. Her folks had gone to the temple that evening, and she was watching Nate. "I'll get it," came his shrill little cry. As he raced through the room, Darcy was reminded of a speeding Trans Am and bolted to her feet.

"Hi, Randy," she heard Nate say, and she shrugged off the fear that now accompanied any thought of that car of Shad's.

With a smile, she greeted Randy, who was dressed strikingly in the brown and grey uniform of the Utah Highway Patrol. She offered him a piece of cake she had just finished baking and icing an hour earlier.

Randy whooped with delight, picked Darcy up like she weighed nothing, spun around with her, and then, laughing with delight, gently lowered her until her feet touched the carpet. "I sure do pick the best times to come visit," he said, still chuckling as he helped himself to the cake, refusing the chair Darcy offered.

Darcy grinned and said nothing as Nate took the opportunity to add a piece of cake to his already bulging stomach. She thought how fun and unreserved Randy was when he was with just Nate and her. She silently thanked the Lord, as she had done a thousand times the past three weeks, for preserving Randy's life.

"Thanks, Darcy," Nate said with a mouthful of pilfered cake.

"Yeah, thanks," Randy agreed. "Your mom said they were going to the temple tonight. I was just passing, so I thought I'd check in on you two. Glad I did," he said before stuffing another bite of rich chocolate cake into his mouth.

Suddenly, one hand flew to his forehead, and he began to choke. A partially chewed gob of cake flew from his mouth and lit on the floor. He reached for a chair and sat down. Darcy gasped and ran to his aid. "Randy, what happened? What can I do?" she asked in alarm.

"Nothing," he said after a moment. "I'm sorry. I'll clean that up in a minute."

"I'll get it, but, Randy, what happened just now?"

"Oh, I still get a little pain once in a while in my head. It's getting better, though. Now, don't you worry, kid," he said, and he reached for his cake again as if to prove his point.

"Does the doctor know?" Darcy asked fearfully.

"No, but I'm fine, really. Let's forget about it, all right?"

"Randy, you shouldn't be working," Darcy persisted as a compelling terror for him pressed down on her, and she too had to seek a chair for support.

Then Darcy spotted Nate, so small, so vulnerable, standing with his eyes wide, staring at his uncle as if he were a freak. And fear for him, that dear little brother, crushed and mixed with her fear for Randy, and in a weak voice she heard herself say, "Nate, Shad'll be out of jail soon. You stay off the highway with your bike."

# Chapter Sixteen

QUIN SELTZ REFLECTED on the status of his heart. No longer was it his alone, but it was shared equally with Darcy Felding. Never had anything but his love of God and the Savior been stronger than the love he felt for that beautiful girl.

He lay in his bed late on Christmas night. They had celebrated much of that special holiday together, and the sweet scent of her perfume and soft feel of her tender lips on his still lingered. He thought with delight of the beauty of her voice when she sang and when she spoke. He reflected on the hours they had spent together these past weeks at the piano. She played while they both sang.

"A blend of voices created in Heaven," his sister Stacy had remarked after the two of them performed a duet at the Christmas program in his ward on Sunday.

For a moment, Quin thought of Stacy. How she had matured the two years he had been gone. But even more, she had developed a deep spiritual maturity since he had been home. Most of that could be attributed to the powerful influence for good that emanated from the angelic person of Darcy Felding.

Quin threw the covers back, climbed from his bed, and walked to the window. Outside, gently falling snow veiled the neighbor's house, and a covering of white glowed faintly from the lawn. As he watched, a soft wind came up and the snow began to dance and swirl before his eyes.

How like Darcy it is, he thought with a swelling in his breast. Truly, it could be said of the girl he loved that she was almost as pure as the driven snow. Oh, he knew she was not perfect, but she worked very hard at doing what was right. A light came on in the neighbor's house and cast a startling shade of green through the swirling snow. An effect, he realized, of the green curtains in the neighbor's window.

Instantly, he thought of the startling green of Darcy's eyes beneath her crown of chestnut hair, and Quin yearned for her. An eternity with that girl, that blossoming woman, would never be too much. Quin dropped to his knees and thanked the Lord for bringing her into his life. And again, as he had done several times these past weeks, he asked if she could be his through eternity. A sweet feeling of peace swelled in his bosom, and a tingling began at the top of his head and penetrated his body clear to the bottom of his bare feet. And Quin knew, yes, he truly knew that Darcy would be his through the eternities if he would stay worthy of her.

He stayed on his knees for a long time, savoring the sweetness of the influence of the Comforter. When he finally rose to his feet, all semblance of sleep had fled, and he tiptoed from his room, down the dark hallway, and into the kitchen. There he flipped on a light, took a glass from the cupboard and peered into the refrigerator. He debated briefly between milk and orange juice, finally choosing the milk.

After toasting a slice of bread and spreading it thickly with straw-berry jam, he sat at the table. Quin had barely begun to enjoy his midnight snack when he heard light footsteps behind him.

"After all you put away at dinner tonight, I didn't think you'd be hungry again for days," the lilting, teasing voice of Stacy called out softly.

Quin twisted on his chair. Stacy's tousled blonde hair outlined the clear features of her pretty face as she stood framed in the doorway. She was wearing a long flannel nightgown and furry slippers. "Hi, sis," he said, rising to his feet. "Come sit down and I'll fix you some."

"Sit down, Quin," she responded mildly. "Your toast will get cold and your milk warm. I'll fix something for myself and then join you. I couldn't sleep and saw a light. I suspected it was you."

"I couldn't sleep either. I'm glad for the company," he said, watching her as she moved gracefully from the doorway to the refrigerator.

Neither spoke as she reached for a glass and filled it with orange juice. She was remarkably pretty. She didn't look at all like Darcy, but she was gorgeous in her own special way. It would not be long, he suspected, until some lucky young man would fall in love with her the way he had fallen in love with Darcy.

How wonderful it is that relationships can be never-ending for those who really want it to be that way, he reflected soberly. Anything less seemed empty, he decided as Stacy placed her glass of juice on the table and gracefully sat down opposite him.

"Just a small glass of juice?" he asked.

Stacy smiled and brushed a wisp of golden hair from her face. "Yeah. I'm not hungry, just wide awake."

She sipped her juice, and he polished off his toast. "I should have toasted two," he said as he rose to correct the error.

"When are you going to ask Darcy to marry you, Quin?" Stacy asked unexpectedly when his back was to her.

"Why do you ask that? She's young and I'm not terribly old. There's no hurry, is there?" he asked, pausing to look at his sister for a moment before depositing a slice of bread in the toaster.

"I don't know. You two just seem so right for each other. I hoped you'd give her a ring for Christmas, but it's too late now," she said with an impish grin.

"Not really, there's always next Christmas, or the next," he said with his customarily sober face.

His flippant answer brought a look of alarm to Stacy's face, and her smile vanished. "Oh, don't wait, Quin. Please don't."

A faint shiver of alarm passed through him. "Stacy, why did you say that, like that?" he asked as his toast popped up. He failed to notice it.

"I...I'm not sure, Quin. I'm sorry. I know it's none of my business, but I just feel this...this urgency. Silly, huh?"

"I don't know, sis. I...we...it's just too soon, I think. She's still in high school, and I'm..." he began falteringly.

"Not getting any younger, big brother," Stacy interjected. "You do plan to marry her, don't you?"

"Of course," he said.

"Have you prayed about it?" Stacy asked. Then, before he could respond, she said, "That was a dumb question. You pray about everything."

"Everything of importance," he agreed.

"And?" she inquired.

"Let me put things away here, and then I'll share something with you," he said as he felt again the tingling he had experienced earlier.

After telling Stacy of his prayer and the answer he had received, she said, "Wow!" and a tear wet her cheek. "Just like that, huh?"

"Not exactly. That wasn't the first time I asked, just the strongest answer," he said.

"I wish I had faith like yours," she said after a moment of silence.

"You do; some of it's just still dormant, Stacy. You're a great kid, and I love you. You will be the queen of some lucky guy's home someday. But before that happens, if you but ask in faith, you will know he is right for you, just like I know Darcy is right for me," he said. Then, after a significant pause, he added, "For eternity."

"I love you, too, big brother," she said, and once more there was a moment of silence. Then with a puzzled expression on her face, she asked, "Why did you ask that way—pray that way?"

"What do you mean?" he asked.

"You said you asked God if she was right for you for eternity. Why not just ask if you should marry her?"

Quin looked for a long moment at his sister with her tousled hair and half-full glass of orange juice. Finally, he said, "I guess I asked that way because that's what I wanted to know. I love Darcy very much, but I love her for more than just a few years on earth. I know now that she can be mine forever!" he said with more gusto than the lateness of the hour dictated.

"Thank you," Stacy said, almost reverently.

"For what?" Quin asked, puzzled.

"For sharing this with me. It's all so...so very special. You and Darcy are both so lucky. No, not lucky, blessed," she said.

"You're right," he agreed.

"Quin," Stacy said a moment later.

He looked up quickly from the milk he had just placed on the table after taking a drink. He had detected an urgency in her voice.

"Quin," she repeated, then went on. "Darcy's afraid for you, I think."

"I know," he said somberly. "Actually, she has this persistent fear. It's the only unreasonable thing about her. She thinks something awful will happen to me, or Randy, or Nate, or somebody else she is close to. She won't talk about it to me anymore. She tries to repress it, but I can see it in her eyes."

"Me too. Jill and Todd are worried, just like we are. Todd thinks it's all because of Shad Cleverly and the awful things he's been doing. He says Randy's wreck should have made her quit worrying, but instead she worries more," Stacy said. As she spoke, her eyes grew misty.

"I agree with Todd, but there's more. Darcy has this great capacity for love. She loves everyone in a truly Christ-like way. She can hardly bear to see others suffer. She dwells on it too much, I think. I've got to help her overcome this," he said with feeling. Then he chuckled without smiling. "Not that it's really bad," he went on, absently picking up his milk again. "All she does is love too much."

Stacy smiled. "Yeah, I guess you're right, Quin. She really is a good person."

"And I love her so much it hurts," Quin said, his voice suddenly full of emotion. "Oh, Stacy, what did I ever do to deserve such an angel?"

"You're pretty good yourself," was Stacy's simple reply.

"And what am I ever going to do with her here and me at the university?" he asked, already experiencing a taste of the loneliness to come.

"Come home every chance you get, and then marry her this next summer," was Stacy's next simple, but direct answer.

"Think I should?" he asked, feeling a tingle of excitement at the thought.

"Of course," Stacy said firmly.

"But in the meantime, what will I ever do while we're separated?" he asked, his excitement giving way to thoughts of loneliness again.

Stacy smiled. "Imagine this, me giving you advice. But, since you ask, here's some. Just compare the time you are apart with eternity. A little separation is nothing when compared with eternity," she said profoundly, more profoundly than either of them really understood, for eternity is a very long time.

❈

Darcy awoke to four inches of new snow the day after Christmas. It was the first significant snowfall since the Thanksgiving storm that had been partially responsible for Randy's accident.

She smiled to herself as she looked at the blanket of white that graced her bedroom window. She had kept after Randy until he finally went back to the doctor. Now he was getting a much deserved rest for the holidays. His concussion had been worse than the doctors thought at first, and he was ordered to take it easy until he was better. That would not be until at least the new year, his doctor insisted.

Darcy was relieved, but still she worried. Maybe Quin was right. Maybe she worried too much. She would try to worry less, she decided with resolve and turned from her window with thoughts of the man she loved lifting her spirits.

At breakfast, Nate asked, "Darcy, will you play in the snow with me?"

"Of course, Nate, but only for a little while. I promised Quin he could pick me up at one o'clock," she said.

"But Darcy, you're always with Quin. Don't you love me anymore?" he asked with downcast eyes.

"Of course I do, you silly boy," she said with a shiver of apprehension.

"Then why can't you play in the snow with me all day?" he asked after gulping a huge drink of milk.

"Because you'd both catch your deaths of cold if you did," their mother cut in firmly. "I told you just a few minutes ago that you could play outside for one hour, and I meant it. You got more toys than any boy should have for Christmas. You may play with them most of the day."

"I'll spend the whole hour outside with you, Nate. And after that I'll still have time to read one of your new books to you before I have to start getting ready to meet Quin," Darcy said, eyeing her little brother fondly.

"But Darcy, this afternoon we could..." he began again with a mouth full of cereal.

"That's enough now, young man," Kerry broke in with a gleam in his eye. "Don't you know your sister's in love and her beau will be leaving in a few days?"

"Dad!" Darcy said sternly, but she could not restrain a smile. Her father understood her so well, and she loved him so much for it.

"What are you going to do when Quin goes to school, Darcy?" her mother asked.

Darcy chewed a bite of eggs silently for a moment and then swallowed. "Study, I guess, and play with Nate," she said, and was pleased at how her little brother brightened. "And I'll be lonely," she admitted wistfully.

Quin, as was his habit, was at the door several minutes early. "I hate to be late," he had told her once. "So I set my watch ahead five minutes and go by it. That way, if I'm a few minutes slow, I'm still on time."

She was amused by his reasoning but agreed that it made sense. So, at precisely five minutes before one o'clock, the doorbell rang.

Quin greeted Darcy with a quick hug and a grin from that usually sober but very handsome face that she hoped to gaze at in the eternities. He slipped inside and shut the door. "Bit chilly out there," he remarked.

"I'd say," she teased. "After the storm went past, it dropped to twenty-five degrees. Yeah, that's a bit chilly, all right."

"Lots colder in Moscow," he reminded her.

Quin had told her all about Russian winters, and she hugged herself and shivered at the thought.

After greeting Kerry and Sharon and thoroughly mussing Nate's hair, Quin helped Darcy into her coat. He promised to be back in time for dinner, which Sharon promptly invited him to share with them, and to which Quin equally promptly agreed.

As they had earlier discussed, Quin drove directly to the old rundown Albright house. Inside, they found that things were not so drab anymore. Darcy scarcely recognized Todd's father. Besides putting on some much needed weight, he was clean shaven, cheerful, and seemed very happy and content.

He greeted Darcy with a hug, which surprised her. And then he said, with tears in his eyes, "Thanks for coming by, both today and that other time."

Darcy felt awkward and couldn't think of a thing to say but, "Sure," which she knew was not sufficient. Maybe it was because he was sober.

Ed Albright was not through, and as he spoke again, Darcy was aware of Todd standing right behind his father. His eyes were shining and he had a huge grin on his face. "Young lady," Ed said slowly, "I'll have you know that you knocked more sense into me with that old shovel than you could ever know."

Darcy's face reddened at the unexpected reference to her desperate act, and she stammered, "I'm...a...I'm...sorry about...that."

"Don't be sorry, young lady. Please don't be. You stopped me from doing the worst thing I could ever have done. I love my wife and my son. I was hurting her. I might have killed her," he said with a horror-stricken face. "You came along and stopped me from destroying my soul, girl, and I thank you. And I also thank you for the change you made in my boy, Todd. And I'm even going to start back to church myself. Now if that ain't something, then there just ain't nothing!" he exclaimed.

Todd came to Darcy's rescue at that point. "Dad's a new man. I can't believe how much they helped him in that hospital," he said, circling around Ed and giving Darcy a friendly hug.

"But the shovel knocked something into place that ain't been in place since I quit going to church when I was sixteen. Thank you, girl, thank you."

"You're welcome," she said awkwardly.

Again Todd tried to rescue her. "Dad, you are embarrassing her," he said firmly.

"She can handle it, boy," Ed countered with a good-natured laugh. "Any girl who can swing a shovel with such gusto can stand a little bit of embarrassment."

For the first time since entering the house and being confronted by a much reformed and very grateful Ed Albright, Darcy noticed Quin. He was still standing at the door, which he must have closed, and was nearly doubled over in mirth.

Ed noticed him, too, and began pumping his hand firmly, bringing him out of his silent laughter. "This your young man?" Ed asked.

Darcy nodded, red-faced, but happy.

Then Ed Albright unwittingly brought back Darcy's haunting fears. "Sure is a fine boy," he said. "And so's my Todd. Fine, fine men. Young lady, I just wish you would take that there shovel of mine over to the Cleverly house and clobber Todd's old friend, Shad. Heaven only knows that kid needs it."

Darcy suddenly felt ill. In Ed Albright she had discovered just one more person she loved and now worried about. What if Shad hurt him in some way? The thought made her shudder.

# Chapter Seventeen

QUIN'S DEPARTURE TO the university to resume his studies was a difficult thing for Darcy to handle. He was leaving on a Sunday afternoon, and try as she might, she could not hide the pain his leaving inflicted on her tender heart. Tears flowed and her voice failed. For a long time they stood together in the bitter January air in a warm embrace.

At last he said, "I'm sorry I have to leave."

"It's okay," she said with a sob.

"I love you, Darcy. I'll come back as often as my studies and job will allow, for I shall miss you desperately."

"Me too," was all she could force from her quivering lips. She hoped he knew she meant that she both loved him and would miss him.

Almost poetically, he spoke again. "You have become the morning star in my life, Darcy. I look to thoughts of you to get me started each day and to sustain me throughout. Write often, if you can."

"Every day," she promised in a broken voice.

"If I can't make it home before your birthday in two weeks, I left a little token of my love for you with Stacy," he said, and for the first time his voice broke, too.

He kissed her, and the warmth of his lips drove away the bitter cold, but it returned when he finally pulled gently away. For a minute, he gazed into her eyes, and she saw in them an eternal flame of love, and she knew, somehow she really knew that theirs was an eternal love.

"It will be but a moment, Darcy, and we will be together again," he promised. "I'm sorry, but I really do have to go now," he said as he climbed into his car.

"It's okay," she sobbed again.

And then he was gone, down the lane and out of sight. Darcy stood watching the empty road until the bitter cold drove her into the warmth of her home.

As the next few days passed, Darcy did not allow her loneliness to slow her down. Rather, she masked it by digging into her school work with a passion, practicing the piano diligently, and singing at least a half-hour each day. When called, the Sunday after Quin's departure, to be the Laurel president, she put her soul into the calling. And her mother never had to ask for help with the meals or dishes, for somehow, Darcy always managed to be there.

And Nate. How Darcy cherished her moments alone with him each day. On the evening before her birthday, she overheard him say, "Darcy's an angel, Mom. I love her. She's never mean to me anymore. What will I do next year when she's gone to school with Quin?"

"Now, Nate," his mother scolded lightly. "We must not assume where Darcy will be next year. That is for Darcy and Quin to decide."

"And God," Nate added innocently.

"Yes, and always God, son. I suspect that Darcy and Quin are letting God guide them both. They are both so good," Sharon agreed.

"She's like Jesus, isn't she, Mom?" he asked as he brushed away a tear.

"Almost," Sharon agreed. "Yes, Nate, almost."

And then Darcy fled to her room in tears. She felt so unworthy of the love and praise heaped upon her. When the tears finally dried, she spotted the package, wrapped gaily in silver and gold, that lay upon her bed.

It had been given to her that evening by Stacy. She had brought it to the house with an apology that Quin called and asked her to deliver it. "His boss got sick today, and Quin had to go in to work tonight to cover for him," Stacy said. "So he could not drive home tonight like he hoped to. But he promised he would call you tomorrow. So be at home at four. You may open the present early—tonight," Stacy concluded.

With trembling hands she picked it up. It was flat and nearly sixteen or eighteen inches square. She could not imagine what it was and held it to her breast as though it were something she would love and cherish. And somehow she knew that it was.

Finally, with fingers that were shaking, she carefully pulled free the silver lace and set aside the silver bow. Next, she loosened each strip of tape without allowing a single tear in the heavy gold wrapping paper. As she lifted the paper away to reveal the contents, she chuckled. For there before her lay a very large pizza box!

On the lid, written in Quin's neat and familiar handwriting was a brief message. She could almost see his sober face and hear his clear baritone voice as she read, "My darling, Darcy. Happy eighteenth birthday. Sorry about the box, but it was the best fit I could find for what is inside. I made it just for you, but you may share it if you like as He has shared with us." It was signed, "Love, Quin."

Puzzled, she read the inscription again. Quin made it? she thought. But whatever could it be? And she could share it? Then she would, she decided suddenly and burst from the bedroom carrying her extra large pizza box and calling to her family.

Curiously, they gathered around the dining room table. "What's the pizza for?" Nate asked. "We already had supper."

"It's what the gold wrapping contained that Stacy brought just before we ate," Darcy explained. "In it is a present from Quin. Listen, all of you, to what he wrote."

She then read the inscription again. "What beautiful penmanship," Sharon remarked.

"I wonder why he capitalized the H on He. Usually that is reserved for Deity," Kerry said with a puzzled expression.

"Open it, Darcy," Nate urged impatiently.

So she did and gasped at what she saw.

Beneath the lid of the pizza box and under a layer of tissue, the face of Jesus, painted in oil, gazed reverently at her, casting a bright light, it seemed, throughout the room. For a moment, the eyes of the Savior held her spellbound. Never had she seen such love burst forth from painted eyes! And there was something familiar about them. Finally, as her family also studied the painting in awe, her eyes sought out the artist's signature in the lower right-hand corner. There, in the same neat penmanship that was on the pizza box, was the name of the man she loved.

"Quin painted it for me!" Darcy cried, her voice full of love. Then she paused for a moment before exclaiming, "But he can't paint!"

"At least he did not let you know he could," Sharon said gently. "He must have wanted this to be a complete surprise."

"And it is! It is!"

"Darcy," Nate said in a timid little voice, his eyes still glued to the painting of the Savior.

Darcy glanced at him. "Yes, Nate?" she coaxed gently.

"His eyes—they're like your eyes," he said, and it hit her; Quin had painted the eyes of the Savior the same startling green as hers.

"They really do remind me of you," Sharon agreed.

Kerry shook his head in wonder and then pointed to the upper left hand corner of the painting. "Look," he said. "He has written something here. It is very small."

Darcy leaned eagerly over and, squinting, read aloud, "That when he shall appear, we shall be like him, for we shall see him as he is. Moroni

7:48." Then she cried.

For several minutes, they all emotionally gazed at the beautiful painting, and Darcy's love for her Savior grew. And so did her love for Quin Seltz. Finally, her father broke the spell. "We must hang it in your room, Darcy. I'll get a hammer and a nail."

"Dad, couldn't it be...couldn't we hang it in the living room where we can all see it?" Darcy asked hesitantly.

"Of course," Kerry said. "If that is what you'd like."

"I would. Very much."

While Kerry hung the magnificent painting of Christ in the most prominent spot in the living room, Darcy made a phone call.

She spoke with Stacy. "Stacy!" she exclaimed. "Have you seen it?"

"I watched him paint it," Stacy said. "Isn't it just the best?"

"Yes it is. But I didn't know he could paint," Darcy said.

"He wanted it that way. He swore us all to secrecy. He said the surprise would be better."

"Oh, Stacy, I can't wait until he calls."

"Four o'clock tomorrow. Right after school."

"I'll be here," Darcy promised.

"Darcy, did you notice the eyes?" Stacy asked.

"Did I! Why, Stacy? Why did he use my eyes?" Darcy asked.

"Because you try so hard to be Christ-like," Stacy answered.

"Oh, but I don't do very well!" Darcy exclaimed.

A few minutes later, as the whole family again stood and viewed the magnificent portrait, Nate asked innocently, "Is that what Jesus really looks like?"

"We don't know that, son, " Sharon answered. "Each artist that paints Jesus has his own idea of how he might look, but each is beautiful."

"And you can always tell who it is when someone paints the Savior," Kerry added. "That has always amazed me."

"But this one is probably really Jesus," Nate said.

"Why do you say that, son?" Sharon asked curiously.

"Because it reminds me of Darcy," Nate said.

No one noticed the tears that slipped from her shining, startling green eyes, those so like the ones in the face of Jesus on the canvas on the wall.

At five minutes to four o'clock in the afternoon of the fifteenth day of January, the day Darcy Felding turned eighteen, she stood by the phone with her shaking hand poised to answer it the moment it rang.

At that moment, as she was expecting to hear the phone, there came a light knock on the front door. Then a clear baritone voice rang out, "Darcy. Darcy. Calling Darcy."

Darcy almost tripped over herself in her haste to reach the door. She did send a chair sprawling but did not take the time to upright it. As she swung the door open, there stood the man she loved, his face sober, but his eyes a blue sea of sparkling mischief. With a shout of joy she threw herself into his outstretched arms.

"Why didn't you tell me you were coming?" she asked a few seconds later.

"Stacy asked me the same thing when I made her promise not to tell you. I just kind of like surprises, I guess."

"You must. You're full of them. Oh, Quin, I love the painting! It is just—well, the best."

"So you like it? I was worried. I haven't really painted very much."

"Of course I like it, Quin. It's beautiful. It is the most beautiful painting of the Savior I have ever seen. Thank you so much," she said, and she punctuated her gratitude with a lingering kiss.

Then, as they moved together toward the glowing depiction of Christ, Darcy said, "Quin, I thought you had classes this afternoon. You shouldn't have driven here so early."

"I cut a couple of classes," he confessed.

"Quin, your grades!" Darcy exclaimed.

"Seeing you was more important. Anyway, I did speak to a guy that has both classes with me. He promised to share his notes and let me know what the assignments are. I do have to go back tonight, though, for I have a test in the morning at eight," he explained. "So I can't stay long."

"Thank you, Quin," she said softly.

"Where are your folks?" he asked, looking around the room.

"Dad went out to chore before you came. Mom took Nate grocery shopping. They said they wanted to give me some privacy when you called," Darcy explained as she boldly wrapped her arms around his neck and pressed her lips to his.

When, breathless and with a rapidly beating heart, she released him, Quin said, "So we're alone, I hope."

"For a little while."

"Good, for I have a little something in my pocket. It is for your birthday," he said with his customarily sober face.

"But Quin, you already gave me the most wonderful gift," she protested weakly, wondering, but not daring to hope, at what small gift his pocket might contain.

"This is different, he said, fishing in his pocket and coming out with a closed fist. "First, Darcy, there is something we need to discuss."

He was so serious that her chest constricted. "What?" she scarcely managed to whisper.

"Well, I've decided that I need to take a few classes this summer. And my boss will give me all the hours I can work," he said.

Darcy was sick at heart. She had so looked forward to his being at home this summer. It had never occurred to her that he might go to summer school. But she was not about to admit her disappointment and hurt him in any way. So she said, "That's nice, Quin," with downcast eyes.

Quin put two fingers beneath her quivering chin and gently lifted. "Hey, Darcy, don't be so glum."

It showed! She forced a smile in an effort to compensate.

Quin went on, "It's sure lonely without you, Darcy."

To that she readily agreed.

"And I don't know if I can stand it, being alone all winter and spring and then having to be alone again during the summer," he said sadly.

"But your education is important," she pointed out half-heartedly. "You are going to be an important doctor some day."

"I don't know how important I'll be, but my education is important for both of us. Darcy, my classes don't start until the last week of June. I know this is rushing things, but I wondered…" He let his thought linger and again lifted her sagging chin.

"Darcy, I love you. You know that, don't you?"

"Yes, of course. And I love you," she said very quietly.

"Well, I was wondering, do you love me enough to marry me right after you graduate?" he asked.

Darcy yelped in delight and threw her arms around his neck while murmuring, "Yes, oh yes, oh yes."

"Then you'll need this," he said, and as she stepped back, his left hand came open. In it was a gold ring with a glittering diamond, set in a heart-shaped framework of several more tiny diamonds.

"Quin, it's beautiful!" she exclaimed and quickly held out her trembling left hand.

The ring fit perfectly, and like her own heart, a glow came from within the heart-shaped pattern of diamonds as she showed it first to her family, then to Quin's family, then to Todd and to Jill, and to others. The short evening of her birthday would have been perfect but for one thing.

When they went to Randy's house to show Randy and Sandy the engagement ring, Randy was not at home. He was on duty.

❋

Shad Cleverly, despite his drinking and carousing about, did not forget the birthday of the girl he believed he loved. "Darcy doesn't want to see you, Shad!" his mother scolded with an aching heart when he walked into the house that night and announced his intentions.

"Maybe, maybe not, but I'll let her decide that," he raged as he grabbed his coat. "I got her something and I'll take it to her."

"Shad, you've been drinking again, and you don't have a license to drive. I refuse to take you out to Darcy's house," Paula cried.

"I hadn't planned for you to," he said with a snarl.

"Well, your father won't be home until nearly midnight, so that settles it," Paula concluded.

"Not quite, Mom," he taunted as he pulled out the keys to the red Trans Am from his pocket. "I've been driving all evening, so why shouldn't I now? See ya."

"Shad, please don't!" Paula cried as he slammed the door.

Shad tossed the package he had bought for Darcy on the seat beside him and roared up the street. On a sudden impulse, he turned down the street where Todd Albright lived and slid to a screeching halt in front of the run-down old house.

He had just decided that he wanted Todd with him when he gave Darcy her present, for he did not want a scene. If there was one person in the world whom he did not want to hurt, it was Darcy Felding, for he loved her with a hopeless love.

Todd seemed surprised to see him. "Shad, what's going on? You've been drinking, and you shouldn't be driving, "Todd said with undisguised disgust.

"Todd, I didn't come for a lecture. I need your help."

Todd's face softened, and he said, "You know I'll help you if it's possible."

"Good. Come with me to Darcy's house. I have a present for her birthday," Shad said with a distinct slur.

"No, Shad! That's impossible. You can't go..." Todd began in alarm.

"I can and I will!" Shad interrupted. "I just wanted you there so there wouldn't be a scene."

"Shad," Todd said, seeming quite agitated. "Darcy ain't home."

"How do you know?"

"Cause she was just here, and before that she'd been to Jill's," he said. "And they were going to several other places, too."

"They?" Shad asked suspiciously.

"Yes, they," Todd said.

"Who's she with, man?" Shad demanded.

"Quin, who'd you think?"

"That jerk's supposed to be at school. What's he doing here?"

"Well, since you ask, I'll tell you, Shad. She's not for you, and you know it. You've said so yourself. She is wearing a ring. She and Quin are engaged, so you see..."

Shad roared with rage. "Engaged! To Quin Seltz? That jerk! I oughta bust him right in the mouth!" he shouted, and he ran from the house in a rage.

Todd ran after him, shouting urgently, "Shad, don't do nothing stupid. Come back and let's talk. I'll even drive you home, Shad."

But Shad was not listening. He was seeing red, and he hopped into his Trans Am of that same bright color and left with a screeching of tires and roaring of the big engine.

❋

Randy Hutchins was feeling better. He still got occasional headaches, but nothing that a couple of aspirins couldn't handle. He'd seen Darcy just after school and admired the magnificent painting of the Savior that Quin painted for her. He had been deeply touched. He left her a small gift and went on duty. He had last seen her standing in the living room, staring at her painting as she said with a bright smile, "Quin's calling at four."

He had smiled in delight himself when he passed Quin a few minutes later. "Looks like he's calling in person," he had said aloud as the blue Buick headed up the highway toward the Feldings' farm.

That had been several hours ago. With a grin he waved when he spotted the blue Buick, a somber Quin at the wheel, pulling out of the Conoco station. Must be going back tonight, Randy thought, and suspected that he knew what Quin had driven all the way home to do on Darcy's birthday. It was about time for a break, so Randy thought maybe he'd just drop in on the Feldings and see if Darcy had any exciting birthday news.

Suddenly, Quin slammed on his brakes, narrowly avoiding a collision with a rapidly-traveling, wildly-weaving red Trans Am. Shad's angry face was clearly visible under the street lights as he passed Randy, who flipped on the overheads and siren.

With a groan, Randy turned to pursue Shad, grabbing the mike as he did so. "I'm in pursuit of a red Trans Am which is driving recklessly just east of the Conoco station," he told the dispatcher. "The driver is Shad Cleverly. I repeat, Shad Cleverly is driving."

As soon as dispatch had acknowledged, Sarge came on the air. "Careful, Three-fifty-six," he said urgently, using Randy's call number. "I'm close by and will try to intercept."

Shad cursed aloud and jammed down his foot when he saw the lights on Randy's new patrol car. "You asked for it, copper," he shouted, and he followed Main Street east, heading for the open highway just a few blocks ahead. But as he approached the last intersection of town, another patrol car with lights flashing and siren screaming a warning, careened into the intersection, and the officer driving it bailed out, jacking a round into a shotgun.

Shad cursed again, ducked low behind the steering wheel, and whipped around the city cop car. As he did, a sheet of flame a foot long burst from the shotgun just as he recognized Sarge. At almost the same moment he heard the boom of the exploding cartridge and felt the tug of a blown right front tire. His powerful Trans Am refused to obey his frantically turning steering wheel as it slid on through the intersection and plowed into a snow bank in the borrow pit a hundred feet or so short of the city limit sign.

Jamming his foot to the floor, the rear tires shrieked as they spun, shoving him even deeper into the snow bank before the engine finally killed. Shad Cleverly, tough, young, and drunk, began to cry as Trooper Randy Hutchins angrily ordered him out of his car. Shad attempted to run, but both cops were on him like gang-busters, and before his woozy brain realized it, he was handcuffed and being dragged off to a patrol car for another trip to the now familiar county jail.

# Chapter Eighteen

D ARCY WAS LYING IN BED with the lights out when she heard the phone ringing. Tears of joy stained her pillowcase. She felt like she was in a dream. Over and over in her mind she repeated the phrase, "Mrs. Quin Seltz." She was going to be married to the man she loved in the temple of the Lord on June 10th. Wow! she thought.

"Darcy," her mother's voice called gently as a simultaneous tap came on her bedroom door. "Are you awake, dear?"

"Yes, Mom. I don't think I can sleep tonight. I'm too excited," she answered.

"You're wanted on the phone."

Darcy's stomach lurched. "This time of night?" she heard herself saying as she glanced at the alarm clock. "It's almost eleven thirty!"

"I know, dear. It's Quin."

Darcy bolted out of bed at the mention of that magic name. "Is something wrong?" she cried as she jerked the bedroom door open.

"He didn't say. He just apologized for calling so late and asked for you."

Darcy left her mother standing by her door and raced to the phone. "Quin! What's wrong?" she asked the instant she had the receiver in her hand.

"Nothing, sweetheart. Nothing. I'm sorry I alarmed you," he said quickly.

"Oh, Quin. I was so worried when Mom said it was you calling."

"I'm okay. But I had to call and make sure everything was all right there," he said. "I was..."

"Why wouldn't it be?" Darcy cut in with alarm.

"Darcy, take a deep breath and be calm," Quin instructed. She did and then he asked, "Are you calm now?"

"I think so, but Quin, why did you call? You know something," she insisted.

"I'll explain, but don't be worried. Shad nearly ran into me when I was pulling out of the Conoco," he began.

"Oh!" Darcy gasped.

"He didn't hit me or anything, Darcy. But, Randy had just gone by and waved at me."

"Randy?" she interrupted again. "Oh, no! Did he chase him?"

"I don't know for sure, but I did see his lights come on. The farther I drove the more I worried, and I just had to call and make sure Randy was okay."

"I don't know!" she exclaimed.

"You'd have heard by now if he wasn't," Quin reasoned calmly. "I feel a lot better now. I'm sorry if I upset you, Darcy."

"Quin, if you'll hang up now, I'll call you right back. I have to find out for sure."

Quin agreed, and she put the receiver down. Her parents were both standing there, casting her inquiring glances. She quickly explained, and Kerry reached for the phone. "I'll call the dispatch center," he said decisively. "You just sit down there, Darcy, and relax. I'm sure Randy's okay or Sandy would have called."

It only took a minute and Kerry hung the phone up with a sigh of relief. "Shad's in jail. Randy and Sarge arrested him after he tried to run Sarge's roadblock. Sarge blew a front tire out on Shad's car with his shotgun when he tried to go past," he explained quickly.

"Is Shad hurt?" Darcy asked fearfully.

"No, but I think he's in trouble this time. Deep trouble. Even that shyster MacArthur shouldn't be able to get him out of this one. Now Darcy, Shad is not your concern. You think about Quin and your wedding plans and let Shad Cleverly rot in jail if he must," Kerry said vehemently.

Darcy nodded, for she knew she must shut Shad from her mind and savor the blessing Quin was in her life. But she still worried. Always Shad was there. And always her loved ones seemed to be at risk.

Back in her bedroom, after calling Quin back, she knelt and prayed for Shad, that he might yet repent and do the things he knew were right. And she prayed that the Lord would protect her loved ones from him if he did not change. Feeling some better, she went to bed and dreamed that night of Quin Seltz.

✳

The next morning, Paula Cleverly lit into her husband, Bill, with a passion. "Don't you dare bail that boy out of jail, Bill!" she shouted.

"Can't you see that we've got to quit protecting him. He'll never learn if he's not allowed to take his medicine for what he does."

"You mean, can't I see that I've got to quit protecting him?" he shouted.

"Yes, that is exactly what I mean. As long as you keep bailing him out when he gets in trouble and paying that creepy MacArthur guy to defend him, Shad will keep getting into trouble."

"Shad's trouble is that Hutchins guy!" Bill countered. "He's out to destroy our son. Bishop Olsen ought to do something about him."

"Bill! What an awful thing to say. Randy is doing his job, and you know it. Shad is at fault, and it's time you face up to it and start trying to really help him instead of backing him in his wrongdoing. He was drunk last night. I begged him not to drive, but he did anyway. How can you keep blaming others?"

Bill's face was dark with rage. "Say what you like, Paula, but if it weren't for Randy Hutchins this whole thing with Shad would not be going on."

"This conversation is absurd!" Paula countered tearfully. "Randy did not cause Shad's wreck."

"No, but old man Burrows' cow did! Randy Hutchins blamed Shad! Now I don't want to hear another word of it. And when I bring the kid home, so help me, Paula, you better lay off him! You hear?"

She heard, and she cried, and she grieved, and she felt pain that only a mother can feel. She loved Shad, despite all that he had done. And she desperately wanted him to change.

Bill Cleverly backed his son, cursed Randy, threatened to sue Sarge for shooting at the Trans Am, and dished out more money to Mac MacArthur. And Mac was only too happy to take it. But the prosecutor would make no deals this time, and a jury of two men and two women convicted Shad of driving under the influence of alcohol, driving while his license was revoked, and for evading the police.

Judge Galen Simper, on the last day of January, ran his hand through his thinning grey hair and peered through thick glasses down from the bench at a glaring and angry Shad Cleverly. Paula Cleverly shed more tears from what must have been an endless reservoir, but she was silently grateful, for someone had to help her son before it was forever too late.

❉

"Missed you at school yesterday, Todd," Darcy said as Todd and Jill met her and Stacy for lunch.

"Sorry, but it was Shad's trial. I couldn't stay away. Did Randy tell you what happened?" Todd asked with a long face.

"No, he doesn't like to talk to me about Shad anymore. Not that I blame him," Darcy answered.

"So, tell us," Stacy insisted. "Darcy will be an emotional wreck until you do."

"The jury found him guilty," Todd said simply.

"Of everything?" Darcy asked.

"Yup. That hot-shot MacArthur ain't so hot after all. He was so mad that he actually screamed at Judge Simper. Almost got himself throwed in jail for contempt of court. So did Shad's dad," Todd said with a shake of the head.

"What did the judge say to Shad?" Stacy asked.

"That was good," Todd said with a half-grin. "He just peered through them thick glasses of his like he was looking down the barrel of a gun at Shad. And he says kinda' mean like, 'Young man, you are out of control. I have no choice but to confine you to jail for a healthy term.'"

"How healthy?" Darcy asked, trying to match Todd's lighter mood, but truthfully feeling nothing but profound sorrow for Shad.

"I'm getting to it," Todd said, his half-grin blossoming into a full one. "Anyway, when the judge says that, that lawyer interrupted and started screaming something about a reasonable fine being plenty." Todd got into the theatrics of his story by throwing his hands wildly in the air.

"Then Judge Simper, he says, 'You've had your say, Mr. MacArthur. Now I'll have mine, and mine is final! One more outburst like that and you'll be sitting in the jail yourself, for contempt.' Well, Mac, he shuts up then, but he ain't liking it none. His face was red as Shad's Trans Am. Then Simper, he says, 'There won't be a fine, because Mr. Cleverly pays Shad's fines!' At least he says he figured Shad's dad had paid his other fines since Shad couldn't keep a job," Todd said as he suddenly jumped in the air.

"What was that for?" Darcy asked, grinning despite herself at Todd's antics.

"That's what Mr. Cleverly done when the judge said that. So he got told about contempt and jail and stuff. And poor Mrs. Cleverly, she hung onto Mr. Cleverly's arm after that, just a crying and trying to hold him down."

That brought more pain to Darcy's tender heart, and all semblance of a smile was erased from her face. Todd said, "I'm sorry, Darcy, but it was kinda' funny how it happened." But then he continued with less theatrics. "Anyway, Judge Simper, he told Shad that he'd have a year in jail."

"Ohh," moaned Darcy.

"Not so fast, Darcy. He did suspend most of it. All but four months, to be exact. Ordered him to stay in jail through the end of May."

"That's just a few days before Quin and I are getting married," Darcy observed and felt a tremor of apprehension flow through her.

"Darn it, Darcy. Quit fussing so much. When Shad does get out of jail he won't have a lot of time on his hands. He has to perform community service for forty hours a week for two months!" he said fiercely. "That'll keep him busy!"

"That's three hundred and twenty hours," Jill clarified. "Think what a guy could earn in that time if he were getting paid."

"Wow!" Stacy exclaimed.

"Yeah, and that ain't all. If he screws up again in the next year, he gets to sit out the other eight months in jail," Todd added. "That'll make him behave."

When Todd had finished, Stacy turned to Darcy. "Well, now we know. Sounds like maybe he'll get a lesson this time. At least you can quit worrying now."

Darcy did not quit worrying. She did, however, forge ahead with her life. Quin came home every time he could and they planned, then they planned some more. Darcy continued to excel in school and graduated as valedictorian just two weeks before her wedding day.

She accepted a full scholarship to the university where she and Quin, as husband and wife, would both study in the fall. She also spent hours helping her mother sew a stunning white wedding dress that was acceptable to be worn in the temple.

Stacy and her mother helped Darcy and her mother plan the wedding reception, address invitations, and the myriad of other things that needed doing during the final days of May. Then, at last, the day of her wedding drew near. Quin came home for a short four-week break, eager to return to school as a married man.

*

Shad Cleverly got out of jail.

Shad Cleverly was a bitter young man. Each day, he performed his community service, even though it was hard work, but he did it only to avoid an instant return to jail. But he still drank, though he did so with more discretion. And he seldom drove his fast Trans Am, but that added to his frustrations. His anger and hatred toward Randy Hutchins knew no bounds. And as talk of the upcoming wedding of Darcy and Quin could be heard being discussed everywhere as the social event of the year, his hatred for Quin Seltz also festered like an angry boil.

Yet still he thought fondly of Darcy Felding and told himself that he'd never do anything to cause her pain. From time to time, he saw her halo of long chestnut hair, and he dreamed impossible dreams of getting her back—of rescuing her from the clutches of Quin Seltz.

❋

Nate worried his sister to death every time he rode his bicycle on the highway. And thoughts of Shad Cleverly were a constant source of agitation and worry as she and Quin prepared for their temple wedding. But, despite her concern for her loved ones, she was as excited as any prospective June bride had ever been.

Her love for Quin continued to grow, and there was no doubt in her mind that theirs was an eternal love. Each time she gazed at the painting of Christ that Quin had created for her, she cried, and her powerful love for her Savior also grew.

A week before her wedding, Darcy's parents and Quinn took her to the temple where she took out her endowments and felt the Spirit of the Lord like she had never experienced it before. From that day, Darcy felt nothing but peace. Even thoughts of Shad no longer disturbed her. She placed her trust in the hands of the Lord and was more filled with love than she had ever been.

The evening before the wedding, Darcy tried on her completed wedding dress. "See, Mom," Nate observed smugly. "I told you Darcy was an angel. She looks just like one."

"Thank you, Nate," Darcy said with a smile.

Then, more seriously, Nate asked, "Why ain't Quin here so he can see you in your new dress?"

His mother chuckled and explained, "The groom mustn't see the bride in her wedding dress until the wedding. And please don't say ain't. Say isn't."

"Why?"

"Because ain't is not a proper word."

"No, I mean why ain't the groom supposed to..."

"Why isn't the groom..." Sharon cut in sternly.

"Yeah, why ain't Quin supposed to see Darcy till tomorrow?" Nate asked stubbornly.

Darcy chuckled with delight, and Sharon sighed in resignation. "It's just tradition," she said.

The phone saved them from more questions. "I'll get it," Nate volunteered.

In a moment he was back. "It's Quin," he announced.

With a light heart, Darcy rushed to the phone, wedding dress and all. "Does it fit?" Quin asked as soon as she had greeted him.

"How did you know I was trying on my wedding dress?" she asked with a laugh.

"Why else would I be forbidden to come to the Felding house between four and four-thirty this afternoon?" he asked, and she could just picture his sober face lighting into a fluorescent smile, and his blue eyes sparkling like diamonds in the sea.

"I love you, Quin Seltz," she said.

"And I love you, Darcy Felding, soon to be Seltz," he said, and a baritone chuckle followed.

"I want to see you this evening," she said.

"I'll come out. You just tell me when," he offered.

"No. I need some things from the store. I'll come into town, get my shopping done quickly, and then come over for a little while," she said.

"What time will I see you?"

"Give me thirty minutes. About five o'clock, I guess."

"I'll be waiting. And I surely am anxious to see you in that white dress," he kidded.

"You will. When the time is right, you will. I love you Quin Seltz," she said again.

"I love you, Darcy-almost-Seltz," he said and the line went dead.

"Don't be too long in town, dear," her mother said as she skipped lightly to the door. "We still have a lot to do tonight and we must leave for the temple early. Tomorrow will be a very long day. You need your rest."

"I'll get plenty of rest, Mom. I promise," she said. Impulsively, she turned and ran across the room to Sharon, hugged her fiercely and turned away.

"What was that for?" Sharon asked as Darcy skipped back to the door.

"I love you, Mom," she called over her shoulder. "Thanks for all you've done for me. You make me so happy."

"And you make me happy, too, my angel daughter," Sharon said amidst a sudden downpour of tears.

Darcy hurried to the old Ford. "Where are ya' going, Darcy?" Nate called as he raced from the back yard on his bike.

"To town."

"To see Quin?" he asked.

"Of course. And to get you a treat," she added.

"Really? Why?" he asked, his little face lighting up.

"Because I love you, Nate, and because you are such a good little brother. And stay off the highway."

"I love you too, Darcy," he said with a grin big enough to swallow the Grand Canyon.

As she started down the lane, she slowed up as her dad came toward her on his tractor, pulling the bale-wagon with a load of hay. She thought how much she loved him, too. He worked so very hard. Even now, the evening before her wedding, he was determined to get the rest of the hay in from the big field across the highway. "I love you, Dad," she called as he passed.

Kerry waved cheerfully from the cab of his big John Deere, and Darcy drove onto the highway.

✳

Shad got off work at the county garage, where he was doing his community service, at three-thirty. By four-thirty he had downed five cans of beer. "Shad, why are you drinking tonight?" his mother asked in a pleading voice after he rushed into the house, changed his clothes, and started to rush out with a brightly-wrapped package under his arm.

"Because Darcy's getting married tomorrow," he shouted.

"What's that package for?"

"A wedding present for Darcy," he said smugly. "Thanks to that creep of an uncle of hers she never got it on her birthday, so I decided to take it to her tonight."

"No, Shad! Don't!" Paula cried, but he was already stumbling toward his red Trans Am.

✳

Trooper Randy Hutchins had the next day off for Darcy's wedding. He was anxious for this shift to end, and he glanced at his watch. Four-thirty-five, it informed him. He'd be home helping Sandy get ready for their trip to the temple in just twenty-five minutes. He was scheduled to be off duty at five, and he intended to not work a minute of overtime this evening.

✳

The phone rang at the Albright house. Todd's mother called to him where he was sitting in a newly constructed porch swing with Jill. He and his father had built it together—one of the first things they had ever done together.

He hurried to the phone. It was Shad's mother, and she was upset. "Todd, I didn't know who else to call. Bill's out of town until morning, and I just couldn't call the police."

"What is it?" Todd cried in alarm.

"It's Shad. He's drinking and heading out to Darcy's house with a present. It'll upset that poor sweet girl so much."

"I'll try to stop him," Todd promised rashly and hung up. "Mom, call the cops. Tell them that Shad's drinking and driving. He's going to Darcy's house," he shouted in a sudden surge of anger. "Come on, Jill. We gotta' try to find Shad."

A moment later, he and Jill were in the car and pulling into the street.

❋

Quin Seltz spoke to his sister. "Stacy, I can't wait until five. Why don't you come with me and we'll surprise Darcy at the store."

"Love to," Stacy said with a laugh, and together, the handsome blond groom-to-be and his beautiful, golden-haired sister headed up the street in his old blue Buick.

❋

Randy's radio came to life. In quick, crisp tones, he was advised that Shad Cleverly was drinking and believed heading for the Felding farm to cause a disturbance. He headed out of town, groaning to himself, "Not Shad again. Please, why me? Why always me?"

❋

Darcy Felding had never been so happy in her life, and that was significant because she had experienced much joy in her eighteen years. She just wanted to tell everyone how much she loved them. But mostly, she couldn't wait to throw her arms around the man she loved most of all and was prepared in a few short hours to commit herself to for eternity. Of course, in her joyful heart, that commitment was already made.

She selected a favorite tape and inserted it into the cassette player. One of Jeff Goodrich's beautiful songs of the Savior came on. A few tears wet her eyes as the soloist sang the emotional words of "I Heard Him Come."

As she listened to the joyous cries of Christ as described by Jeff, a string of cars approached. The third was a red one, and it kept darting across the center line like the driver wanted it to pass. But Darcy was too contented and happy to be irritated by an impatient driver.

Then, without warning, the red car, Shad's Trans Am, was attempting to pass the other cars, and it was coming straight at her! Darcy screamed and jammed on the brakes.

The last thing she saw was Shad's face, his eyes wide with terror. Then, for the last time she called aloud the name of Quin Seltz. A moment later the powerful crash of two cars coming together with a rending of steel, shrill screech of rubber on hot pavement, and a shattering of glass snuffed out the shining life of Darcy Felding.

# Chapter Nineteen

"C AR THREE-FIFTY-SIX," the dispatcher called, and Randy detected an urgency in her usually calm voice.

"This is three-fifty-six," he responded, using his badge number as was customary on the radio.

"Three-fifty-six, we just received a report by cellular phone of a head-on-crash. It is just two miles east of town. The caller sounded panicked. We are sending an ambulance."

"Ten-four," Randy responded, but his voice cracked and his knees trembled as he went on. "It must be just around this next bend. I'm almost there."

As he rounded the curve, he saw the crash ahead. Steam was still rising, and several cars were stopped on the road. Both of the vehicles involved in the wreck lay mangled and welded together in the center of the highway. His heart jumped to his throat and his head pounded, for as he drew to a stop, Randy recognized the distinctive rear-end of a red Trans Am.

He tore from the car, and his legs threatened to buckle as the harrowing smell of death assailed him. "Hurry, Trooper!" someone called.

Others shouted, but Randy's ears ceased to hear as his eyes took all his attention. They were fastened to the long but matted chestnut hair that was visible in the mangled mess that was the second car. Beyond the unmistakable hair, he could barely recognize the battered face. He then heard someone screaming, "Darcy! Darcy!" But he was at the shattered window and reached in to touch the bloody face of his beloved niece before he recognized his own voice doing the frantic shouting.

With brute force that tore his hands, Randy attacked the crumpled door of the wrecked Ford, but it would not budge. Someone grabbed his arm and jerked, yelling, "Officer, this one's dead, but the other one's not!"

"Darcy," Randy cried again, and tears ran like rivulets of rain down his cheeks.

"Please, Officer," the man at his elbow pleaded.

In a trance, Randy let go of the door with hands that now were stained with the blood of an angel. Slowly he turned. "This is my niece," he sobbed. "He killed her!"

"Officer, please. I'm sorry, but the kid's alive and needs help desperately."

With an iron will and a strong sense of duty, Randy moved toward the twisted red sports car. "He killed her. She was so afraid for me, but it was her he killed," he muttered in agony.

Shad was battered and bloody, but at the point of impact, the angle of the two cars had been in his favor. Neither car had air-bags, but Darcy had absorbed the greater shock. Shad had not taken the direct blow that she had. Randy thought bitterly as he began to take steps to save Shad's life, Shad was limber and loose with alcohol. He had refused to learn, and now, for Darcy Felding, it was forever too late.

❖

"Hey, look! There must be a wreck ahead," Todd said grimly as he rounded a sweeping curve in the highway. "Oh, no! I hope it's not Shad again," he added as something cold surrounded his heart and sent tiny spears of ice through his chest.

"Todd! There's a red car all smashed up!" Jill screeched hysterically.

The flashing of another set of lights in his rear-view mirror and the spine tingling wail of a siren forced him to pull over. A police car raced by. "Sarge," he said as he recognized the big patrol car of the veteran officer.

Two men were frantically directing traffic as Todd and Jill slowed down near the wreck. He was studying the red car, or what was left of it, with a growing sense of horror. "It's Shad," he muttered and glanced over at Jill.

She was crying. "I think he must have killed somebody, and probably himself, too." she sobbed.

"Yeah, I just..."

"Hey, kid! Get moving," a man at his window ordered. "There are people waiting to come through from the other direction. You're creating a traffic jam. The cops said to keep everyone moving."

Todd had not realized that he was nearly at a standstill as his eyes frantically poured over the crumpled and steaming Trans Am. He was forcing himself to obey the man's order and speed up when Jill suddenly gasped and grabbed his arm. "Todd, look!" she screamed.

At that moment, Todd needed no further directions to point out what Jill was staring at. His own eyes had also caught a glimpse of rich chestnut hair, and the cold spears of ice in his chest penetrated his whole body.

"Get going, kid! Quit gawking," the man shouted.

But Todd slammed on the brakes, rammed his shifting lever into park and hastily unfastened his seat belt. With a cry like a dying rabbit he burst from the car, shoving aside the man who was attempting to stop him, and rushed to the other car—the one welded to Shad's deadly red Trans Am.

"Darcy!" he cried as he slipped in a pool of oil, falling to his knees beside the smashed Ford. He pulled himself up and reached through the shattered window. No one had to tell Todd that Darcy's spirit had flown, leaving behind a bloody and battered shell.

"Shad, you killer, you," he moaned as he sunk to his knees, his hands spreading blood and oil down the crinkled door of the Feldings' family car. And there, with his head against the hot metal, he cried.

"Todd!" someone yelled. "Todd! Get control of yourself."

He looked up and into the grief-stricken face of Randy Hutchins. "She's dead!" Todd bawled.

"I know," Randy said in a voice choked with emotion. "There's nothing you can do, and your car is blocking any traffic from getting by."

"Jill. Oh, no! I left her alone," he cried, stumbling to his feet.

"She passed out," Randy said. But he quietly added, "Sister Olsen is with her. She was in one of the first cars here. Just pull your car out of the road until you both feel better, then go home."

Todd nodded and let Randy direct him back to his car. "Shad, is he..." he began.

"He's alive, Todd. The ambulance just pulled up and took over. I think he'll make it," Randy said, but Todd detected bitterness in his voice, a bitterness that matched his own feelings toward Shad Cleverly at that moment.

❧

Quin rubbed his forehead. "I know she was coming here, Stacy. She should have been here by now," he said as he looked over the Foodtown parking lot again.

"She must have had something come up," Stacy suggested.

"I guess. Let's just head out that direction. Maybe we'll meet her on the way. If we do, we'll just turn around and follow her back," he suggested.

"Quin, there goes another cop car," Stacy said as a siren wailed by.

"Must be a wreck somewhere out east," he said, and then a terrible thought hit him. "Stacy, let's go," he said in a suddenly tight voice.

"Quin, what's the matter?" Stacy demanded.

"I hope nothing is," he said, but in his heart a deep concern was developing, and he drove much faster than he normally would have toward the Felding farm.

As he rounded a sweeping curve just two miles from town, the concern turned to fear, but he fought to control it, telling himself he was being foolish.

"There's a wreck up there," Stacy said. "Maybe Darcy couldn't get past and...Oh, Quin! It couldn't be!"

Quin could not speak. He had just recognized the fiery red back end of Shad Cleverly's Trans Am, and he remembered Darcy's fears. "I'm afraid he'll hurt someone I love," she had said several times, and he had shrugged it off.

"There's Todd's car, just past the wreck on the right," Stacy said, and from the tone of her voice, Quin knew she was near panic.

He rolled up to the accident scene. A patrolman he did not recognize tried to signal him through, but he had to know!

"Keep moving, folks. We have a bad one here. Keep moving," the trooper said with a stony face.

"Quin, that's Shad Cleverly's car," Stacy said as he pulled forward slowly, his eyes glued to the mass of people surrounding the wrecked cars.

Then he saw Darcy's uncle, Randy Hutchins, looking right at him. And from the look in Randy's eyes, he knew his fears had been justified! He slowly passed the wreck, almost in a daze, and stopped behind Todd's car. He briefly noticed Todd and Jill huddled in each other's arms and crying. Stacy had grown very quiet beside him except for her frightened, labored breathing.

Quin began to open his door, but Randy Hutchins appeared there and held it shut. His eyes looked tortured and streaks of blood smeared his face. Quin rolled down his window and said, in a voice that only faintly resembled his normal baritone, "Is it...is it..." But he could not say her name.

"Quin, don't get out," Randy ordered huskily.

Stacy screamed. "It's Darcy! I saw her hair!"

"Randy, let me see her!" Quin demanded as his voice returned in the panic that overcame him.

"No, Quin! There is nothing you can do, and you don't want to see her like that."

But Quin did want to, and with a rush of adrenaline, he forced the door open, tore past Randy and into the small crowd of people who had gathered around the wreck. He then saw the crown of chestnut hair, matted and bloody, and Quin's world came crashing down upon him. "Darcy! Darcy!" he screamed in helpless horror.

Strong hands pulled him away, and Quin had not the strength left to resist. He was unable to catch another glimpse of the girl he loved—that almost perfect angel of his dreams.

Quin broke down and cried an ocean of tears from his sea blue eyes. Todd and Jill, who had been comforting one another, encircled him and Stacy with their arms and tried to give comfort. Stacy's tears mixed with his, and more fell from the red eyes of Todd and Jill.

Deep in this moment of intense grief, Quin slowly began to realize that Darcy had been right all along. Shad Cleverly had indeed, in the most devastating fashion, brought pain to those she loved most.

❈

Kerry Felding shut off his tractor and jumped to the ground. The last load of baled hay was in. He headed for the house. Before he began his evening chores, a cool drink of lemonade was in order to soothe his parched throat.

Suddenly, Nate sped up on his bike and stopped in a miniature cloud of dust. "Dad, I keep hearing sirens like Randy's. And two policemen went past. They was going real fast!" he said with youthful excitement that had his eyes as wide as silver dollars.

"Nate, have you been on the highway on your bike?" Kerry asked sternly.

"Nope, just by it," Nate responded proudly.

"Good, now quit worrying about the sirens and let's go see if Mom still has some cold lemonade for us boys."

"Ah, Dad, you're a man, not a boy," Nate said, and Kerry fondly tousled his son's curly hair.

"Hi, Sharon," Kerry said upon following Nate into the kitchen where his wife was busy at the stove. "When's supper? It sure smells good."

"Not until after Darcy gets back. You've probably got time to chore first," she said, smiling as she placed a lid on the pan in front of her and turned away from the stove.

"Where did she go? She sure looked radiant when she waved at me," Kerry said, remembering how pretty Darcy had looked when he caught his last glimpse of her smiling up at him as they passed one another on the lane.

"She went to the grocery store, and she was going to stop by Quin's for a few minutes," Sharon said. "Kerry, I need a bottle of peaches from the basement. Would you mind?"

"Glad to," he said. "Then Nate and I could sure stand for a cold glass of lemonade, couldn't we, son?"

"Yup," Nate said importantly.

"I'll pour it," Sharon said with a tired smile.

"Darcy's gonna' get me a treat," Nate said as Kerry headed for the door.

"She is?" Sharon asked.

"Yup, cause I'm such a good brother," he said and beamed.

Someone rang the doorbell. "Get that, will you Nate?"

"Yup," he said and tore out of the kitchen in that direction.

"Kerry, Darcy seemed so happy and full of love when she left. She hugged me before she went to town!" Sharon said.

"She's a good girl," Kerry said, stopping at the doorway that led to the basement. "I sure don't know what we'll do without her around here. Hope she and Quin can come home often. Well, I better get those peaches so I can earn my lemonade." He grinned and his wife smiled in return.

"Dad. Mom. Bishop Olsen and a policeman like Randy want to talk to you," Nate said from the door to the living room.

Kerry Felding suddenly felt faint. He looked at Sharon, and in her eyes he read the same apprehension he felt. Why would the Bishop and an officer, other than Randy, come here at this time of day? he wondered with a strangely sinking heart.

"Kerry. Sharon," Bishop Olsen's kindly voice said from the doorway. "Why don't you both come into the living room and sit down?"

The bishop's eyes were red. He had been crying. Something was terribly, horribly wrong, and Kerry knew it. Another glance at Sharon told him that she knew it, too. He reached for her hand and led her through the door and straight to the sofa where they both sat rigidly.

"This is Sergeant Ball, Randy's sergeant," Bishop Olsen said. Then with only a tiny pause, he went on. "I don't know of an easy way to say this, but we have some very bad news."

"Randy?" Sharon gasped.

"No, Randy's fine. But, I'm so very sorry," Bishop Olsen said, and his voice broke. "Darcy...she's been in an accident."

"Oh, no!" Sharon screamed.

"Bishop," Kerry said before Bishop Olsen could go on and as he threw a protective arm around his wife's trembling shoulders. "Is she hurt badly?"

Bishop Olsen's eyes erupted in an uncharacteristic flood and he tried to speak, but his voice broke.

Stern Sergeant Ball, a veteran in such matters, took over instantly.

"Your daughter has been killed," he said bluntly.

The next few minutes were the worst Kerry and Sharon Felding had ever experienced. So shocked and weighed down with grief were they that neither one noticed little Nate. He had heard every word.

But not until Bishop Olsen said, "Nate, my boy, come here," did Kerry think of Nate, and he immediately turned to his son, his only living child.

Nate did not move. He stood in the middle of the living room. His eyes were on the picture of the Savior that Quin had painted for Darcy's birthday. "Is Darcy with Him now?" he asked in a broken little voice.

Bishop Olsen raised his eyes to the painting. And even as he said, "Yes, Nate, Darcy is with Jesus," a look of wonder passed across his rugged face. "His eyes!" he exclaimed.

"They're like Darcy's eyes," Nate sobbed, still staring at the picture as tears eroded tiny ditches through the dirt on his little cheeks.

Sharon rushed to him and took him in her arms as Kerry approached the painting. Aloud, with a voice full of emotion, but also full of faith, Kerry read the inscription Quin had printed on the painting. "That when he shall appear, we shall be like him, for we shall see him as he is. Moroni 7:48."

It was silent in the room then, except for sobs and sniffles. Crusty Sergeant Ball, unnoticed by Kerry, had also walked to the painting.

"Your daughter's eyes?" he asked.

"Yes," Kerry responded. "Her fiance painted it."

"I wish I'd known her," he said reverently. Then, "I must be going now. They'll be needing my help."

After the sergeant had gone, Bishop Olsen prayed with the little Felding family. Only after they had completed their pleas for help and comfort did Nate ask, "Was it Shad that done it, Bishop Olsen?"

Kerry was stunned, but not nearly as stunned as when Bishop Olsen answered, "Yes, Nate. I'm afraid it was."

Randy refused to leave the scene of the deadly crash while there was still much to be done there. When Sergeant Ball returned and informed him that his sister and his family had been notified, he insisted that Quin, Stacy, Todd, and Jill leave. They all informed him that they intended to go to the Felding house. He offered no argument, because somehow, it seemed right.

"Now, Sergeant, will you please come with me to tell my wife and boys?" Randy asked. "If I wait much longer, they might hear it from someone else. But, I'm not sure I can do it without some support. They adored her, just like I did."

"Sure thing," his sergeant answered.

Randy walked over to his patrol car, then paused to turn and look once more at the terrible carnage that still littered the highway. Darcy's body had been removed and Shad was being life-flighted to a hospital over a hundred miles away. Sadly, Randy shook his head, then without warning, he became violently ill. For nearly five minutes, he retched in the grass at the edge of the road. Sergeant Ball stood by and said nothing in all that time except, "Best this way, boy. Just heave it out of your system."

❋

Quin Seltz saw Darcy's wedding dress the following Monday evening when her casket was opened at the chapel for a viewing. As part of her temple clothes, it was perfect, he thought. And with an aching heart, he sobbed over her silent body.

So vibrant had she been in life. So still was she in death.

Quin's head ached, and he was weak and dizzy. He had slept very little since the accident of Friday evening. He was confused and angry. Why? he wondered. Why did the Lord let her die? He had prayed so earnestly, and the Holy Ghost had borne undeniable witness to him that she would be his for eternity. But now, even before they were married, she had been taken.

As he stared through misty eyes at her face, something suddenly came to his mind. He remembered Stacy asking why he had prayed to know if Darcy could be his for eternity. He had told her that he guessed that's what he wanted to know. And he did, but what about now? he wondered desperately as he viewed her silent body.

Quin had not noticed Stacy as she moved to his side and was surprised when she spoke. "She was too good for this earth, Quin."

"I suppose you're right. She worried about all of us being hurt, and I scolded her because I saw that as a flaw in her character. She was right all along, Stacy. We are all hurt. Everyone she loves is so terribly, tragically hurt," he said.

"But remember, big brother, you asked me for advice that night, and I gave it to you. Well, as much as it hurts, please remember what I told you."

When she parted her lips to go on, Quin put a finger there to silence her. Then he said, "'A little separation is nothing when compared with eternity.' Oh, Stacy, it was so easy to think that then, when all we were concerned about was a few short months. But now...now it is so very hard. I loved...no, I love her so, and I will forever.

# Chapter Twenty

RANDY LIFTED HIS HEAD as he, along with the rest of the family of Darcy Felding, entered the large stake center the day of her funeral. Everyone in the whole county must be here, he thought as he saw people standing in every doorway and against the walls in the cultural hall. Randy was not far wrong. Darcy had touched many lives in her eighteen short years. And all of those she had affected for good were there.

Yes, she would be missed, and she would be grieved for, but she would also be remembered. And he was grateful for that, for Darcy was worth remembering. He still wondered at the events that had led up to her death, but many hours on his knees the past few days had brought a measure of peace to his soul. And he saw in his sister and her husband the same peace and faith that he felt, and he wondered how anyone could go through such a tragedy without the faith the gospel brings.

He who grieved the most was Quin Seltz. But time has a way of healing even the worst wounds, and as the days passed following Darcy's huge and emotional funeral, Quin began to heal. His faith in God was strong, and his knowledge that Darcy really could still be his for an eternity was a comfort. Slowly, he was coming to accept her leaving.

But there was one thing from which he found no relief. That was a bitter and growing anger toward the young man who had caused her death, Shad Cleverly. At first he felt justified, for Shad had been warned about the terrible dangers of drinking and driving and had openly ignored them, but then Quin felt guilty. He knew that he had no right to judge, and that of him it was required to forgive.

But he could not.

Even though he knew that his anger would eventually canker his soul, he still could not find the strength to forgive. He fought the bitterness without asking the Lord, with faith, for help, for he was ashamed.

As a result, he found no success.

Quin was not alone in his hostility. The whole community seemed bitter. Blame was thrown about like leaves in the wind. In silence, Quin listened to criticism of Shad's parents. He grieved for them, especially Shad's mother, but he could not bring himself to face them with the bitterness he bore in his soul toward their son.

Some folks railed on and on about Mac MacArthur and condemned him and all those of his profession. Quin found himself nodding in agreement. And poor Judge Simper was even criticized by the press, both local and statewide, for not keeping Shad in jail for a full twelve months or more. One editorial read in part, "If Judge Galen Simper had conscientiously examined the Cleverly boy's drinking and driving history, he would have done the only responsible thing and ordered a maximum jail sentence."

On the other hand, Quin was assaulted with reports of gossip among those few who felt Shad was being unfairly condemned. They were said to be making excuses for his behavior. Condemning Shad was taken by those as a judgement on anyone who drank, and they took offense. Quin knew that he should not be angry with those people, for they had the right to their opinions, although he felt that many of them were only defending Shad because they were guilty of doing the same things he had done. They had just been more lucky.

The result of all the controversy and anger surrounding Quin, and his own bitterness, was a deep depression. Summer school was due to begin at the university in a couple of days, and his part-time job was awaiting him. But Quin had no desire to return to school or to work. Yet he felt the need to leave town and the bitterness and controversy that raged there.

That night, after a half-hearted prayer, Quin slipped into bed. He was so disturbed and depressed that sleep was elusive. He lay with his hands behind his head, staring at the dark ceiling, wishing he could forgive and forget and get on with his life, what there was left of it without Darcy. He could not change the reality of her death, but he feared losing her in the eternal sense if he did not get his feelings under control.

As he lay in troubled thought, a dim light began to glow on the far side of the room. At first, Quin thought it was just his imagination, and he shut his eyes. But when he opened them again, it had become much brighter, and he sat bolt upright in bed, trembling.

Then, to Quin's astonishment, a figure appeared, obscured and unclear at first. As he stared, it became more pronounced, and Quin finally recognized the beloved person of Darcy Felding! She stood surrounded by light where the wall should have been, and was a couple of feet above the floor. He gazed at her in reverent awe.

After a few moments, her features became very clear and he recognized her wedding dress, or at least it looked exactly like the dress she had helped to make and in which she had been buried. Now, however, it was whiter and glowed with a light of its own. Darcy's rich chestnut hair also glowed, as did her startling green eyes, and a celestial smile lit her exquisite face like the sun at noon.

Quin gazed in rapture at the woman with whom he shared an eternal love. "Darcy," he called in a broken voice he scarcely recognized as his own.

"Quin," she responded. Then, almost without hesitation, she said, "It's okay."

"I miss you!" he cried.

"It's okay," she repeated. Then, "I'll be waiting. Please don't let me down." And with that, the beautiful image of Darcy faded and the light receded, plunging Quin's bedroom into somber blackness.

Quin sobbed and stared at the spot where Darcy had stood. Her image, so perfect and so beautiful, filled his mind. He reflected on her words, and that reflection dragged him to his knees beside his bed.

This time, when he prayed, it was with real intent and great faith. For several hours he was on his knees, but Quin Seltz, that night, found the strength to forgive. The sweet influence of the Comforter filled his soul with love and drove from him all trace of bitterness. Nothing, he resolved, would stand in his way of becoming worthy of the girl the Savior had called home.

The next morning at breakfast, Stacy was the first to comment on the change she saw in Quin. "Your eyes are sparkling the way they used to when you would look at Darcy," she said. "You look like the weight of the world has been lifted from your shoulders,"

"It has," he said, but he refused to comment further.

A few minutes later, as he stepped from his room to begin the task Darcy had inspired during the night, Stacy confronted him gently. "Quin, please tell me what happened. You are happy again. It is like the difference of night and day in your eyes and on your face."

For a moment, he stared at her, thinking how sweet and pretty she had become, then he said, "Come in," and he beckoned for her to follow him into his room. He closed the door and she sat on his bed when he pointed to it. "Stacy," he began, standing over her. "You must promise to tell no one what I am about to share with you. I will tell Dad and Mom some day, and maybe others, but not yet."

"I promise, Quin," Stacy said breathlessly.

He took a deep breath and glanced to the far side of his room where Darcy had appeared. He allowed a smile to cross his somber face, then he said, "I saw Darcy last night."

Stacy gasped and her hand flew to her mouth.

"Where!?" she asked.

He smiled again, for she did not doubt him. "Right here in this room. She stood over there," he said, pointing. "She spoke to me."

"What...what...did she say?"

"She said, 'It's okay.'"

❋

Paula Cleverly rarely left the house, and visitors came even more rarely since Shad had taken Darcy's life. So she was surprised when the doorbell rang. She rubbed her eyes, eyes that were almost always either full of tears or right on the verge, and approached the door with apprehension.

She moved so slowly that the bell rang again before she had placed her hand on the door knob. When she opened the door, she was stunned, for there on the step stood the one person she most feared to face. Tall, blond Quin Seltz, holding one hand mysteriously behind his back, said, while favoring her with one of his rare smiles, "May I come in for a moment, please?"

"Why, yes, of course," she said awkwardly and threw the door wide.

"Is your husband at home?" he inquired as his eyes scanned the room.

"No, he's out of town for several days."

"I hope he won't object," Quin said, his face sober again as he withdrew his left hand from behind his back. "This is for you."

"Oh, my!" she exclaimed as he extended to her a single, long-stemmed yellow rose. She accepted it with a trembling hand.

"I've missed you at church," he said. "Please come back."

"I...ah...just can't face anyone," she stammered.

"Sister Cleverly, I hope you will forgive me for not coming sooner," he said. "Please accept my apology. I know this has been very difficult for you and my behavior hasn't helped."

"But...but...why? Why did you come? You have done nothing wrong. And why did you bring me this...this beautiful yellow rose?" she asked, flustered and embarrassed.

"Because I wanted you to know that I bear no ill will, Sister Cleverly. Neither Darcy or me have any bitter feelings. You must believe that."

"D...Darcy?"

"Yes, she bears no malice, and I know she would not want you to stay away from church."

"She...she was such a good child," she said, remembering when Darcy had come bearing cookies and a smile for Shad when he had been so bitter at her and she had done nothing wrong.

"I know, Sister Cleverly. Please now, for me...for both of us, don't let what has happened to us cause you further pain," he begged.

"But, my son, Shad...he took her life...took that darling girl's life," she sobbed.

"He is forgiven. I bear him no bad feelings, anymore," Quin said. "Thank you for seeing me. Please tell Brother Cleverly I was here and what I have told you."

"Thank you for coming, Quin," she said, and she awkwardly showed him to the door.

After he had gone, she stared at the beautiful yellow rose she still held in her hand, and she shed the first tears of joy she had known in many months. In Quin Seltz there was still a bit of Darcy and her goodness, she thought with pleasure.

❖

Quin, after leaving Sister Cleverly, called on Judge Simper, who seemed mighty surprised to see him. "I just had to clear my conscience," Quin told him. "I was one of those who questioned what you had done with Shad. I'm sorry."

"Thanks, Quin," the judge said, leaning back comfortably in his large black chair. "I have questioned myself these past few days. I felt mighty rotten when a reporter called me and asked, "Judge, how do you feel, knowing that someone is dead who would not be had you locked Shad Cleverly up for a longer term?"

Quin shook his head. "I'm really sorry," he said again.

"Don't be, Quin. It has made me think. Maybe there is more I can do. And, Quin, I was mighty fond of that little gal of yours."

Quin's next stop was at the plush law office of Mac MacArthur. He extended his apologies again, but Mac just snorted and said, "It doesn't make a lick of difference to me what people say or think about me. When they get in trouble, they come running like deer to a salt lick. And in case you came to ask, the answer is yes; I will be representing Shad in court again, as soon as he is well enough to stand trial."

"I hope things work out for him," Quin said sincerely.

"I'll just bet you do!" Mac said with a snarl.

"Mr. MacArthur, I bear no malice toward him, and I do hope that through all this, he will come out a better person," Quin said.

His conversation with Mac did not get any better, and he never did get the feeling that Mac cared for his apology, so he left. Quin was glad he had gone though, for he had done what he could to let Mac know that he did not hold bad feelings for him. And despite the cold treatment he had received, he felt a deep contentment, for he had done what Darcy would have done in his place.

Finally, Quin raked together all his courage and drove to the hospital for the most difficult visit of all. Shad had been transferred back to his home town hospital after the doctors determined that his life was out of danger. He was badly bruised and had a dozen broken bones, but he was on the mend.

From the look on his puffy face, it was apparent that he had not expected, nor did he welcome, a visit from Quin. "Hello, Shad," Quin began awkwardly. "How are you feeling?"

Shad glared at him for a moment before saying, "I've felt better."

"You're looking pretty good," Quin said.

"Well, I don't feel it."

"I hope you soon feel better," Quin offered.

"Why'd you come? Think you can make me feel any worse? If you do you're crazy. She was my girl first, you know."

"Shad, I came to tell you that I'm sorry for the feelings I've had against you since the accident. I know it was not something you did intentionally, and I came to tell you that I forgive you," Quin said.

Shad was a little taken back, but not for long. "Well, a lot of this is your fault. If you hadn't come along and took her from me, she'd still be alive. So how do you feel about that?"

Shad was not making this any easier, Quin realized, but he was not about to let Shad ruffle him. "I loved her. I still love her. And what's done is done. I just want to put it behind me, and if I can, to help you put it behind you, too. That's why I'm here today, Shad. You can be angry if you want, but I am not. Not anymore."

"Sure! Mac warned me that you'd probably be suing me. Well, sue away. I ain't got nothing anyway."

"Shad, please. You don't understand. I'm not going to sue anyone. It's okay, really it is."

"That's what she always said," Shad said. "She always said 'It's okay,' when things didn't go right."

"I know. And she always meant it, Shad. And so do I. Hope you get better soon. See you around."

"Yeah, okay," a suddenly subdued Shad said, and Quin left, both saddened by the hardness of Shad's heart and encouraged that his task was finished. He had forgiven, and he would never look back.

Oh, he would be lonely, and his heart would ache for Darcy's company, but he took comfort in knowing that this life was but a short time when compared with eternity. And he was grateful that eternity was a very long time, and he could spend it with Darcy.

❊

It was several months before Shad stood trial. True to his word, Mac MacArthur was there, but the evidence was overwhelming, and Shad Cleverly was convicted of automobile homicide and sentenced to prison for a term of not more than five years.

Todd Albright, just a few days before departing on a mission, visited Shad at the Utah State Prison. "I hope you will be out before I get back," Todd said sadly. And he wondered if, without Darcy Felding's sweet influence, he might be someplace like this instead of embarking on the Lord's errand.

"I'll be out a lot sooner than that," Shad assured him. "I shouldn't be here in the first place."

Todd shook his head. Would Shad never learn to accept responsibility for his own actions? Then he remembered his father, and he had hope.

❊

Shad's prediction was correct. He was ordered released by the parole board after serving only eight months. His father's money and Mac MacArthur's persuasive skills served him well, and he returned to his home town with a chip on his shoulder and fire in his eyes.

Shad had tasted the bitter dregs of prison life and wanted no more of it, but he had not lost his taste for beer nor his hatred for Randy Hutchins and every other officer he saw. In prison he had rubbed shoulders with the worst of the bad, and their influence had not been good for him.

One year to the day after Darcy's death, Shad came out of his bedroom with a package under his arm. It was torn and slightly bent. "Shad, where are you going with that package?" his mother asked apprehensively.

"I gotta' take it to someone," he said.

"To whom?" she asked.

Shad ignored her and opened the door just as his father came into the living room. "Where are you headed, son?"

"Just out for awhile," Shad said, hesitating in the doorway.

"Isn't that the package you bought for Darcy, the one that was in the wreck with you?"

"Uh, huh."

"I didn't realize you still had it."

"I kept it," Shad said. "Thanks for not letting the cops destroy it. They would have, you know."

"Yeah, you're right, but what good is it now?"

"I gotta' take it somewhere," Shad said evasively.

"Is someone coming to pick you up?"

"No, I guess I'll walk."

"It's too hot out there, son. Here, take my truck," he said and tossed Shad the keys.

"Bill, he doesn't have a license," Paula protested.

"But at least he hasn't been drinking," Bill said sharply. Then, turning to Shad, he said, "Watch for the cops, son, especially Hutchins. I don't want you in any more trouble."

"Then let him walk, or take him yourself to wherever it is he's going," Paula suggested.

Bill threw his wife a disgusted glance and said, "He's served his time, Paula. Give him a little space."

Shad left with the argument between his parents unfinished. He was used to it. His mother just didn't understand.

In his father's shiny new truck, Shad took the back streets across town to a low hill overlooking the valley. There he parked, took the package, and stepped out among the headstones of the city cemetery.

A warm breeze rustled the branches of the trees as he looked for a certain grave. He had meant to come here before, but he needed an excuse. The anniversary of Darcy's death provided one. After five minutes, he finally found the small, flat piece of granite that marked the earthly resting place of Darcy Felding. He stood looking at her grave for a long time. Then he muttered, "I never meant to hurt you, Darcy. I loved you, you know. You are the only good person I ever knew."

He fumbled with the package in his hand, tearing off the wrapping to expose a small box. It was bent at the corners, but when he opened it, the present he had bought for Darcy's birthday eighteen months before was unbroken in its bed of styrofoam.

He took it out gently and knelt in front of the headstone. "I brought this for you," he said. "I wanted to give it to you a long time ago, but things kept getting in my way. Here it is now. It's yours to keep," he said, placing it gently on the headstone.

Shad Cleverly then bowed his head and cried. His life was such a mess, and he knew it. And Darcy Felding had been so good and he had taken her life. At least Quin Seltz did not get her, he thought with grim satisfaction, but even that thought did not stem the flow of tears.

When he finally stood and turned to leave Darcy's grave, Shad looked at his watch. He'd been there for an hour! "I'll come back," he promised and shuffled away.

Back in his Dad's truck, he muttered, "I gotta' have a drink," and he went in search of Dwight Arnot.

❖

"Stacy, I'm going out to the cemetery," Quin said early that same evening. "It was a year ago today, you know."

"Yeah, I remember. It's all I've thought of all day," she said as she rubbed at her eyes. They were red.

"Still miss her, do you? I sure do," he said.

"We always will, until we meet her on the other side," Stacy answered. "Yes, I'd like to go with you, Quin."

Stacy was home from school for the summer. Quin was home for a week. Together, they rode out to the cemetery in his old blue Buick. Quin parked near the grave and got out. Then, arm in arm, he and his sister approached the hallowed spot where Darcy's body awaited the resurrection.

"What's this?" Stacy said, pointing to a small glass object on the headstone that gaily reflected the rays of the sinking sun.

"It's a glass figurine—an angel," Quin said. "That's most appropriate. I wonder who left it here."